The Pyronian Prophecy

By Robert Rotondi

Prologue

Thunder boomed and lightning crashed into the muddy plains of the castle courtyard as the powerful King Flint's army made their way toward a distant agitated mob that stood by the towering gates. Flint's men were an army of around one hundred, marching in unison. They wore dark metal armor and wielded sharpened spears. Shouts rang out as the army grew closer to the large grouping of people. A slender figure led the battalion, standing calmly before the enormous mob of people. Pandemonium occurred among the mob.

"Stand down, civilians. We would prefer this not be violent." Instructed Argus, the king's loyal servant. Argus' directions had no effect on the mob, as they continued shouting back.

Many years before, a man had murdered the king of Pyronia and claimed the throne for himself. In the years after the death of the tyrant and his firstborn son, a rebellion had developed in his wake. The tyrant's second son Flint had been inaugurated in the years since. The political tensions had already grown heavy after the great global collapse, leaving the newly founded Pyronia in a techno-medieval state of frenzy. The people had grown increasingly upset at the cruel and tyrannical royal family, longing to return to the peaceful monarchy they served previously.

As tension rose before the towering castle, a rioting couple who stood toward the front of the conflict, Ted and Nancy Larson, grew worried. Wearing a pair of dark shoulder pads and grey pants, with black boots worn from many years of rough use, Ted stood beside his partner Nancy, who wore a similar getup with lighter brown pants, grey shoes and her hair tied behind her head to avoid inconvenience in battle. Nancy had just given birth to their son William, whom Ted had been calling 'Will', and the new parents were afraid they wouldn't make it out of this battle alive.

The King's men began to slowly approach the citizens with each ticking second, and the rioting crowd grew increasingly tense. Suddenly, lightning struck the muddied ground in front of the castle offering distraction, allowing the army's spears to strike the mob fiercely. The bodies descended quickly, and Ted knew he had to do something. He looked into Nancy's dark eyes that he had cherished for many years. The two silently communicated as Ted stared into the window of his wife's soul. She nodded in understanding.

Using only a gaze, Ted directed Nancy and she fled while holding young Will. Ted's golden blade, a special weapon that carried immense weight with each swing, cut down royal soldiers valiantly. After fighting hoard after hoard of men, Ted was eventually overpowered by a group of soldiers and brought to his death.

Overwhelmed with heartache, Nancy stopped in her tracks at her husband's death and screamed her lungs out in agony as she dropped to her knees in defeat. Her mourning quickly converted to rage as she handed baby Will to one of the remaining civilians as they ran to safety. Nancy picked a silver blade from the ground, ran into the conflict as her husband had, and began to slash upon the swinging blades of the men who had killed her husband. She was quickly overpowered as well after slaying close to a dozen men, and baby Will watched from a distance in confusion while his mother was slain before him just as his father had been.

King Flint, now entering the conflict, wielded a long, blood red blade in his right hand. His greying, uneven beard blew in the wind of the storm before him as men dropped to the earth all around. He took a deep breath in reluctance before seemingly forcing himself to approach more of the armed conspirators, and with only a few swift swings of his bloodthirsty sword, the massacre was over, and the castle courtyard returned to silence.

With achievement, he stood neutrally in tranquility. King Flint had won the fight that ended the lives of Ted and Nancy Larson. As he was escorted into the city streets further from the castle gates, baby Will looked upon the courtyard as the burly, gray-bearded King Flint stared back at him coldly from afar.

Chapter 1

The blaring sound of horns startled Will, whose eyes shot open at the noise.

"Come on soldiers, up and at 'em!" A familiar voice rang in his ears.

Will slumped out of bed and rubbed his eyes. He had been exhausted from constant tossing and turning. *Another nightmare*, Will thought as he stared out his small window, and the voice rang again:

"Get the hell up, men!"

Will leaped off the creaky futon bed of his dorm and stepped toward the door. The loud, angry woman was Darla, current leader of the Rebellion. The Rebellion was of great importance. Ever since the tyrant Flint and his family took over the throne, the whole kingdom was trapped in a cloud of despair. The Rebellion was the only bit of hope that the world had, and Will was a part of it. Will's family had been in the Rebellion since it was established.

Will wasn't too eager to leave his dorm, but he knew that he had no choice. Another thieving mission was sure to await him, despite openly despising stealth related deployments. Will understood, however, that it was the easiest way to both be trained for combat and stay hidden from royal eyes. He just wished there were some other way to make a difference in secret. Making up his mind, Will approached Darla with a smug grin on his face.

"Morning. 5:30 in the morning, precisely." He spoke in a mocking tone, and Darla frowned.

"Exactly. We have a big plan for today, and the earlier we get ready, the more prepared we will be. Speaking of getting ready, you should do that."

Will looked down. He was still in his night clothes.

"Yeah, I'll get to that. See you." Will turned to re-enter his dorm, and Darla glared fiercely into his eyes.

"That's 'yes ma'am' to you." She smirked. "But yeah, we'll catch up later." Will entered his dorm again, and Darla went back to waking the others.

When Will's parents passed away in battle, Darla's family took him in as their own. Will and Darla had done everything together, from pretending they were in the roles of their parents with stout wooden swords and killing the king, to being equally confused over homework the rebellion professor had assigned in a class neither of them had paid any attention to. Will quickly got dressed and hopped into his thieving gear. Will had something to be slightly excited for in the least, as he knew that Darla would have a city mission for him this morning for the first time in months.

Today is my chance. He thought confidently.

Today, he would finally prove to Darla that he could be a warrior. The first opportunity he was given, Will was going to take on a soldier himself, whether she wanted him to or not. He would finally be able to live up to the childhood games Darla and him had grown up with, and fill the shoes of his late parents.

The entire Rebellion hideout was disguised in a mountain beside the capital city of Thanatos. They were always incredibly careful to keep hidden, and it paid off. The mountain being right next to the capital made it easy to pull off heists, as well as being right beside the castle. And in the scenario that they were followed by enemies, the Rebellion always had many pre planned safety measures, and a few tricks up their sleeves if all else fails.

Will looked around at the beautiful Rebellion capital as he made his way to Darla's meeting room. Older rebels whispered between each other as he walked by, trying to hide their glares. The trees were wonderfully tended to by Terri, the Rebellion's head gardener, and the buildings shone brightly, reflecting the artificial light just past Will's eye. The dirt roads were perfectly level, almost as flat as the asphalt in the city. Not that it mattered how bumpy the roads were, however, because none of the rebels owned a car. Cars were not something a rebel would simply own.

Will examined the great wall that stood as the gateway between the gigantic capital city of Pyronia and the rebel base that Will had called home for the last 3 years. The rebellion moved around from base to base quite frequently in the past, but for the last few years they had stayed in the mountain base, and it had worked out well for them.

About 2 hours later, Darla met Will and his group of thieves in her meeting room. They all gathered around a planning table, and Darla laid out a map.

"Listen up, men." She ordered. "Here's the plan. Louie, you and Bella are going to dress as citizens and go to the town square at 9:00, right when the main crowd builds. Bella, you throw one of your powdered bombs to distract the guards and cause chaos in the crowd of people, then Louie, you take as many guards out as you can with your shocker bands. Will, that's when you come in. When the guards are all outside dealing with the distraction, you charge into the Town Hall and into the back room where they keep all of the classified files. Grab as many as you can and evacuate the premises. Louie and Bella, look for him and follow. You all got that?"

"Yes, sir!" Louie shouted. Darla glared at him, and Louie flushed before coughing in embarrassment. "Yes, ma'am."

Louie was a tall, thin boy with skin slightly paler than Will's and strawberry blonde hair. He was generally quiet, but felt more comfortable around Darla and Will, having grown up with them. His dulled hair blew over his eyes which had seen many sleepless nights as he cracked a grin toward Bella, who scoffed. Bella was only a year or so older than Louie, but had matured much quicker than he ever could. She had long, black hair and a warm smile that brightened the room around her.

When the three were dismissed, Will sat and leaned against the gigantic metal wall that divided the city outskirts and the rebellion base. He put his hands over his eyes in distress, and Louie knelt beside him.

"Another sleepless night, huh?" He said, and Will nodded. "I get it."

"I've just been having these nightmares recently. Of my parents." Will spoke, and Louie looked down.

"You know..." He said after a moment. "I never got to know my dad, but you remember my mom." Will looked up at his remark.

Louie's mom had been one of the most caring people Will had known when he was a child, besides Darla's parents. He remembered one day when he and Louie were close to eight years old. They had been pretending that Will was the king and that Louie was going to defeat him, and Louie accidentally slashed Will too hard with his wooden toy blade. The cut on Will's arm began to bleed, and Louie's mom ran over as quickly as possible with a bandage that she had carried in her pocket at all times. While she wrapped it around his arm carefully, Will felt more loved than he had ever before.

"I used to have nightmares a lot, back when my dad passed." Louie spoke, bringing Will back into the present. "She used to have me meditate every day for a few minutes. She called it mindfulness. I thought she was full of shit, but she was also a nurse, so I couldn't argue. It ended up really helping me. It's nice, too. You get some time to reflect. I recommend it."

"Yeah..." Will said in thought over Louie's suggestion. "Thank you. That actually sounds really nice."

"What can I say, she always used to have the best remedies." Louie smiled, and Will grinned back. "Besides, you don't need my advice. You have Darla watching out for you like a hawk. What else could you need?"w

"Thank you, man." Will said, and Louie gave him a fist bump while he chuckled.

"Of course. Anytime."

•••

A few minutes later, Will entered the weapons hall of the rebellion's east wing. Louie and Bella already stood inside the door waiting for him and Darla followed behind. Will grabbed his Thieving Armor from off the shelf and strapped it on. The two metal shoulder plates slipped right over his arms, while he stuck his arms through the fabric chest straps that looped around his chest in the shape of an 'X'. He'd worn this suit a million times, but he still admired the simplicity of the protective gear.

As the thieves walked down the hall to leave, Darla stopped them.

"You guys know not to do anything stupid. Be safe." She looked at Will. "Seriously. I know that look on your face. You're planning something. Don't. I'll see you later."

Darla walked away, and Louie grinned.

"We got this. Another easy heist. No problem." He walked out the door, and Will looked toward Bella.

"This isn't going to be as easy as he thinks, is it." Will spoke, and Bella smirked.

"He thinks every mission is 'Another easy heist!', and knowing Darla, it definitely won't be."

Bella walked out the door, and Will looked back one more time at the base as he walked out. The giant metal doors slowly closed and locked tightly behind him.

Chapter 2

Will, Louie, and Bella left through the gateway, and entered a large forest pathway that leads to the city. Will looked around him and admired the beautiful trees that hung above, and the lovely sound of birds singing that he was never able to enjoy inside the mountain fortress. Will closed his eyes and took a deep breath of fresh air. Louie turned to Will, with an unusual look of seriousness on his face. He wore a thin, dark coat that he kept his hands inside the pockets of, and black running sneakers that had been worn by use.

"Do you think we'll ever win? Like, I understand that taking the kingdom's special files is a nuisance for them, but what is it doing to the king? Will we ever have enough men to actually attack the castle?"

Will looked at the ground in deep thought.

"I'm not sure. We've been doing this together for 3 years now, and although Darla has said that what we do is important, I've always wondered if there was something more we could be doing." He responded to Louie's interest.

Bella cut in between them with a stern look on her face. She wore a gray long sleeve shirt and brown boots with scratches from wear.

"Alright, alright. Look, Darla has been leading us for a while now, and it may be best just to let her plan everything out. Let's just keep doing what we can for now, because at least we know that we are helping this way, even if it's not as direct." Will nodded and kept walking forward.

The capital city of Thanatos was enormous. If Will and his group hadn't had a map to guide them through, they most likely would have gotten lost. The buildings were very diverse, some being made of stone or wood, while others were made of glass and metal. Some buildings barely reached 30 feet tall, while others soared past 200 feet tall. The entire city was built on a slowly inclining hill, with some buildings even being built into it. Of course, at the top of the hill resided the Royal Castle, which was a behemoth in size. The stained-glass windows reflected the sunlight upon the city, gleaming a white shine across the streets.

In front of Will stood a steep downward hill, going down about six feet, leading to a side entrance to the city. Louie, without hesitation, leaped over the mini cliffside, landing on the asphalt with a thud. Bella slowly climbed down the rocky dirt wall, barely making a sound when she touched the ground. Will hopped off the edge of the hill, landing on the floor in a roll.

"All right, let's get moving." Will said with a sigh.

The three thieves started towards their destination, which was the city's town hall, home of all the city's most important documents.

Will gazed up at the towering church clock as its large hands revealed the time, which was 8:14. They had exactly 46 minutes until the big heist. Will wasn't nervous. He'd done this many times, and every time it got easier. The kings' guards were very vulnerable to sneak attacks, and that's what they had done every time. Will looked around at the citizens of Thanatos as they lived their daily life. Even with the direct terror of the tyrant king constantly looming over, these people had somehow managed to live a decent life with what freedom they had. He observed as the citizens around him shared greetings, while others gave embraces to loved ones. A father waved farewell to his children, dressed in a well kept suit. It was easy to forget the throne's constant grip over every citizen's life. *We'll free you all, I promise.* Will thought with hope.

By the time they reached the town square, it was 8:54. 6 minutes until the heist. The crowd had already started to build, and Will listened in on the many diverse voices.

I needed those files yesterday!

What do you think? Isn't this city the best?

Oh man! I'm going to be late!

Move along!

Will's eyes went toward the direction of the last voice, when he saw him. A royal guard. Multiple guards, who were leading a shackled man in the direction of the royal dungeon, located right next to the grand castle building. The guards wore shiny metal armor and sported long, sharp spears for protection. One of the two guards had long, brown hair, while the other had short black hair. The man they were moving was in poor condition. His clothes were torn at the seams, and his shoes were falling off his feet. Will took a step toward the guards when Bella grabbed his arm.

"I know. We can't stop this now. Come on." Will knew she was right, and he followed her and Louie to the waiting point.

At 9:00, the church bell rang in the distance, nine strong waves of noise that reminded Will that the time had come. He nodded at his partners, and the plan went into motion. Bella threw her powder bombs right into the middle of the gathering crowd. Clouded with thick fog, the mob of people panicked, causing chaos. As the royal guards ran into the crowd, desperately trying to stop the commotion, Louie followed them in and slapped his shocker bands on the guards one by one, causing them to convulse violently as they fell to the ground with a thud. A shocker band was similar to a taser, but it slapped on one's wrist in a bind so there was no escape from the attack.

Then it was Will's turn. He beelined it for the entrance of the town hall, and safely made it inside. Will heard guards shouting from the outside;

"It's a sabotage!"

"Alert the lieutenant!"

He ran through the lobby, leaping over the front desk, where the recipients were hiding under. The filing room was the last room on the left of the main hall. Will opened the door, and grabbed as many files that looked important as he could.

Will left the town hall and observed his surroundings. The smoke from the bomb was beginning to clear, and from the corner of his eye he saw Bella and Louie waving towards him. They were hiding around the corner of a building, anxious to escape. Will ran over to the two of them and handed Bella the files.

"Alright, let's get out of here!" Louie shouted. Will was about to run when he heard a vicious yell.

"HEY!"

Will looked towards the shout and saw an angry and confused guard leaving the thick fog, chasing after the man that he had seen shackled earlier that morning.

"Please, let me go! I promise I'll have the money sorted out for the taxers in a week! Please sir, I have a young daughter at home!" The man is cornered by the guard.

Will recognized the guard as the one with long brown hair. He turned to Louie and opened his mouth.

"I'll be right back."

Louie looked back at Will with shock as he began to walk towards the guard.

"No! Will, come back! What the hell are you doing?" He shouted. Bella ran back to Will and angrily whispered;

"Get back here! WILL!"

Will ignored them and stomped up towards the guard.

"What the hell does he think he's doing?" Bella shouted in a whisper to Louie, who returned the same confused and frantic glance she gave.

"I don't know, but we have to leave now!" He shouted as more soldiers began to enter the plaza, looking for the rebel terrorists who had disturbed its peace.

"The maker has a plan." Bella said with a sigh. "I just hope he'll keep Will safe." She finished lamentingly, as she and Louie slipped out of sight.

Will approached the taunting soldier with rage and pushed himself between the soldier and the man.

"Get away from him!" He spoke, and the guard turned towards Will with disgust.

"What the hell did you just say to me?

Will took a breath of courage and stepped closer to the towering soldier.

"Get. Away. From that man." Will said sternly, and the long-haired guard chuckled before responding.

"And what gives you the authority to tell me that, scum?" Will began to boil inside, furious at the soldier's insult.

"That man is clearly too poor to pay your rich ass. You're the scum for bullying him over it." Will said coldly.

The guard's face turned red, as he grabbed Will by the arm.

"Alright dipshit, you are coming to the courtrooms with this filthy peasant. Happy now?"

The guard turned back to look at the poor man, but to no avail. During Will's distraction, the man had run away. *Just as planned.* Will thought cheekily. Will looked back towards where Louie and Bella stood before, but they had disappeared as well.

Will punched the guard in the face to escape from his grip, knocking the large man to the ground. Will tried to run in the opposite direction but found himself face to face with the short-haired guard from earlier.

"Look at him." The guard said mockingly. "He thought he would get away just like that."

Will noticed that the short-haired guard was surrounded by supporting soldiers. All the guards had woken up from the shocker band attacks.

"Hey, I saw him earlier!" One of the guards exclaimed. "He's in cahoots with the rebels! He helped them attack!"

Shit. Will thought nervously. Before he could escape, the short-haired guard grabbed Will by the arm and handcuffed him immediately.

Oh man. Will thought. *Darla's going to kill me.*

Chapter 3

King Flint stared into the distance. An eerie silence echoed throughout the palace, as Flint sat alone on his throne. A flurry of footsteps awoke Flint from his gaze, as he watched as one of his loyal guards frantically ran into the throne room and knelt by Flint's feet.

"Your majesty, there was a rebellion attack near the town hall today. Most of them escaped, but we were able to capture one of them." Flint sat courtly and stared down.

"Very well. We'll interrogate the prisoner tomorrow."

Flint stood up from his grand chair and began to walk toward the stained-glass window.

"Leave me be." Flint said solemnly.

The guard left the room, and Flint gazed down over the gleaming city of Thanatos, named after his very own father. His father, King Thanatos of Pyronia. Many looked up to his father as an inspirational figure, striving to stand up against the rich and powerful. But most saw Flint's father as a monster. He drove through with his army many years ago, burning buildings and landscapes throughout his quest for new power. He slaughtered his way through the crowds and crowds of royal supporters. He single-handedly killed the beloved King Atticus of Pyronia and took the throne for himself. And now, Flint was forced to live with the consequences of his father's tyranny.

"My King?" Spoke Argus, loyal servant to the throne, as he entered the room. The hanging fabric behind his dark suit fluttered in the light breeze, as did his ghoulish long hair. Flint turned his attention to him at once. "The west sector is having a famine of wheat supply. We have done what we can do with our rations, but we need to make a decision quickly to prevent the worsening of the famine."

"Invite the lord of Spiral City to the castle for a formal meeting next week. I will discuss potential redirection of product distribution until the problem is eliminated." Flint spoke after a moment of thought, and Argus nodded as he left the room.

Some time after he left, a higher ranking soldier entered the throne room and knelt before King Flint before stating his business.

"My lord, a riot has broken out in the Northern edge of the city." He started. "What are we to do?"

"Arrest those who cause damage to city property, and take necessary means of action." Flint started, and the soldier stood in agreement. "Just be mindful. Don't cause any unneeded damage. Do only what must be done."

"Of course, my lord." The soldier said as he left, and Flint sat again upon his throne.

After an hour or so of tranquility, Argus re-entered the throne room and stood before Flint with urgent news.

"My King," spoke Argus. "The terrorist that our soldiers took prisoner during the attack by town hall... There's been an issue." Flint bit his lip in conflict and stared sternly at his servants' news.

"What kind of issue?" He said, and Argus took a step back nervously.

"Well, we were unable to find any record of him in the city archives. He must have been raised with the rebellion."

Flint thought for a moment.

"Interesting. Were you able to get any information out of him?" He responded, and Argus gazed downward.

"That's the problem. He hasn't talked in hours. We are unable to get a word out of him."

Flint let the words he had heard process in his head for a moment.

"What exactly did he do today?" Flint asked in curiosity.

"Well, my lord, from the reports I had read it seems as if he participated in the terrorist attack in the city square today." Argus responded.

"And?" Flint pushed, wondering if there was any extra information. Argus opened the field report, and began to skim through it.

"He assaulted a taxing officer. It says that the tax officer was arresting a man after failing to receive payment from him, and the boy intervened. A *Robin Hood*-esque situation, it seems." Argus continued, reading from the file in his hands.

"Hmm." Flint spoke quietly in thought. "Place him in cell #27." Flint turned away from Argus and walked slowly back to his throne.

As Argus left the room, Flint sat in his grand seat, which had used to carry honor and dignity. Now it carries tyranny and bloodshed. Flint flinched. He could not be thinking such things. He sat and thought of his late brother. Jonah Strife, older brother to Flint, was well beloved by the city. But most of all, he was beloved to Flint's father, Thanatos. It was obvious that Jonah was a favorite child to him, and Flint lingered on that fact every day while Jonah still lived.

Prince Jonah was a prodigy, instantly incredible at everything he'd done. In the great fight for the throne of Pyronia, Jonah was Thanatos's greatest weapon. Flint was always number two. But eventually, Jonah passed on to an incurable disease, as did Thanatos to age. Now Flintlock, 2nd son of King Thanatos, oversaw the entire city.

In his final days, Jonah had been acting strange. He would speak with Thanatos in the throne room for hours. He began to bring home these strange objects, but Flint always believed that they were meant to attempt to heal his sickness. One of which was a glimmering blade, which Flint had only seen from the corner of his eye as Jonah held it in his grip. Despite its enigmatical presence, it carried a sense of odd familiarity as well.

Later that night, Flint watched as the sun set over the shining city of Thanatos. His city. He thought about the rebellious prisoner that was captured. Something felt off about him as well. Zero personal records, no trace of even existing anywhere. It was almost as if the Rebellion had been trying to keep him hidden for all these years.

Flint called for his servant, Argus, who hurried into the room as fast as possible.

"Bring me to our new prisoner in the morning." He spoke, to Argus's obedience. "I would very much like to speak with him."

Chapter 4

"Yep, he's definitely dead."

Will laid on a cold, hard surface, motionless.

"He's only been down here a couple hours, give him time." Another voice said in conflict with the first. Will attempted to open his eyes, but to no avail. He tried again, shooting straight up with a loud gasp.

"Shit!" The first voice, who Will now saw as a young man, around his age, jumped back in surprise.

His sweat stroked hair was strewn about, and his pale skin grew flushed in the heat. His crimson shirt and red scarf were tattered and torn, paired with worn gray pants and dark hiking boots. The second voice, who was also around Will's age, was a girl. The girl stood up and held out her hand for Will to grab. She had long, brown hair, and wore a worn purple dress. She sported a rough and completely purple hat, which stood up in a bent cone shape with a small hand sewn star dangling from the tip.

Will took in his new surroundings. He was in a cold and dust-stained dungeon cell, seemingly deep underground. The walls were made of freezing stone, and the floor made of flat concrete.

"Where the hell am I? What happened?" Will exclaimed.

He grabbed the girl's hand and pulled himself off the ground. The young man took a step towards Will and crossed his arms.

"You were knocked unconscious by one of the guards. He said something about you not speaking up." Jack threw his arms out to the side welcomingly. "Anyways, welcome to our humble abode, or as everyone else calls it, King Flint's dungeon. The name's Jack, newbie. Put 'er there."

Jack stuck his hand out welcomingly, and Will shook it firmly. The girl stepped in front of Jack and introduced herself.

"My name's Becky. I'm a witch, or at least I'm trying to be." Becky languished downwards for a moment. "I don't really know how to cast spells yet."

Will spoke boldly.

"My name's Will. I'm with the Rebellion-" He paused, losing the light in his eyes. "At least I was." Will tried to wipe the notion of abandoning the Rebellion from his mind, turning away from his newfound acquaintances.

Hours later, Will leaned against the wall with boredom. He gazed his eyes towards Jack and Becky, who were whispering in the corner, seemingly staring at a clock of some sort. Suddenly, Becky waved Will over. He slugged his way towards the group and knelt.

"10 seconds." Jack whispered.

"10 seconds until what?" Will responded.

And then the lights went out. The entire dungeon was covered in a huge sheet of darkness. Becky took something out of her pocket and made her way towards the back wall. She put a key-like object in an opening between two stones, and the wall began to move. The stones, which were seemingly stuck together, began to slide apart creating an opening. A large door was unlocked, revealing a stone staircase.

"Come on," Becky spoke. "We want to show you something."

"Where did you get that?!" Will said, left in complete shock by Becky's key-like item.

"It was stuck in the wall when I first got here." She responded. "Apparently, this entire dungeon used to be an elaborate tunnel system for immigrants, and this was a leftover piece of it."

The three of them sneakily stepped down the bumpy stairs, which descended in a helix shape. The air was thick and dusty, and Will could feel his throat closing. Becky grabbed an unlit torch from the wall and pulled a nearby lever. Two dark stones scraped together quickly enough to create a spark, lighting the torch.

At the bottom of the staircase, there was a large metal door. It stood tall and imposingly, and Jack took a curved dagger from his pocket and attempted to pick the lock, while Will looked at him disapprovingly.

"What are you doing?" He said in monotone.

"Picking the lock, what's it looks like I'm doing genius?" Jack responded, and Will reached for the dagger.

"Give me that." He said, as he tore the blade from Jack's hand. Will knelt and began to pick the lock himself.

"What's wrong with you? That knife was my grandfather's personal hunting knife! It's a family antique! I can't believe you would just-" Jack was interrupted by the creaking of the opening door. "Oh. Would you look at that." He said in awe, and Will turned to Becky.

"You guys have never opened this door before, have you?" She blushed and looked away. The party of three stepped through the pathway of cobblestone, peering through the gaping doorway at the expansive interior.

The entrance to the ancient tunnel was filled with weaponry, with blades of gold and steel, as well as armor. Will stepped into the room in awe. Jack approached a golden chest plate, with one shoulder cap remaining. He strapped the chest plate around his torso and held his golden knife to the air in a heroic pose. Will advanced towards the center of the room, while Becky moved to the left side. The left wall was filled with objects that were unknown to Will, and he watched as Becky pulled a thin, cylinder-shaped item from the wall.

"Do you know what these are?" She turned excitedly.

"They look like a couple dusty sticks to me." Jack said cheekily, and Becky frowned.

"These are wands. Like, real wands. I've always wanted one..." She started to quiet her voice as she reached for a wand.

Will turned his attention again to the center of the room, where there was a platform with a strange shape sticking out of the middle. He grabbed the shape, which was in the form of a pole, and pulled on it a bit for play. Gazing downwards, he noticed a message on the platform below the object.

"He who wields The Blade of Atlas shall carry the weight of the world"

Will thought carefully, before Jack pushed him aside and began to pull on the object, which had been revealed as a sword.

"It's a sword in a stone!" Jack exclaimed as he gave it a tug, but to no avail.

Jack pulled as hard as he could, but the blade's gripped hilt hadn't moved. Will stepped in front of Jack and tugged on the sword.

"You have to pull it. Give it all you got!" Jack encouraged. Will thought of the warning listed below him.

Do I really want to carry the weight of the world? he asked himself. He thought of Darla, and the Rebellion. Anyone else would have agreed instantly. He thought of his parents, who had died in battle for him. Would they have pulled the sword? No matter what, he owed it to them. To everyone, for abandoning them out of his own selfish wants. Will closed his eyes and his muscles trembled as he placed every ounce of his weight into the force he exerted.

The platform under Will began to rumble just enough that only he could feel it. Before he could react, the sword slipped out of the stone beneath him, and Will held it in the air. The blade shined brighter than the torch Becky held, as it reflected a bright golden gleam.

"Congratulations, pal." Jack snarkily remarked. "You now hold the world's weight in your hands. Is it heavy?"

Will couldn't take his eyes off the tip of the blade.

"Shut up." He mumbled, as he walked towards a sheath and began to strap it onto himself. He slipped the sword into its sheath and regrouped with the others.

Will opened the exit door, which led through a long tunnel. Picking up his torch, he led the group down the ancient hallway. As they entered the ruined tunnel, Will noticed a switch of sorts on the wall.

"What do you think this does?"

Jack approached the switch.

"Let's find out."

Before Will or Becky could stop him, Jack flipped the switch, and the room made a groaning noise. The walls from either side of where the trio entered the hall began to close together, making an unopenable door.

"Now." Will started. "How are we supposed to get out if there's not another exit?"

"My bad." Jack flushed, cheeks rosy.

The three captives made their way down the hallway, and as they reached the end, it led to a turn. The turn led to another hallway, which led to more turns.

"We're going to die down here, aren't we?" Will stated negatively.

"Give it time. There must be some kind of exit here somewhere..." Becky replied.

For the next hour, the group wandered throughout the abandoned halls, in search of light.

Desperate to end the awkward silence in the seemingly endless search for escape, Will turned to Becky, attempting to start a conversation.

"So, Becky. Where are you from?" She looked over.

"I used to live with my family in the city. My dad was a wizard, so I always had a lot of pressure to live up to his abilities. One day, the stress was too much, and I ran away. By the time I had gotten over myself and I returned home..." She looked down. "They were gone."

Will turned his gaze over to Becky.

"I'm really sorry you had to go through that." He looked back in front of him. "I… Never knew my parents. They died before I was old enough to remember them. I was raised in the Rebellion."

Jack joined the conversation, stepping between Will and Becky.

"I never knew mine either. My dad died before I was born, and my mom… Went missing a long time ago. So, I was raised by criminals. They showed me how to survive off nothing but the ground beneath my feet, and how to make do on my own. Never ask for help, always keep on your feet, never…" He faltered. "Never trust anyone."

Will looked down as he processed Becky and Jack's lives. Maybe he hadn't had it so bad after all.

"Wow" Will spoke quietly, and Jack remained silent. Turning to face him, Will noticed an expression of confusion across Jack's face as he stared past him. "Jack? Is everything ok?"

"Look." Jack responded, pointing ahead. "Does that look like a light to you?"

Will looked forward and noticed a faint spark of shine in the distance. The three of them made their way to the light, which grew larger into a beam of sun, shining through a crack. The light led upwards a flight of stairs, and it shone through a crack in a rock door.

Will, Jack and Becky used all their might and cooperatively moved the rock and touched the dewy grass for the first time in seemingly ages. The sun shone brighter and more beautiful than Will had ever seen, as he watched it set before his eyes. Its golden glare buzzed in an orange tint as the sky surrounding it grew darker in its descent.

"Oh, sweet nature!" Jack exclaimed, as he dropped to his knees, feeling the dirt beneath him. Will realized that the other two had been in the dungeon much longer than he had, and that they may not have seen the outside for quite some time.

"So, what now?" Becky asked the others.

Will thought about how he had been missing from the rebellion for around a day at this point, and realized how much he missed his simple dorm and the rebellion's environment. It was so minimalistic in comparison to the rest of the kingdom, from the lumpy bed to the dying lamp in the corner, to the untreated gray plaster of the walls. Despite its flaws, seeing the cozy middle class houses before him, Will missed it. It was his home nevertheless, and in its absence it felt as if a small part of Will's soul had vanished with it. He turned to Jack and Becky, who looked toward him questioningly. With the shame of abandoning his friends, maybe bringing these two back with him could be enough...

"You three want to get back at the king, right?" He asked, and the others nodded confidently. "How would you guys feel about joining the rebellion?"

Chapter 5

Will, Jack, and Becky climbed over the hill to their right, and got a good view of their position. They were around five or six miles from the city, and a small town sat at the bottom of the large, mountain-like hill.

"Perfect." Jack stated. "We'll stay there for the night, and then make our way to the rebel base."

Will looked around.

"I don't think there are any hotels, and even if there were, we have no carchans to spend."

Becky looked carefully through the houses and spotted one in particular.

"Hey, that house still has lights on and smoke coming from the chimney. Maybe they could help."

Will and Jack nodded in agreement.

"It's worth a shot." Jack said.

Once they reached the town, the sun was already gone, and the sky was dark. The road and buildings were worn, as if they had not been cared for by the kingdom for a long time, yet the nature and atmosphere of the town was thriving.

There were street lights that lined the tattered road, flickering in the night from their dying light bulbs. The houses that surrounded the one still living had their own bit of life as well. One house stood out, being painted a shade of light blue with a wooden sign beside the door that read; *Doorbell broken - yell for entry.* Jack opened his mouth to shout, before Becky caught wind of his plan and threw her palm over his mouth.

As the trio reached the house, Will began to doubt that they had a chance at receiving generosity. In his past experiences, the people of Pyronia hadn't been the most kind.

Becky gave the door 3 careful knocks, and stepped back so that it could be opened. A woman stood in the doorway, holding her baby in her arms.

"I'm so sorry to bother you ma'am, but we've been traveling for a long time and need a place to stay for the night. Would you be so kind as to let us stay here?" Becky asked politely. The woman observed the three escapees with a seemingly shocked expression for a moment, before she smiled and responded.

"Say no more. Come in, all of you." She opened the door welcomingly, with a warm smile.

The woman's house was uniquely decorated, with pink wallpaper, and woven pillows gently laid on a cotton filled couch.

Two more young children ran through the halls of the pampered building, bursting with energy.

"Sit, please." The woman said, gesturing towards the couches. They all sat, and the woman left the room.

"What a kind woman." Becky stated. Will looked between the two of them and Jack butted in.

"Ok, what's the game plan now?"

Will looked down, solemnly.

"I actually don't have one."

The group stayed quiet for a bit, and the woman walked back into the room, with teas in uniquely colored mugs for each person. Her children ran into the room behind her, and one of them, a small boy looking to be around 8, stopped in front of Will.

"My mommy thinks you are the prophecy people." He whispered; however, his mother heard the comment.

"Finley!" She yelled orderly, and he sat down.

The rest of her children sat around him, and the woman sat in front of them all, facing Will, Jack, and Becky.

"Tell the story!" Her children shouted, and she smiled.

"Ok, Ok." She grabbed a book from off a bookshelf behind her and opened it to the first page.

"Once upon a time, the kingdom lived in peace. Everyone lived in unity, and Pyronia was safe. One day, the kingdom was taken over by a tyrannous man, who killed the king and crowned himself in his place. The kingdom of Pyronia was very sad, because now our beloved kingdom had fallen to chaos. But from the shadows, three heroes will arrive at the devil's doorstep. With the aid of a ghostly prince, and the Blade of Atlas, they will vanquish the tyrannous rule from the castle, and bring peace back to Pyronia." She closed the book.

"Again, again!" Her kids called, but she smiled and nodded her head.

"Not tonight, sweethearts. Come on, go off to bed."

They ran up the stairs to their room, and Will took a minute to process the story. *The Blade of Atlas...* He thought. Will pulled the Blade of Atlas from its sheath and placed it on his lap.

"No. Way." Jack exclaimed, looking at the sword.

"Are we...? No, we can't be..." Becky grabbed the sword, and inspected it carefully. "Guys... What if we are these heroes from the prophecy? We might be able to stop the king and save Pyronia from tyranny!"

Will put his hands up defensively.

"Woah, guys, come on. It's just a story." The woman re-entered the room, eavesdropping.

"But it's not. This is a story that has been told for almost 20 years. And it's true." She grabbed the blade from Becky. "This weapon has special abilities, some which people may consider supernatural. This weapon... It changes people. It can change its surroundings." She thinks for a second and grabs the book from the bookshelf once more. "'With the aid of a ghostly prince'..." She closed the book. "The grave of the late Prince Jonah is around 50 miles west of here. I can give you resources for the trip, but you must go. The kingdom is in dire need of you three."

Will looked between his newfound friends, who each seemed unsure.

"We'll do it." Will blurted.

The next morning, the woman had prepared days worth of food and water for the trip. Will slipped his clothes on, which the lady had so kindly washed. She had also packed him a few extra outfits, which would be nice for Will, considering he had worn the same outfits for the last 19 years of his life. As he stepped out the door to meet Becky and Jack, the woman came out behind him.

"Good luck, all of you. And thank you." She shook hands with Becky and Jack, who smiled in thanks to her hospitality. When she approached Will, rather than shaking his hand, she took something from her pocket, and held it out to him.

"What is this?" Will asked, taking the charm-like object.

"I was never sure. But it's an heirloom, meant to be given to a traveler found worthy enough to take it." She smiled warmly. "Perhaps it's a symbol of hope." She finished as she went back inside, and carefully closed the door.

As the trio left the outskirts of the town, Will looked back at the small village. So little to work off of, yet they had made such a nice community. It reminded Will of his home back at the rebellion, and he smiled. He hoped that one day every place in Pyronia would end up like this.

At this moment, he realized that the fate of Pyronia was now laid in his hands. He realized that alongside Jack, Becky, and whatever being they would soon meet, they would decide the futures of every man, woman, and child living in Pyronia. His smile faded away at this thought, and he wondered if he would be able to handle this responsibility. But he swallowed his indecisiveness, and stepped forward alongside his newfound friends.

Chapter 6

King Flint sat at a large, impounding golden table, thinking to himself. The royal dining hall was enormous, yet it only ever sat one man. The air was frigid, and the echoes of the chambers had been silenced. The wind was frozen in time, and the purple curtains which surrounded the windows hung still. The king was the only man in the room, left alone with his thoughts. He put one hand on his chin and rubbed his buzzed yet lively beard.

The castle had been empty for ages hence. Since the death of his brother Jonah, the castle had been practically uninhabited. Jonah had exceeded everything Flint had done and was more successful than him in many ways. He was a skilled fighter in battle and was highly intelligent in military strategy. Most of all, he was beloved by his father's followers. Even some citizens loved him, although they despised his father. Flint could never understand how Jonah achieved his status. All he knew was that he had a mysterious way with people. Until he had passed away, of course.

When Flint was close to 20 years of age, Jonah had fallen under a terrible illness. Flint's father brought doctors from across the kingdom, but to no avail. When Flint's father eventually died as well, Flint was forced to take the throne in Jonahs's place. In the present day, Flint still sits on the throne of the despised, living daily with the burden of his bloodline.

Suddenly, a ringing broke out. It got increasingly painful, and Flint dropped to the ground, gripping his ears. His sharp, golden crown fell to the floor with a clang as it touched the concrete. As the ringing grew quieter, a grisly voice grew louder.

I CAN HEAR YOU...

Flint's head felt fuzzy. He keeled over, wrapping his arms around his head. He began to breathe heavily and yelled to the voice;

"GO AWAY!"

The ringing grew higher, and he groaned as he hunched over.

OUR BLOODLINE IS NOT A CURSE... YOU ARE THE RIGHTFUL HEIR TO THE THRONE... YOU HAVE DISAPPOINTED ME...

"I apologize, father! Have mercy!" Flint pleaded with the voice, and the ringing began to slow. The fuzziness in Flint's head began to clear, and the voice spoke once more.

THAT BOY THAT YOU HAVE IN YOUR CUSTODY... HE IS THE SPAWN OF THEODORE AND NANCY LARSON... HE IS THE CHILD IN THE FORSAKEN PROPHECY... HE HAS ESCAPED YOUR COMPLEX... HOWEVER, HE WILL RETURN... WHEN HE DOES, YOU WILL KILL HIM...

"OK! I will obey your wishes, father!"

At last, the ringing and the fuzziness were gone, and Flint was left to silence once more. He breathed heavily and got up off his knees.

"My Lord?" Argus, standing upright, walked into the dining hall.

He stared at Flint with a concerned look.

"I'm fine, Argus." Flint spoke. "What is it?" Argus fixed his stance.

"My Lord, Kronos was looking for you."

Flint looked up, now focused on the news.

"He can wait. I will speak with him in the throne room later." Argus nodded and turned to leave the room, and Flint stood before he could be left in silence once more.

"Argus." Flint spoke, and his servant spun back to face the king. "Stay, won't you mind?"

"Oh, my lord, I'm sure you would rather eat alone. Besides, I have much to do, and-" Argus started, and Flint interrupted by sticking out his hand.

"Stay. Please." Flint ordered, and Argus nodded as he sat upon the opposite side of the table. Flint stood from his chair, and grabbed a spare plate that sat beside his own, waiting for a guest to use it at last.

He began to place food onto the plate from the center of the grand table, making sure to grab the most delicate food when he passed by it. When the plate was full, he walked over to Argus and placed the plate before him.

"My lord, I couldn't-"

"Eat." Flint interrupted. "You look exhausted. Take a break."

Argus wanted to argue against the king's order, but it was to no avail. He had to serve the king's every wish, even if he did not agree.

"A-As you wish, my lord." He began to eat slowly, savoring the food that had been given to him. "If you don't mind me asking, my lord, why did you ask me to stay with you here?"

Flint clenched his fist underneath the table to avoid thinking of why he didn't want to stay alone. After a moment of thought, he looked back up to his loyal servant, who awaited a response.

"I just enjoy the company, that's all." Flint spoke deeply, and Argus nodded.

Flint took the crown from his head as he watched his most loyal servant finally enjoy a meal before him. As he set the ornate crown down next to him on the table, he smiled for the first time in many years, seeing the joy upon the face of his faithful servant.

Chapter 7

Darla sat in the strategy room with Louie and Bella. She had gained faint strains on her cheeks from stress, and her red hair had been tinted gray. The past week has been a catastrophe. Louie broke the silence:

"Maybe they'll let him go. He could plead forgiveness or some crap, and they'll ditch him."

Bella kicked Louie from under the table, and he yelped.

"What the hell was that for? I'm right!" Louie said in defense.

"You know that he has no chance of being set free." She whispered. "It's already hard enough for Darla. Don't give her false hope."

Darla held her hand in the air, and the two were silenced.

"Listen." She spoke. "Will is incredibly arrogant, but he's innovative. He'll figure something out. That's not what I'm worried about."

She sighed and put her hand on her forehead. Bella looked at Darla concernedly.

"Darla... What happened?"

Darla looked up disappointedly.

"After Will was arrested, one of our members... lost faith in the rebellion. They left to live in the city. If they rat out to the king, which they have a great chance of doing..." Bella and Louie's hearts dropped.

"Holy shit... we could lose everything..." Louie said, slumping in his chair.

"So, that's why I brought you two here." Darla said, standing up with her hands on the table. "I want you guys to find this guy and take care of him. Try talking him into coming back or moving far away from the kingdom. If he won't listen... make sure to bring something sharp."

Bella looked shockingly at Darla.

"You don't expect us to... he was a member!" Darla looked coldly at Bella and walked slowly towards her, stopping right in front of her face.

"This rebellion is my life. This was the life's work of my father, and my father's father, and I will not let it crumble under my hands. If one man needs to die to save the entire rebellion... so be it." Darla turned around and left the room with her hands behind her back.

In the weapons hall, Bella and Louie prepared for their task. Louie observed the daggers, then moved on to the guns, but shook his head.

"I don't want to take a gun. It'd be too easy, y'know? I'm looking for something with a little pizazz." Louie spoke, and Bella growled.

"I don't give a shit what Darla says. We are not killing this guy."

"Come on. She had a point. If we ignore this guy, he could rat us out any day he wants."

Bella looked downward angrily.

"Let's just get this over with." She responded, and Louie grabbed an 8-inch blade from off the shelf and slipped it into a sheath.

"Perfect." He grabbed a gun and slipped in his pocket as well. "Just in case." He smirked.

The capital city of Pyronia was quiet at night. Bella and Louie walked through the empty streets, which were dimly lit by lamp posts. When they reached the house of the deserter, Bella knocked carefully. The two waited for a minute or so, and the door was opened by a young boy around the age of six.

"Hello!" He shouted enthusiastically.

Bella and Louie stood uncomfortably. Moments later a woman came up behind him and held his shoulder.

"How can I help you?" She asked, and Bella stepped up.

"We need to talk to Dave. Is he here?" The woman flinched.

"I don't know what organization you're part of, but Dave is not leaving again!" Bella looked back at Louie, who shook his head subtly. A man appeared behind the woman and grabbed her hand calmly.

"It's ok. Let me talk to them." The woman whipped around to face Dave.

"You are not leaving us again!" Dave's wife screamed. Dave looked at his wife solemnly and held her face carefully.

"I won't. I promise." He stepped outside and shut the door behind him. "Lou. Bella." Dave said as he nodded towards them. "Why are you here?"

Louie met Dave face to face.

"You're gonna have to come back with us, man." Dave clenched his teeth.

"My wife already told you. I'm not leaving."

Bella stepped in between Louie and Dave.

"We're worried about your safety. We... we could take your family back as well." She spoke.

Dave looked down.

"No. I won't put them in more danger. It was stupid of me to ever join the rebellion."

Louie intervened once more.

"Look man, if you don't come with us, it's gonna get gnarly."

Dave put his hand over his pocket, where a sword sheath sat hanging down his leg.

"The rebellion is even more corrupt than the monarchy. Do you know how many letters from my wife were intercepted by Darla? She wrote to me every day for 6 years. 6 YEARS. And I never got one. She thought I was dead. My only son thought I was dead. And for what? According to Darla, it was 'For the greater good of security'. You can't make me lose my family again. I won't let you."

He unsheathed his sword and held it out. Bella looked at Louie.

"Don't do it. Don't fight him." Louie ignored her and unsheathed his sword.

"I'm sorry, Bell." Louie swung the sword over his head and clashed with Dave's. All Bella could do was stand back and watch.

As the swords swung, the two men scrambled all over the place. Louie pulled his blade upwards, and it ricocheted Dave's sword in his house, leaving a huge chip in the stone wall. Bella heard a noise from behind her, as she saw Dave's wife, holding a gun. She aimed for Louie's head and held her finger on the trigger. Before she could fire, Bella tackled her, and the gun slid across the driveway.

"You bitch!" Dave's wife yelled towards Bella, as she threw rapid punches at her.

The two women were wrestling on the ground, as Dave and Louie continued to lunge at each other. Louie flicked his sword and disarmed Dave, knocking him back. Dave fell to the ground and grabbed his sword again, and threw his sword at Louies, knocking it from his grasp. Dave leaped up and punched Louie in the nose, and as he went for a second blow, Louie grabbed Dave's fist and threw him back to the ground aggressively. Meanwhile, Dave's wife beat Bella down to the ground, lifted her up by the shirt and slammed her into the wall of the house. Dave called for his wife, who was limping and covered in blood.

"Grab the walkie talkie in my room!"

Bella went pale. *Oh shit.* She thought. *He's already in contact with them.*

She stumbled back onto her feet and wiped her bloody face, just in time for Dave's wife to reappear. Dave kicked Louie to the ground and grabbed the walkie talkie from his wife.

"This is Dave. There are two rebels at my house right now. We were able to hold them off, but they are trying to kill my family-" Louie interrupted, punching Dave in the head with all his might, and he fell to the dirt. Louie caught the walkie talkie and smashed it on the ground.

"It's too... late..." Dave heaved. "They promised my family safety. They said if I helped them catch you all... they would be safe." Louie chimed in.

"We... didn't want to kill you... you... betrayed us..." Louie teared up. "We... are supposed to be... like family..."

Dave yelled in anger at Louie's childish comment.

"YOU ARE NOT MY FAMILY... THEY ARE..." He pointed to his wife, who was also tearing up. "When you lost the kid... Will..." Dave continued. "I knew... It was the end of the rebellion. You knew how... important he was to the cause." Dave coughed. "When I joined the rebellion, I thought... I was doing the right thing. But we... are no better... than them..." He pointed at the castle, and Louie stepped up.

"Dave, listen-"

Suddenly, an ear-piercing bang shook Bella's ears, and Louie yelped in pain. Dave's wife stood in the doorway with her gun aimed at Louie's heart. Her aim was shaky, so the bullet had lodged in Louie's side. Louie stepped backwards, holding his wound, and fell over.

Bella screamed in anger, as she ran over to Louie and knelt by him. Dave's wife gave her gun to him, and he held it loosely.

"It didn't have... to be this way. You could have left me alone... with my family... I'm sorry." He held the gun up to her head and began to remove the safety.

Suddenly, Dave's seven year-old son ran out of the house and saw the blood and destruction. Dave's wife put her hand to her mouth in distress.

"Daddy? Wh... What happened?"

Dave began to break down in tears and looked at his blood covered hands, and then to his son.

"My boy... don't look at me... I'm so sorry..."

Bella grabbed the gun from Louie's pocket. Louie had a busted lip, but he was able to mouth the words "*Do it.*". Bella removed the safety and held it towards Dave. Dave dropped to his knees in front of his son, dropping his defense, and Bella held the gun to the back of his head.

"I'm sorry..."

Dave whimpered to his son, who was pale at the bloody sight of the driveway. Bella began to tear up, and her arm was shaking like hell.

"No. I am." Dave's wife screamed, and Bella pulled the trigger.

BOOM.

Dave's lifeless body slumped to the ground, and his wife dropped on her knees sobbing. Bella lifted Louie on her shoulders and held Dave's wife at gunpoint as she limped away. She could see the lights of the royal army approaching the house from a mile away. She slid between an alleyway and sat Louie down behind a building. She used the rest of her drinking water to clean an old trash bag, and she wrapped it around Louie's wound. Louie looked up to her, and grinned.

"I'm gonna be fine... are you ok?" He coughed. She grabbed his hand and fell into his arms sobbing. He caressed her hair and comforted her.

"It's not... your fault." Bella took a shaky breath. "I know... I was worried that... I lost you." He pulled her in closer and kissed her chapped, bloody lips.

"Well, I'm still here, aren't I?" He chuckled, then coughed. She laid her head in his arms, and spoke.

"We're not like the monarchy, are we?" Louie looked down for a minute.

"Nah. Wanna know why?" She looked up. "Because they fight for the castle. We fight for the kingdom. What happened to Dave wasn't your fault. It was his."

After the sirens of the royal guard silenced, Louie got up, and lifted Bella up by the arm. While stumbling back up the hill to the secret rebellion entrance, Bella looked back one more time to Dave's house. She thought of the little boy's ghost-like face as he watched his father's death and shed a tear. She knew that boy would never be the same. Maybe the rebellion really was evil. If so, what was she fighting for?

Chapter 8

Meanwhile, Will, Jack, and Becky had been walking through the boiling desert searching far and wide for the grave of the late prince Jonah. They had almost run out of water and had run out of food a few hours before. At last, out in the distance, they saw a small desert village. The houses, unlike the ones in the previous town, were very run down. It was almost night, and they needed a place to stay.

As they approached the town, it became increasingly clear that it was a ghost town. All of the houses were broken down and abandoned, and there wasn't a person in sight, until Will spotted someone. There was an older man, who sat in a worn lawn chair by himself. His face was completely empty except for a scar going down his left eye. In his lap, he held an old, curved blade, which was etched with the words "Night Howler".

As the trio approached the man, he looked towards them slowly.

"Excuse me sir, do you know where everyone is?" Becky asked.

"There's no 'everyone'." He responded. "Only me out here." Will chimed in;

"Do you know a place we can sleep? Just for tonight?" The older man looked Will in the eye and spoke;

"Well, y'all can sleep anywhere you want. If you're looking for somewhere safe to sleep however, I guess you can stay in my barn out back for the night."

The man spoke in slurry words through his battle worn mouth as he pointed his thumb behind him towards a large-in-stature building, which was surprisingly not rotting. The doors were tall, wooden gates that slide open and shut, and the roof was made of carved tree bark.

"Phew! Finally!" Jack shouted as he threw his bag to the ground. The air is the barn was humid and dusty.

"Y'all can sleep on the hay if you please, there's bags you could stuff as a pillow if you really care." Said the man as he followed them in the barn. "I'll let you all get settled, and there's dinner in the kitchen if y' please."

Becky set her bags down.

"Thank you, sir!" The man left the room, and the three grouped up to make a plan.

"So, we get one night here, and then what?" Will asked.

"Maybe this guy knows where the cemetery is?" Jack contributed. "If he doesn't, then what?".

Will thought for a minute.

"I'll talk to him. Maybe he'll know directions to the next town, even if he doesn't know where the graveyard is."

Later that night, after dinner, Will set off to find the old man. He walked into his house and got a feel for the place. While seemingly rotten on the outside, the inside was surprisingly well kept. There was a rocker with an antique pillow, which seemed to be hand sewn. It sat next to a stone fireplace, and ancient paintings were hung in modern frames around it.

Above the fireplace, a long and jagged blade was hung. In curiosity, Will took the blade off its stand and observed it. There were words written across the handle, which read *Lupus Noctis.* He turned the blade in his hands, and gently felt the sharp curves of the bladed side. While he was mesmerized in the craftsmanship of the sword, Will heard a thump from the front porch. He set the sword carefully back in its stand and went to investigate.

The old man sat in an old wooden chair on the front porch, staring at the sunset. Will approached him, and sat next to him. The old man ignored him for a few minutes. Will eventually grew sick of the silence and broke it.

"I know it's not my place to ask, sir, but why do you live out here all alone?" The old man looked towards Will and chuckled.

"I know it'll be hard for you to believe young man, but this town used to be full of life. Children runnin' all over, mile long farms behind each house. It was nice." He remarked with a smile. "I used to live here with my wife, before she passed." He frowned. Will looked towards him with sympathy, and the old man looked back towards Will.

"I used to work for the old king, before he was killed. I was Chief of security for the king back in my day, and I led a group of men. They called me Wolf, because my men and I would travel like a pack of wolves in the night. My real name's Mike, but I haven't gone by that name in a long time. I used to be a master swordsman. That is why the king hired me in the first place. I've got blades out my ass, but each 'n every one's special to me." He looked down in shame.

"I retired around a month before the king was assassinated by that tyrant. If I'd only been there on that day..." He paused and looked curiously towards Will. "What're you three doing out here anyways? I haven't seen a single visitor out here in years, let alone three of 'em." Will smirked with confidence.

"We are trying to take down the tyrant king of Pyronia once and for all."

Wolf snickered in amusement at this ridiculous statement.

"You three? You've gotta be kiddin' me."

Will looked hurt.

"What's so wrong about that?" He asked. Wolf got up from his chair and looked at Will's sheath. He did a double take at the golden tip of the Blade of Atlas.

"Son... What's in that sheath there?" He said questioningly.

"What, this?" Will asked, taking the blade out of its sheath.

Wolf took it from Will's hands carefully and examined it with a gaping mouth.

"You..." He mumbled in shock. "How'd... how did you find this?" Wolf asked. Will shrugged.

"I found it in an armory underneath the castle while the three of us were escaping the royal dungeon." Wolf looked up in even more surprise.

"How on earth did y' three escape the royal dungeon? That place is impenetrable!" Wolf yelled, and Will sighed. This was going to take a while.

••

After about 30 minutes of explanations later, Wolf understood the situation.

"I can't believe I'm holdin' the Blade of Atlas. I searched for this for 30 years." The two sat in silence for a minute, and Will finally broke it.

"I've actually been meaning to ask you something."

Wolf looked towards Will.

"Go ahead, son." He spoke.

"We read this prophecy about the sword, and it says we need to find this ghost, but we have no idea where it might be. Could you help?" Wolf stroked his beard, for a moment, and responded.

"I know where it is alright." Wolf said, and Will smiled in excitement.

"That's great! Where is it?" Wolf had a dead expression.

"I'm not going to tell y'."

Will's excitement instantly disappeared.

"W-What? Why?" Wolf kept his dead expression and turned away from Will.

"None of you 're anywhere close to ready to fight King Flint. He is incredibly skilled with blades, and incredibly strong. They say his blade is so large, he can break an average man's sword in a single strike."

Wolf picked up the Blade of Atlas once more. "But this isn't an average man's sword. This blade is special. It carries powerful magic inside, magic that can potentially match the pure force of a meteor. But the wielder must be equally skilled. The power of the sword always matches the skill of the user. And you, son, are hardly skilled."

Will looked down in disappointment at the news.

"Isn't there anything I can do?" He asked, and Wolf smirked.

"Well, you're standin' right in front of a master swordsman, aren't you?" Wolf said. Will dropped to his knees and held his hands together in a praying motion.

"Please teach me your ways!" He pleaded, and Wolf chuckled at Will's childish gesture

"Go the hell to bed, son. Be up and ready by 6 am."

"Yes sir!" Will said, leaping to his feet, and running back to the barn.

Inside the barn, Jack was dead asleep, and Becky was reading a book with a small night light coming off the tip of her wand. Will stepped inside gleefully and laid back on the hay with a huge grin on his face. Becky looked over in surprise at his cheerfulness.

"So, does he know where it is?" Becky asked, and Will spoke.

"He sure does."

Becky sat up in excitement.

"Great! Did he tell you where it is?" She asked, and Will kept his goofy smile.

"Nope!" He spoke, and Becky frowned.

"So, what's making you so happy?" She spoke in confusion. Will sat up to face her, and filled her in on the story excitedly.

"Wow, that's great!" Becky said in support of Will's sudden enthusiasm. Will scooched over closer to Becky to see what she was reading.

"'Advanced spells and curses.' Huh." Will said in curiosity, and Becky smiled.

"I found this book at that kind woman's house back in that town. She let me keep it, so I've been trying to make good use of it." She said proudly, and Will grinned.

"Cool."

They sat in silence for a few minutes, and Will piped in.

"You said your dad was a wizard, right?" He asked.

"Yeah, why?" Becky said looking over, and Will responded.

"Well, what you said about them disappearing made me think. We have had a few wizards come in and out of the rebellion while I was growing up. Do you think one of them could be..."

He paused, and Becky bit her lip and looked the other direction.

"I don't know."

Will looked around for a second awkwardly.

"I bet he would be super proud of you. Y'know, for coming along. I was kinda forced into this with that whole sword thing, but it means a lot that you and Jack are coming along." Spoke Will. Becky smiled and responded.

"It's nothing, it's been nice being able to freely practice spells without being arrested or yelled at."

Will grinned warmly and laid on his back.

"Goodnight, man." he spoke as he shut his eyes.

"Night." Becky responded. But she didn't go to sleep.

Chapter 9

In the morning, Will woke at exactly 5:30 just as he had always in the rebellion. He took his last pair of clothes that the woman had packed him and found Wolf's downstairs shower. As he stepped out, he brought his old clothing to Wolf's washer, which was an antique, rather than an electric one like in the rebellion. It took a minute to get used to, but Will eventually finished and hung the clothes to dry. By the time he was done, it was 5:58. He walked back towards the front door, and was met face to face with Wolf, who had already gotten ready, and was sipping a coffee calmly.

"I would've shown y' where the shower was, but I see you've made yourself comfortable here. C'mon, let's get to work."

Will gripped the Blade of Atlas firmly and waited for Wolf to be ready. At last, Wolf left his house, gripping his blade that sat above his fireplace.

"My crew called this one *Lupus Noctis.* Have you ever taken Latin, kid?" Wolf asked, and Will shook his head. "It means 'Wolf of the night', because it moves swiftly and sharply, and if you aim for the right spot, your opponent won't even be able to make a sound." Will gulped in slight fear and got into a fighting position.

Wolf charged forward surprisingly fast, and with one light flick of his slick blade, the Blade of Atlas was knocked 6 feet from Will's grasp. When Will looked back over to Wolf, he was holding *Lupus Noctis* towards Will's neck.

"I guess I still got it." Wolf sneered.

Will embarrassingly walked over and picked up his sword as Jack left the barn, rubbing his eyes.

"Will," He spoke. "What are you doing?"

"Hey, Jack! I'm training with Wolf on how to use the blade!" Jack looked at Wolf with interest.

"What a sick name, man." He looked back at Will. "I think I'll watch, if you don't mind." Jack sat legs crossed on the ground and watched keenly.

Will charged towards Wolf aggressively and slashed down on his sword.

"That force was good, son. But remember to focus on your defense." Wolf flicked his blade upwards and twisted it to the right, disarming Will.

"What's your name, son?" Wolf asked and Will looked up.

"Will." He responded.

"No, your last name." Wolf stated.

"Larson." Will said, slightly confused. Wolf picked up the Blade of Atlas and tossed it to Will.

"Come on, Larson. Show me some spirit!" He said, charging at Will and slashing downward.

Will almost lost grip of the blade, but kept his firm grasp and slashed upwards, knocking Wolf back. He smiled in satisfaction, but Wolf broke his defense and whacked his sword from his hands.

"Don't let small successes get to your head, Larson. Focus! Again!"

Becky sat in the barn, completely exhausted. She had only slept 2 hours the previous night and couldn't rest a minute more.

She was on page 76 out of 207 in the spell book, and she had barely learned the curses from the last ten pages. She could only successfully perform around 20 of the 49 spells and curses so far, and it was clear that she would need training.

I'm not going to give up now. She thought confidently. She stood up, held her wand in the air, and aimed it at a bale of hay.

"Ok, here we go. Crystal thunder!" She focused all her magic on the wand, and a small shock came out of it. "Damn it!" Becky exclaimed, kicking the dirt.

Will fell on his ass for what felt like the hundredth time, and all he could hear was his sword clanging against the solid ground. Jack snickered from the background, and Wolf walked up and held out his hand to help Will up.

"Don't worry kid, you'll get it eventually." He said, but Will didn't believe it.

He'd been working all day and had no success. It was now one o'clock, and Will was exhausted. He looked up to Jack and saw that he had made some sort of snack.

"You think this is funny, huh?" Will asked Jack, offendedly.

"Hilarious." He responded.

Later that night, after six more horrendous hours of failure, Will slumped back in his hay bed. He breathed out with a heavy sigh and turned to his side. Jack was already snoring away, and Will was left in silence.

Maybe I'm just not meant to be a swordsman. Will thought to himself. *Maybe I would have been better off just leaving the sword.* He looked towards the Blade of Atlas, which lay right beside him, and sighed.

Suddenly, Will heard a scream of frustration coming from outside the barn. He shot out of bed and looked around. Will turned towards Jack, who slept through the noise easily, but Becky wasn't in the room. Will stood up from his hay bed and started toward the door.

As he snuck around the outer barn wall, he saw Becky, sitting with her head in her arms.

"Hey." He said, and she jumped.

Now looking at her face, Will noticed that she had drooping bags under her eyes. As he looked into her eyes, Will realized that he hadn't seen her all day.

"You good? I haven't seen you anywhere today." Will asked as he sat next to Becky, and she looked at him.

"I can't... do this. I can't get any of these stupid spells right." She said angrily as she threw the spell book into the ground. She lowered her head and wrapped her arms around her knees. "What if... what if I just wasn't meant to be a witch? What if I'm not capable?" She teared up a little, and Will grabbed his arm.

"Hey, uh, I think you're a great witch." He began to say. "I mean, I've only known you for like a week, but I've seen you practice a little, and I know I could never have the focus and patience for that stuff." She looked up and smiled a little.

"Thanks." She looked back down. "But... I've been practicing for years now... and I barely feel like I've improved at all. My dad was perfect at casting. He had been since he was a kid... he had a talent for it, I guess. I always had this pressure from my family to live up to him... but I just can't..." She said, tearing up again, and Will grabbed her arm.

"Hey, come on. I honestly don't give a shit how good your dad was, because he's had like 40 years to perfect it. No matter how much he wanted to say it, I don't believe for a second that he always knew what he was doing. No one does at first. All I care about is how skilled you are, and considering you've only been doing this for a couple years, you're way more advanced than kids your age should be."

He got up and grabbed the book.

"Look at this." He pointed to a label on the front. "This book is recommended for experienced wizards and witches over the age of 28. Dude, you're doing advanced adult level spells right now, while your peers are probably still working on High School level advanced spells." Becky looked up and into Will's eyes.

"I guess I never thought about it like that before." Will stood up confidently in front of Becky.

"Another thing, your dad isn't the one out here saving the world. YOU are." He grabbed her by the hand and lifted her off the ground. "It doesn't matter how long it takes, because I know you have the drive and skill to master every spell in that book. Hell, every spell in the world." Will said inspiringly, and she smiled.

"Thank you, really." She gave him a hug and went into the barn. "Goodnight." She called. Will waved his hand up and followed. *I'm damn good at giving advice.* He thought. *Maybe I should take my own advice...*

In the morning, Will got up bright and early again. He showered, made himself a coffee, and got into armor in record timing. Will had never been a scheduled person much, but when he really wanted something, he would well prepare for it.

By the time Wolf got out of bed and ready for training, Will had been half an hour ready.

"Now that's more like it." He chuckled. He unsheathed *Lupus Noctis* and held the tip towards Will. "You ready, Larson?" he asked slyly.

Will smirked confidently and gripped The Blade of Atlas. The gold sword shone brightly in the morning sun, and Will stepped his right foot backwards in a defensive motion.

Wolf charged first and Will seamlessly blocked his downwards strike. Wolf attempted to disarm him, but Will stepped aside and flung his blade upwards. It clashed against *Lupus Noctis,* and the two swords stayed idle, pushing against each other with equal force.

Wolf dropped some of his force, and Will stumbled forward in shock but was able to catch himself before Wolf could disarm him. He allowed for his blade to catch Wolf's as he tried to disarm Will again. Their blades were stuck idle again, pushing against each other, and Wolf cackled.

"You're gettin' real good, son." He said smiling. "But not good enou-"

Will interrupted Wolf by using his technique from earlier and stepped backwards as Wolf stumbled forward in shock.

He quickly flicked his blade up through Wolfs and disarmed him. He held the tip of his blade towards his neck in pride, and Wolf laughed excitedly.

"Haha, yes Larson! Perfect use of strategy! You learned from your mistake the first time we came together, recognized my technique, and used it on me in my most defenseless moment! Brilliant!" He exclaimed.

Wolf stepped backwards and pulled the Night Howler out from its sheath. Will remembered Wolf holding the blade when he first saw him on the porch.

"Listen up, son. If you can disarm me of this sword, you're ready to face the king. Also, I'm tired of having squatters in my barn. However, I am a sucker for a good sword fight, and this here's my greatest weapon. So, better get ready kid."

Wolf stepped back into his fighting stance and Will wiped the sweat off his forehead. The Night Howler was long and curved, like a crescent moon. Wolf spun it between his fingers, and Will realized that the curve would make it nearly impossible to collide with, as his blade would slide around the curve.

Wolf wasted no time and charged towards Will. Without hesitation, Will swung his blade upwards with all his might and collided with Wolfs swift sword, sending his hand upwards with the curved blade. Wolf sidestepped at the unexpected move, and lashed at Will while his back was turned. Will was barely able to reflect the blow, as Wolf continued to circle him.

Will continuously swung, missing each blow. It seemed that Wolf was very skilled in causing confusion and exhausting his opponent, and Will tried to think of a solution. Wolf jumped in the air and slashed down on Will's blade, and the tip of the curve almost pierced Will's forehead.

"Hey, be careful with that thing!" Will shouted in shock.

"The king won't be careful with you, will he?" Wolf responded snarkily, as he swept his leg under Will, tripping him.

He swung downwards again, clashing and pushing against Will's blade. Will was now on his back, placed in a position of disadvantage. He was sweating buckets, and Wolf grit his teeth.

"Come on, Larson! Think of how much you want this! Imagine I'm the king! He'll kill you!" Will gripped the sword as hard as he could.

"He'll kill your friends!"

Will thought of Jack and Becky, then of Darla and his loved ones in the rebellion, who were waiting for him back home.

"He'll kill your family!" Wolf barked.

Will thought of his father and mother, who he'd only heard stories of, because of the king.

"Everything you know and love will be gone!" Wolf pushed harder, and his blade came closer to Will's neck.

All Will could think of was the king, and how much wanted to hate him. He could feel himself almost connected with the sword, as he began to push upwards.

"No!" Will screamed as he pulled the Night Howler to the ground next to his head with his blade and used the pulling force to kick Wolf back with all his might.

Wolf grunted and flew, landing on his back on the dirt with a thud. Will shakily stood up, while Jack and Becky ran outside to see the commotion.

"Holy shit, Will, your eyes!" Jack exclaimed, pointing at Will's eyes.

Will felt his face, which felt sort of tingly. He looked at the Blade of Atlas on the ground, which almost looked like it was glowing. Jack and Becky ran up to Will concernedly.

"What's wrong with my eyes?" Will asked.

"Are you ok? There was this light coming out of them. You looked... furious." Will grabbed his arm in slight shame. He didn't mean to get that worked up.

Wolf coughed a bit, and Will ran over and knelt by him.

"You..." He wheezed but smiled. "You did good kid. Knocked the wind straight out my stomach, but y' did good."

Will slowly helped him to his feet, and Wolf put his hand on Will's shoulder.

"Well son, I had my doubts for sure. But I think I can say for sure that you're ready to fight the king. That thing you did with your eyes... It's like nothin' I've ever seen before. That right there is the magic of that sword, Larson. Don't lose it."

Will listened keenly to his advice and grinned.

“I won't, sir. Thank you.” He said and Wolf chuckled.

“Here you go, son. This here’s a map to the ancient graveyard you kids are looking for.” He said as he gave Will an old map. “Now get on out of here, I’ve got some cleaning to do. A lot more cleaning than I’ve had to do in 10 years.”

Will, Jack, and Becky grabbed their belongings, and let Wolf and his ghost town return to silence at last as they departed.

Chapter 10

King Flint sat at a large meeting table. Across from him sat the lead general of militia, Kronos. Kronos wore a battle-worn armor-suit of iron and technology, with straps and weapons all over. He wore heavy, dark boots, and metallic leg coverings. He wore a demonic gas mask-like covering over his face, and he made an audible wheezing noise through the mouth vent. Steam constantly came through the bottom, and the mask was heavily strapped around the back of his head. He sat in complete silence at the other side of the table.

To his sides, stood two low-level military men, standing at Kronos's side as support, even though he clearly didn't need it. Across his back, a long, jagged, and blood-stained scythe was strapped carefully.

"We have urgent news for you, my lord." One of the support guards said.

"The rebel has escaped. He took two prisoners with him." Flint sat up in his chair in interest.

"Inform me on these two." The second soldier walked up to Flint and placed two folders in front of him.

Flint opened the first one and read it in his head.

Jackson Murray: Level B12. Status: Escapee. Flint gazed downward towards the information section. *Knife user. Arrested for the theft of goods on Jasper Street. Stabbed personnel in the arm.* Flint closed the first folder and opened the second.

Rebecca King: Level B12. Status: Escapee. Flint looked closely at her description. *Mage. Arrested for use of witchcraft without a license.* Flint shut the folder quickly.

"Bring me the folder of the third escapee. Now!" Flint ordered.

The soldier ran and grabbed Will's file and presented it to Flint. He opened it and observed it.

NAME UNKNOWN: Level B12. Status: Escapee. Flint quickly moved towards his information. *Terrorist. Attacked personnel.* Flint slammed his hand on the table in distress.

"Is this all you have on this man?" He bellowed, and the guard flinched.

"Y-Yes, we don't know anything about him. He... doesn't have a birth certificate here. Or anywhere." Flint clenched his fist.

"Show me what they did." He ordered, and the guard showed him the evidence file. Flint read it carefully.

"A secret underground armory..." He observed.

Flint's eyes locked on a specific detail. *A stone slab sat in the middle of the room. It said that there was a "Blade of Atlas" which once sat in the stone. It was missing.*

"The Blade of Atlas... of course..." Flint said quietly, rubbing his beard softly. "This escapee is the child of Nancy and Theodore Larson. He wields his father's blade, the fabled Blade of Atlas." Flint said standing up. He looked at Kronos, who still sat dead still.

"Kronos. You have served me well for many years. This may be your greatest task." Kronos looked up slightly towards Flint, locking eyesight through the dark eye holes of his mask. "I want you to find these three. And I want you to kill them. No mercy. I trust you will bring me proof." Kronos nodded and stood up.

"Yes... My... Lord..." He gasped in an almost ghoul-like, raspy voice. Steam poured from his facial vent, and he left the room, followed by his two guards.

Flint sat alone in the meeting room, and he sighed. He knew how powerful that blade was and was doubtful that Kronos could beat the child if he understood the power of the Blade of Atlas. Reluctantly, the king knew what he must do. He got out of his large chair and left the room. He entered the lower hallway outside the throne room, and met Argus, who was walking out.

"My lord, the people need our assistance. Power is continuously going out in the east sector, and we don't know why. Crime has also spiked in the central sector since the terrorist attack earlier in the week. What will you do sir?"

Flint opened his mouth to speak and felt the horrible ringing in his head once more.

THAT IS IRRELEVANT... STAY FOCUSED...

"I will do nothing right now." Flint responded, turning away from Argus, and Argus walked away.

Flint turned towards the wall and pulled a secret lever that looked like a torch. The stone wall split and opened, creating a downward staircase. He went down slowly, grabbing a torch from off the walls. The castle had hundreds of ancient, secret rooms, which weren't connected to the power system. Most of the castle servants had no clue they existed, while some came across them by accident.

Flint reached the entrance to the room and held his torch up. His blade sat on a hanger on the wall, and he took it off carefully. He held his sword carefully in his large hands and observed it.

It was long, sharp, and forged with fifty pounds of pure ruby. It was around 6 feet in length, so large that it could intimidate a whole army just with its sheer size. Flint had used this blade for decades now, and it had taken the lives of hundreds of enemies. His grim reflection in the shine of the blade echoed decades of slaughter, the ruby tint covering the stain of blood upon its tip.

Flint took a moment to think about the future. The child with the Blade of Atlas holds the power to destroy Flint's legacy. If he didn't act now, Flint's power in Pyronia would be terminated. Flint strapped his large sheath around his back and slipped his massive ruby sword inside. He strapped on protective gear in preparation for battle. He knew it was a matter of time until the three from the forsaken prophecy arrived at his doorstep, and Flint would be prepared.

Chapter 11

One day after leaving Wolf's abandoned town, Will, Jack, and Becky were getting incredibly exhausted from the long trek.

Will unfolded the old map that Wolf had given him for the millionth time and looked for their destination. It seemed like there was another town just before the graveyard. As the sun began to go down, the town was absolutely nowhere in sight. So, without another option, the three of them were forced to set up camp in the desert.

"I hate the desert so fucking much." Jack complained, wiping sweat off his forehead. Becky frowned.

"Come on, Jack, watch your language." She snarked.

"Ok, mom." He responded cheekily.

Will lay on his back and gazed at the sky. For the first time this week the stars were out, and the heat didn't bother him at all. Becky noticed his focus on the sky and mirrored him.

"Stars are out tonight," he said calmly.

"Aren't they gorgeous?" She responded.

Jack laid his head on the ground as well.

"I'm gonna sound like a douche for saying this..." He started. "What if we just don't fight the king? I mean, it's just us now. We can do whatever we want!" He said excitedly, and Will gave him a stink eye.

"Come on man. You know how many people are looking up to us right now. Would you really throw that all away?" Will asked him.

"If it meant I could be free from the king and never be caught? Definitely." Jack responded, and Becky scoffed. "Think about it, guys. I'm just saying, it wouldn't be all that bad." He said in defense.

"You're a dickwad, you know that?" Becky said in disgust, and Jack shut his mouth.

After around 30 minutes of rest, it seemed to be around nine o'clock. Will realized that none of them had eaten dinner yet, and he stood up.

"I'm gonna go catch dinner. Beck, want to come?" But before Becky could answer, Jack leapt up and interrupted.

"Actually, I want to come. We can have, like, a guy's time or some shit." Will was shocked by Jack's sudden urge to volunteer.

"Uh... sure man. I don't care." He responded. Therefore, Will and Jack set off into the desert in search of food, while Becky tended to the fire.

"So..."

Jack started while he walked alongside Will.

"What's up with you and Becky?"

Will jumped in surprise at his question.

"Nothing man. I swear." Jack shook his head.

"You like her, don't you?" He said with a large grin, and Will's cheeks grew warm.

"Hey, shut up! What are we, third graders?" He said defensively. Jack held his head high and closed his eyes a bit.

"I don't blame you, man. You must not have met many women before. It isn't necessarily a bad thing." Jack said passively, and Will looked at him in confusion.

"What's so wrong about Becky?" He asked, and Jack opened his eyes again.

"I knew it! You do like her!" He shouted, pointing at Will, and Will rolled his eyes.

"Come ON, man. I've known you guys for like a week. Not even." Jack looked away.

"Alright man. Whatever you say."

Suddenly, a scurrying noise was made in the distance. It was a meerkat, who ran and dove into a hole. It stuck its head out, and Will crouched quietly. Jack kneeled beside him and stopped him from moving.

"Dude. Are you really gonna catch it with that?" He said, making a gesture towards the Blade of Atlas. "I have this." Jack continued, holding his dagger in the air. "Lemme do it."

Jack started towards the meerkat slowly and quietly. He gripped his dagger firmly and focused.

As he approached the meerkat, it began to slowly climb out of the hole. It kept climbing, until it was clear that it was not climbing, but slithering. As its entire body left the hole, Jack stumbled back a little in surprise.

It had the head of a meerkat, but the long, slithery body of a large snake. It opened its mouth to show its venomous fangs to Will and Jack.

"It's a meerking!" Jack shouted with excitement. "I read about these in a book I found once. Their venom is 3 times as strong as a python!"

Jack held his dagger in a battle stance, and Will gulped nervously before Jack continued. "Well, what're you waiting for? We're gonna need that sword now!"

Will hesitantly unsheathed the Blade of Atlas and took one step forward.

"I got to tell you something man." Will said quietly, and Jack looked over. "I'm like, deathly afraid of snakes." He spoke, and Jack grinned.

"Come on. Let's catch us some dinner." He said, as he charged the meerking.

He leaped over its head, landing behind the tail and stabbing it in the back. It jumped and attempted to bite Jack ferociously. As Will watched, Jack dove on top of the meerking, holding it to the ground with his hands.

"Will, kill it now!" He shouted as he struggled to keep it on the ground.

Will began to sweat uncontrollably and stepped forward reluctantly. He held his sword out shakily and held his ground. He lifted the sword over his head, closed his eyes, and struck it down.

Will opened his eyes and jumped with a shriek when he saw the blood running towards his shoe. Jack broke down laughing and picked up the body of the meerking, which was now decapitated.

"Lookie here." He said, waving the meerking in front of Will. "Dinner."

As Will and Jack turned back to head towards the camp, Jack stopped Will in his tracks.

"Hey man, sorry for being such a douche earlier. Let's save the world together, huh?" He said, holding a fist up for a fist bump. Will bumped his fist.

"Sure thing dude." They began to walk back to camp, holding the body of the meerking they had caught together for dinner.

•••

"What the hell is that!" Becky yelped as she saw the meerking.

“Dinner.” Will and Jack said in unison.

Becky sighed and took it from their hands hesitantly. Jack found a long stick and stuck it through the body of the meerking, and Will created a support for it to rest over the fire with a few stones. As the meat sizzled over the flames, Jack and Will sat next to Becky and watched pridefully.

“At this rate, we should make it to the graveyard by tomorrow.” Will said, looking at the map again.

“There’s a little town next to it.” Becky pointed out. “It looks nice.” They all peeked in to see the small outline of the town.

As soon as the meat was done over the grill, the three wasted no time devouring it. The meerking was divided evenly between the trio, and it had filled them to the point of bursting. After a bit of relaxation, they decided that it was time to get some shut eye.

As Will lay on his back, he thought of the meerking and shuddered. He reminded himself not to get lost in the desert again.

Chapter 12

Darla sat in the infirmary, awaiting Louie and Bella's awakening. Bella slowly opened her eyes and looked towards Darla.

"How long have we been here?" Darla stood up and approached her.

"Two days, more or less." Bella sat up and turned her gaze towards Louie.

"Will he be ok?" she asked worriedly.

Louie was quieter than he had ever been in the last 14 years of his life, as he lay still in the hospital bed.

"They pulled the bullet. Thankfully, it didn't leave any lasting effect." Darla said solemnly, as she looked down on Louie. "They think he might not wake up for a little while. He lost a lot of blood. He needs some time to recover." Bella grabbed his hand and squeezed it, reflecting on what had happened the night before with pain.

After a moment of silence, Rose entered the room quickly, eager to give Darla news. She had short brown hair, sloppily cut with a knife down to her neck. She wore a white shirt under a shoulder strap, and had a pistol strapped to her belt around the back. Up

Bella's left arm, a tattooed rebellion insignia wrinkled from stress. A silver badge hung from her right breast, proving her authority to be just under Darla's own. She sat next to Darla and Bella and crossed her arms.

"We have bad news, Darla." Rose said, and Darla turned towards her. "A few guards are onto our location. After the whole situation with Dave, some neighbors came out and told the army that they saw a few suspicious individuals exit the woods before the attack. A couple hours ago, one of our lookouts spotted six armed soldiers sent to search this area." Darla rubbed her forehead in stress, but grinned and stood up in realization.

"This is great news, actually. I've been looking for an excuse to get out of here and do something fun." Darla said, taking her mace out of its case.

"Rose, go let Kendrick know he's in charge for a bit. Bella, are you up for another mission?" She said, offering her hand to Bella. Bella looked back towards Louie, who still lay sound asleep.

"I don't know... I want to be here for him when he wakes up." she said unsurely.

"I'll have Rose watch over him. She'll let us know if he wakes while we're gone." Darla said as she left the hospital room, leaving the door open for Bella behind her. Bella sat, and turned to face Rose, who stared at her concernedly.

"Is everything alright, Bell?" She asked in her southern-esque accent, and Bella looked away.

"Well, I just," Bella started. "I had something I needed to tell Louie, that's all."

"Oh." Rose spoke, intrigued. "Something good?"

"Yes," She started. "Well, no... I don't know!"

"Just spit it out, sister." Rose pushed, and Bella took a breath.

"I don't want to go into too much detail. But I need to tell him before he gets the wrong idea." She spoke desperately, and Rose leaned in jokingly.

"He gets those a lot, so it wouldn't be too out of the ordinary." She chuckled, but Bella was too preoccupied to laugh. Before she could continue, Darla stuck her head back into the room.

"Well? Are you coming?" She asked, and Bella jumped at her appearance.

"Yes, I'm coming out, don't worry." Bella spoke as she bit her tongue and got up off the bed. She knew that Louie would have wanted her to go, so she followed Darla out of the infirmary.

Inside the weapon hall, Bella didn't hesitate to grab a weapon. Unlike the previous situation, she knew who she was fighting, and she wouldn't allow herself to be put in a defenseless position again.

She grabbed a sickle, and strapped it over her shoulder. She changed into a camouflage outfit, grabbed a container of liquid bandage, and met up with Darla.

"Ready?" Darla asked with a subtle smile. Bella looked down into the reflection of her face in the sickle's sharp blade, and looked back up at Darla.

"Ready."

The forest surrounding the rebellion base was alarmingly silent. The only noise heard for miles was the bristling of the spring leaves atop the gigantic trees that swayed in the noontime breeze. Bella gripped her sickle firmly as she followed Darla's footsteps quietly.

Suddenly, Darla came to a harsh halt, and turned to her right. She made a pointing motion with her hand towards a ditch next to the road. It was blocked from the road by two thick bushes, and Darla hopped down onto her knees. Bella followed, and lay on her stomach next to Darla, with her eyes on the road.

"Do you think they'll be armed?" Bella whispered.

"Considering their job is to defend the wealthiest man in the kingdom, I would bet on it." She responded.

After what felt like hours, but in reality was 45 minutes, three figures began to approach from afar. As they grew nearer, Bella observed them.

There were two tall men with lighter skin, one with black hair and one strawberry blond, and an averagely sized woman with dark skin, as well as dark hair. The men held swords in their respective sheathes, and the woman held a double pointed spear by her side.

"Stay focused, men. This could be the most important day of your lives." The men held their heads up, and followed behind her.

"Yes, lieutenant." They responded.

As the soldiers began to pass the two of them, Darla gestured towards them, and began to count down from three with her fingers. As the soldiers passed, Darla finished counting, and she leaped up through the bushes with her mace, and slashed down the backs of one of the men, tearing through his leather protectant.

He yelled in surprise, and swung his sword towards Darla, who quickly knocked it out of his hands with a strong uppercut from her mace. Bella, eager to help Darla, leaped up and sliced with the sickle. She had a lucky aim, and her blow landed perfectly on the neck of the man Darla had hit, cleanly slicing his head off its stem. Bella screamed in disgust, and jumped back as the head of the middle-aged soldier rolled in front of her.

The lieutenant spun her doubled edged spear between her fingers and grit her teeth, as she charged towards Bella with an echoing war-cry. Bella desperately tried to block the blows from the lieutenant, but she moved too quickly. One edge of the spear scraped along her stomach, and Bella screamed in pain. The woman proceeded to use Bella's distraction to her advantage, and knocked her onto her back with a powerful kick.

"Die, rebel scum." She growled, as she raised her spear to impale Bella through the heart.

"Lieutenant Pandora!" The blond hair man yelled as Darla disarmed him of his sword.

But before Lieutenant Pandora could move, Darla roughly slammed the spiked ball of the mace into the face of the soldier. Pandora yelled in anger, and charged Darla.

Bella tried to get up, but the slash on her stomach stung like hell. She reached into her pocket and took out the liquid bandage she had grabbed in the armory. As Bella put it on her wound, Darla and Pandora slammed their weapons together ferociously.

"I've seen this one a few times," Said Pandora, gesturing towards Bella. "But not you." Darla smirked.

"That's the point, bitch." She said, as she attempted to disarm Pandora, but failed. Pandora grit her teeth in rage at the remark, and charged Darla with a flurry of aggressive attacks. Darla held her stance with her mace, even though Pandora was strong.

Darla attempted to disarm her once more, and failed again. Pandora used her failed attack as a chance to jab at Darla, and stabbed her in the right breast. Darla flinched at the pain, and Pandora kicked her onto the ground.

"DARLA!" Bella yelled, leaping on her feet. Pandora turned towards Bella, and Bella held her weapon in preparation, but Pandora began to sprint down the road instead of approaching her.

"No... NO!" Darla screamed, as she struggled up onto her feet, and began to run after Pandora.

Bella followed behind her, but Darla was much faster than she was. By the time Bella caught up to Darla, she was stopped in front of the entrance to the base. Pandora was gone, and Darla began to walk towards the entrance to the base. As she put her hand on the doorknob, she pulled the door slightly outward, and it opened. The door had been left open.

"I didn't leave the door open..." She whispered, holding her mace ready. Bella and Darla rushed through the door and entered the rebellion hideout. "Where is she!?" Darla yelled to the bystanders inside the walls.

"Where is who?" One responded. Darla dropped to her knees and sighed. She had failed, and the king now knew of their location.

"Everyone..." Darla started, getting up.

"Pack your things. The king knows where we are. We have another base, but it's very far away. It may not be in perfect condition either, but it will have to work. We probably have around 2 hours before the king's men get here. So work efficiently." Darla walked towards her room, soon to be former room, and slammed the door.

Bella entered the hospital, and sat next to Rose and Louie. She held Louie's hand softly, and Rose turned towards her.

"How'd it go?" She asked.

"Pretty bad." Bella spoke in a melancholy tone, and Rose tilted her head in worry. "One of them got away. The king knows where we are."

Rose fidgeted her thumbs in anxiety at the news, and sighed. She and Bella sat for a moment in nervous silence processing what had just happened, and suddenly, Louie began to stir at last and Bella jumped before giving him a tight hug.

"Woah there." He said drowsily. "What happened?"

It had felt like ages since that night in the city, and Bella felt many feelings seeing Louie awake after everything that had happened between them. But despite it all Bella closed her eyes, completely embraced in his arms that had finally stirred from their slumber. And with this silent warmth, just for a moment, she forgot where she was.

Chapter 13

Lights flickered far in the distance. Will, Jack and Becky could see the edge of the desert town in the distance, just as the sun was going down for the night once more. Will held the Blade of Atlas in his hands and looked at his darkening reflection on the golden sword, hoping for a sign that the ghostly grave was near.

The town was run down, but still in living condition. Will looked up from his sword as they grew closer to the town and noticed people watching them from out their windows atop the houses. He wondered if news of their travel as prophetic heroes had spread across the kingdom, and bit his lip in fear of the king's awareness.

As the three of them reached the outskirts of the town, Will observed the land around him. It was very different from the town next to the kingdom they had met that gentle-hearted woman in.

On Will's left, there was what seemed to be a tire, which had been lit on fire through the center. Two men sat around it in old coats, sitting with their legs crossed. Dust swirled around them in the desert breeze, and they tried to ignore its scratchy brush.

On his right, an alley was shoehorned in between two brick buildings. It had art strewn along its surface from top to bottom in a barrage of colors. The names "K & K" were sprayed on top, acting as a sort of signature.

As the sun disappeared from the sky, the trio were becoming exhausted from the walk. Becky decided to approach a nearby house and knock on the door. The owner carefully opened the door slightly and peeked their eyes outside.

"Hello sir, or ma'am?" Becky asked politely. "We aren't from town and have been traveling all day. Do you know anywhere we could sleep for the night?"

The figure behind the door peeked their eyes out more to get a good view of the three of them, and responded;

"Get lost!"

He shut the door quickly, and Becky turned around in shock looking at the guys.

"Second time's the charm, right?" she said enthusiastically.

••

After about an hour of both polite and harsh rejections, Jack stopped Becky in her tracks.

"C'mon, Beck." He pleaded. "Let's just call it quits and sleep on the street tonight." Becky stood her ground.

"No. I refuse to believe there isn't one kind soul in this town." Will stepped up and put his hand on Becky's shoulder.

"I've got to agree with Jack. We shouldn't bother anymore of these people."

Becky sighed, and they walked back towards the tire that Will had spotted earlier. The two men were still sitting there, and Will sat next to one of them.

"Do you two mind if we stay here for the night?" Will asked hopefully.

"Be my guest." The first man responded hopelessly.

Jack and Becky sat down next to Will, and Will crossed his arms. It was early spring, but the end of winter still blew subtly through the air. Papers blew in the chilling breeze of the desert at night, and the golden moon watched as the few plants that grew in the rundown town bent in the poor conditions. The night chill began to reach Will through his chest, as he noticed that his shirt was slightly ripped. He began to shiver audibly, and Jack noticed after a moment, pulling his scarf off over his head and offering it to Will.

"Oh, I don't need-" Will began, but Jack held his arm out sternly. Will took the scarf and wrapped it around his neck. "Thank you. You didn't have to do that." He said with a grin of appreciation, and Jack nodded his head.

"Of course, man." He said, responding, as he laid down upon the ground.

Becky took out her spell book and began to flip through it under the firelight. She stopped on a spell called *Gelida Flamma*, and Will scooched closer in interest.

"You gonna try that one?" He asked.

"Yeah." She said quietly, as she got on her feet.

She turned her aim towards a garbage bag that lay against the wall of a close building and planted her feet firmly. She slowly lifted her wand, and took a deep breath.

"*Gelida Flamma.*"

She said under her breath, as a small blue spark shot from her wand. She clenched her fist in annoyance, and Will stood up to comfort her. She tried a few more times, but to no avail.

On her fifth attempt, Will decided to pick up the book and observe the page.

"What am I doing wrong?" Becky said in anger.

Will looked closely at the imaged demonstration and noticed something.

"It looks like this guy is blowing on the wand as he casts the spell." He said observingly. Becky took the book from his hands and looked carefully.

"It's worth a shot." She said hopefully.

Becky stood her ground firmly, held her wand towards the bag, and shouted.

"*Gelida Flamma!*"

She blew air forcefully against the tip of the wand, and a flurry of blue flames engulfed the garbage bag. The bag began to melt in the pure heat of the flames, but as soon as they stopped coming out of the wand, the entire bag was quickly and sharply frozen over in a fast wave of spiked ice. Becky gasped in excitement and jumped in the air squealing.

"I cast the spell! Christ, I can't believe it!" She hugged Will tightly, and he stepped back shocked.

"Hey, good job!" He replied proudly, and Jack clapped his hands praisingly in support.

"Let's go, Beck!" He shouted, and Becky smiled and sat on the ground beside Jack, and Will followed. Both men who watched sat in astonishment.

"Impressive. Very." The second one said, "But I'd watch your back here. Spell users are very... disliked here."

Becky lost her grin and gave a confused look.

"Why?"

The first man looked over grimly.

"King Thanatos was a sorcerer. This town was the first one he attacked in his raid. Many good men died because of him." He spoke. Will piped in.

"Thanatos... He was Flint's father, right? He... killed the king." The old man nodded solemnly.

"He was the most powerful and feared sorcerer in the Kingdom. When he came here on his quest to steal the castle... Lots of people died. And not..." He paused. "Not just the men."

Will placed his hand over his mouth lightly and grimly.

"After seeing what Thanatos could do 60 years ago..." The second man spoke. "They've been terrified of sorcerers."

Becky looked down upsettingly. After around an hour of mostly silence, Will, Jack, and Becky laid down asleep. The two men followed soon after, and the fire slowly died out in the night.

Will awoke to sounds of screaming. He shot up and noticed the faint sunrise in the distance. He looked to his left and saw Jack, who had also been awakened by the noise. The two men slowly got up from the ground, and Will stood up next to Jack. Becky was missing.

Will ran out into the street and heard screaming from the town square. He and Jack rushed down the empty road, stopping in front of the fountain. The fountain sat in the center of the town square, but no water came out. Twelve men had surrounded Becky and were tying her to a wooden pole. One of the men lit a match, and another poured gasoline around her feet while laughing. Becky screamed for help through a gag wrapped around her mouth, and one of the men yelled ferociously;

"Death to the witches!", while other men laughed around him.

"Hey!" Will screamed as he sprinted toward the men and unsheathed the Blade of Atlas, with Jack following, unsheathing his own sword.

One man, who seemed to be their leader, stepped forward.

"What the hell do you think you're doing, kid?" He asked, and swung his hand in a gesture toward Becky. "This is a witch. She was seen terrorizing our town last night." Another man came up to the leader and whispered something in his ear. "Wait a minute." The leader said loudly. "You two are with her. The witch." He looked at his men. "Get them. I want them dead. And kill that witch already."

The man holding the match tossed it onto the ground and it touched the gasoline. Flames began to rise and were about to engulf Becky completely.

"No!" Will screamed, and before he could do anything, he was moving.

He felt the same tingling sensation that he had at Wolf's house, and he raised his sword. In less than a second, his sword swiftly chopped the leader's head clean off, and Will ripped Becky from off the post with incredible strength. Will had moved so fast that he couldn't feel his legs, and he just as quickly lost the tingling.

"Ugh..." Will said, stumbling as he gripped his head in discomfort. The men stepped back in shock of Will's actions.

Will slowly raised his sword, expecting a fight, but all the men kneeled in front of him.

"That sword..." One spoke. "You are the man in the prophecy..." Will heaved in exhaustion. Whatever the sword had let him do, it had drained all energy from him.

"Yeah." He responded. "Yeah. I am. And that woman you almost just burned alive is my partner." The men looked down horrified.

"Please, chosen one, spare us!" One begged, and Will frowned.

"I shouldn't, but I'll let you off with a warning this time." Will dropped the act for a moment, reminding himself of his uncomfortable position. "A new shirt would be nice though."

One of the men ran quickly into the nearest house, and Will looked back at the man he had killed. His head lay stagnant on the small pool of blood, and Will bit his tongue before he could retch from shock at what he had done. Looking around him, the man's gang were left with similar repulsed and horrified expressions, and Will nearly felt an ounce of sympathy for them.

"Tell the others in this group of yours." Will started, lowering his tone once more. "Let witches live in peace. Sorcerers too. You might fear them after what Thanatos did to your town, but they aren't all like him. Treat them with the same respect you'd treat another citizen with." He said sternly, staring dead into the eyes of the first man. The man stuttered and looked up.

"Y-yes, we'll change, we won't bother witches. We promise!" Will turned around coldly and approached Jack and Becky, before the man stopped him. "There's only one issue. The man you killed was our leader, and now we'll be without jobs."

"Good." Will responded. "Find a better job next time."

"You don't understand." The man pleaded. "The king's forces bring nothing to this land. We are hardly able to survive without the reward the crown gives for a sorcerer."

"Look, I'm sorry, but we really have to be going." Jack interrupted. "We have a kingdom to save and all that."

As Will, Jack, and Becky grabbed the few things they had to continue onward, Will put on a new shirt one of the guys had grabbed him. It was a long-sleeved, dark blue shirt, made of a denser material than Will's previous garment, yet Will was wrapped in the same vibe as his rebellion shirt as it clung around his chest.

He slipped the Blade of Atlas into its sheath, and took 20 carchans out of his pocket, which were the coin-based currency of Pyronia, and divided them between the two homeless men he had met.

"This should be enough to get you two into apartments for a week." Will said. "Use them to your advantage. I trust you guys." He began to walk away, and one of the men stopped him.

"Thank you, chosen one," One of the poor men spoke. "But our town is doomed to repeat itself soon enough. We are poor, without the support of the king. The land is too dry for vegetation, and the enforcers had now been removed from their position. Without steady leadership, there's no telling what may befall our town."

Will struggled in conflict with the reality of what the poor man had told him, and what he would be leaving behind. Would leaving the town to free the kingdom be worth the cost of chaos? Would it be worth the thousands of lives thrown into despair in the lack of leadership?

"He is right, chosen one." One of the enforcers said, approaching the two. "Without some form of stability, our community is doomed."

Will looked up at one of the worn buildings to his left, where a young boy watched him in awe through a second floor window. When he caught Will's gaze turning to him, the boy whipped the tanned curtains shut as if he were to be punished for simply watching.

"We need a new leader." Another enforcer said, and he knelt before Will. "We need you."

The rest of the enforcers began to kneel in unison, and Will was left mouth agape at the action by the men who had been trying to kill him just moments before.

"I..." Will struggled to speak while the enforcers waited for a response. The town had been run into the ground from the lack of royal support and trade. The isolated community had been thrown into a desperate decision, allowing the discriminative enforcement to lead them. Now watching them, powerless, Will only saw pain upon their sagging, tired faces. They needed someone who could be looked up to, and trusted. Even if he didn't feel like much of a leader himself, Will knew that the Blade of Atlas gave these people a spark of hope, even in most desperate times. With that crossed on his mind, Will nodded confidently.

"I will. It's time your town is freed from chaos."

Chapter 14

"What the hell do you think you're doing?!" Jack whispered sternly to Will, taking him aside as the enforcers chatted excitedly amongst each other. "Did you forget that these guys tried to quite literally burn Becky alive like 10 minutes ago?"

"They're misguided, and they need leadership. If I can give them that, then I will. Our job is to protect and serve the kingdom, right?"

"No, our job is to save the kingdom ONCE, and then move on with our lives!" Jack shouted in a whisper, and Will sighed.

"It'll just be for a week or so, that's all. I just need to make sure these people can survive on their own, okay?" Will told Jack, who remained unpleasant, but nodded silently.

By the time the people were dispersed and the streets were empty once more, word had already spread across the community of the enforcement leader's death and the new leader. Every time he turned his head, dozens of faces peeked to see the figure Will through their shaded windows. Some stuck their head out the window for a better view, but were too worried to wave or make themselves noticeable.

When they had finally reached where Will and the others would be staying, Will bit his lip in shame. This must have been the home of the previous leader, as it was the only well kept home in the entire town. There were large, ornate fences that surrounded the perimeter, with a gate unlocked with a key given to Will as they arrived. The walls were dense and soundproof, with the entire territory being powered by a generator. It was like an oasis in an empty, desolate wasteland.

Entering the building, Will's gut sank even further as he saw what their leader had been hoarding. A soft, velvet couch was placed in a fine, rug covered living space with a mahogany coffee table and a flatscreen television, which Will had never before seen in his life. The bathrooms were spotless and lined with soaps unheard of to Will, and the bedrooms were no different. The room where Will would be staying was the old leaders quarters, which contained a large queen sized bed with a lamp and multiple bookshelves beside it. The guest room contained the same, colored differently and without the bookshelves.

"Dibs on the couch." Jack said, throwing himself on top of it in a relaxing position. "I haven't watched TV since I was like nine."

Will couldn't find the energy in him to deny him his wish, or beg Jack to take the large room instead of him. He could only half-heartedly nod, As he dropped his belongings on the floor of the bedroom, closing the door behind him. His body nearly automatically slumped on top of the leisurely mattress, his face pressing into the pillow in distress. Before he could even get under the blankets, his eyes sank shut.

Hours later, Will's eyes opened without command. They refused to close on the thousands of thoughts flooding his mind, and Will was left turning in the dark. When the inner noise became too unbearable to sit with, Will stood and exited his room quietly.

A glass of water. That's all I need. Will thought, opening the steel fridge and grabbing a cold bottle of water. The bottle was the same brand used by the rebellion, but the rebels didn't have a refrigerator to chill them like the head enforcer had.

As he took a sip of the ice cold water, it coated his mouth with a breeze that felt as if his tongue had grazed a glacier. Jack startled Will by yawning behind him, and Will turned to see his friend stretching his limbs in the air.

"Can't sleep?" Jack asked, and Will nodded. "I get it. I haven't slept well since at that lady's house, back near the capital. Before that, I never slept well at all."

Will sat next to Jack on the velvet couch, and spent the rest of the night joking with him and watching the television. Will had never been able to see modern television before, which made viewing it all the more magical. There was one channel that told you exactly what the weather would be kingdom-wide for the next week, using only the power of technological prediction. The concept amazed Will beyond comprehension.

As the sun rose above the town landscape, Will and Jack still sat on the velvet couch beside each other. Jack let his head lay back on the top of the couch, but Will was still incredibly tense. Jack saw that Will was visibly upset, and gave him a light push.

"Well? What's got you all stiff?" He asked, and Will exhaled.

"One week. That's all we'll be here for. Just one week."

"Hey, I believe you. As much as I don't agree with staying to help these guys, I know we'll just be in and out." He responded.

"Right. We'll be out, freeing the prince and saving the kingdom before we know it. We just gotta help these people out. It's the right thing to do."

"I get the feeling you're telling this to yourself, rather than to me." Jack asked, but Will didn't answer. All he could think of was the situation he had wrapped himself in. But he knew it was his responsibility to help the people. He had to bring stability to the discarded town.

••

A week passed in the blink of an eye. Then another. And another. Eventually, without realization, a month had passed in the small desert community. Will had grown fuzz across his chin from the time spent, despite the fact he had been given a razor in the house. He could never find the time to use it.

In time, he grew to know the names of nearly everyone in the community. It was smaller than it had seemed. Only about two-hundred people had been living in the run down land, and they all had grown more comfortable around him as well. The people had begun to stop hiding in their houses, and communicating with each other more. The old enforcers had taken new jobs under Will's administration. Some became officers, some carpenters, and some other servicemen. Many men and women had offered to be Will's personal assistant, but he only accepted the two homeless men who had been kind to the three of them that first night in the town.

The first man, with darker skin and lacking hair, went by the name of Henry. The other, with tan skin and black hair, went by the name of Terrance. Will had used some of the previous leader's leftover carchans to buy the two men suits, and he made sure that they were well kept and housed. In turn, the two men had become incredibly loyal to Will, despite his youth in comparison to them.

Becky had refused to talk to either Will or Jack the entire time. She had been incredibly quiet since that night on the street, and had ceased to practice her magic. Every time Will had tried to approach her to check in, he had been pulled away by other duties. Will could only hope that she was doing okay.

On the twenty-fifth day, Will stood on the corner of Elm Street, watching the reconstruction of a half demolished apartment complex. The light breeze blew his hair while his two sidemen stood behind him. Henry approached, and put a hand on Will's left shoulder.

"It's looking good, man." He complimented. "When this is finished, the homeless population of the town will officially be seventy five percent housed. And after the rehabilitation of Downey Lane from last week, ninety-five percent of the population will have a secure living space, and crime is estimated to decrease by eighty-six percent."

"Thanks for crunching those numbers for me." Will thanked his partner. "You're excused for lunch if you want."

Henry and Terrance left together to grab lunch from the newly opened eatery, and Jack approached Will from behind, standing next to him with his arms crossed. His hair had grown a little longer in the past month, growing from his shorter haircut to a more medium length one. A small, ugly patch of mustache fuzz had begun to sprout on his upper lip, which he had refused to shave.

"Quite the job you're doing here." Jack exclaimed. "Quite the job."

"Yep. The town's starting to look really nice. I'm proud of everyone here." He responded, and Jack exhaled in the moment. After some time, he finally spoke his mind.

"It's about time we leave." He started. "We've been here, what, a month now?"

After a few minutes of thought, Will nodded. Jack was right. They had been here for so long now that Will had yet to realize a lot of things. Not only that they had overstayed their promise greatly, but the toll it had taken on him. Will's eyes now sank into his cheeks from exhaustion, and his limbs constantly ached. He needed more rest than he was getting desperately.

"Okay." Will responded. "I'll let the people know tonight."

Later that night, Will made an announcement to the people that he would be leaving by the next sunset. The news caused more panic than Will had anticipated, and much word of mouth began to spread around the community. The people were worried about what was to come after his departure. Would everything that had been fixed be reversed? Would their weeks of work and hope be crushed by the new leadership? Will assured that he had a plan for a new leader, but in reality he had no plan. He had never planned on replacement, as foolish as it was to not consider. But in his gut, Will knew he wasn't meant to be a leader. Not yet, at least.

Late that night, Will sat in his office room that had been given to him the first week of his leadership. Henry and Terrance stood outside, keeping watch from beyond the door. Will remembered the first order he gave from the office. It had felt uncomfortable at the time, telling people who were mostly older than him what to do. He ordered lessons to be given on indoor gardening, and for each household to contain an indoor garden area for vegetation. Being the prime season for growth, the plants grew rapidly, and by the end of the month vegetation was being donated to farmstands, and used to feed families across the town.

When the clock struck 9:00, the door to Will's office opened and Henry entered, wiping the sweat from his forehead. Without hesitation, he stuck out his hand and Will shook it firmly, thanking his friend for his service.

"We had a good run, Will." He exclaimed. "Shame to see you go so soon. I don't know what I could ever do to repay the life you've given me."

"Thanks, Henry. The least you could do is make sure my house doesn't explode while I'm gone. Or get taken over by those kids I've seen eyeing it all month."

Henry laughed the same hearty laugh Will had enjoyed listening to in his most tiring hours from the past month, and Will put his hand on Henry's shoulder in gratitude to his friend. Suddenly, Henry grunted a spattering choke as the tip of a dagger seeped through the front of his shirt. Will jumped back as the blood of his friend hit his chest, and Henry dropped to the ground in a groan. Will unsheathed the Blade of Atlas in horror as he faced Terrance, who wiped the dark liquid from his weapon.

Chapter 15

Will's hand trembled as he gripped the Blade of Atlas in pure rage. Terrance only stared coldly back, dodging the sight of Henry, who lay in a pool of blood beside him. Will began to breathe heavily, before he stepped forward in confrontation.

"Why." Will asked. "He did nothing to you."

"He wouldn't have left your side. But I can see through you. This was your plan all along, wasn't it? To give our people a taste of hope for the first time in decades, just to rip it away like everyone does. You're no different from them."

"No," Will spoke, gritting his teeth in sadness for his friend. "NO! I care about the people here more than you ever could! I've given up thirty days of the time I could be using to train, or to pursue the prophecy itself, to help this community thrive again, and to give you hope when no one else would give it to you! All I wanted was to help!"

"And now you're going to leave it all behind, and ruin our town just like every other tyrant did."

"I'm not a tyrant!" Will shouted, stepping closer to Terrance in threatening.

"Go ahead." Terrance said, fearless. "Kill me. Kill me and prove to the world that you are exactly the same as everyone else."

"No," Will said, stepping back. "I won't. You were my friend, Terrance. You and Henry gave my friends and I comfort when no one else here was able to give that."

"I didn't give you anything." Henry said. "You just showed up one day, and now you're leaving. Henry never saw it, but I saw through you. Some chosen one. I bet that sword is as bullshit as your care for us."

"No, I-"

"You don't have to say anything." Henry interrupted. "I should have killed you when you were defenseless, all those nights ago. Just like I did to that quiet girl thirty minutes ago. The witch. What was her name, Betsy? Be-"

Will's heart stopped. He couldn't hear anything Terrance said after. All he could feel was his blood boiling warmer, and warmer.

"What." Will muttered, and a slight smile broke out on Terrance's face.

Will gripped the Blade tightly, and it was almost as if it gripped back. His eyes burst in light for just a moment, as he moved in a powerful flash of movement. He wrapped his left hand around the throat of Terrance, and clenched it so tightly that Terrance began to gasp silently. Before he could even get a breath out, Will smashed his body with an unimaginable force through the concrete wall, until the world faded back into view.

Will stood in the center of the street, panting uncontrollably. He looked down at his left hand, which still clenched around the neck of Terrance. His head was twisted in an odd direction, and his face was stuck in a subtle grin. *Broken neck.* Will thought, as he dropped the body to the ground.

"Will!" shouts arose as Will turned to his right to see Jack and Becky running out to see him. "What happened?" Jack cried, and Will dropped to his knees in distress.

"I thought... He said..." Will whimpered, looking at Becky, who stared back in concern. "By the maker, what have I done?" He sighed, covering his eyes. Will remembered Henry, and jumped from the ground in worry. "Henry, he was stabbed by Terrence, he needs medical attention!" The group ran into the office building, and Becky cast a preservation spell on Henry to keep him from bleeding any more.

By the time the three of them reached the town hospital, everyone had heard of what had happened. Henry was now unconscious, and doctors made way for Will who struggled to carry the body of his friend. He entered the first empty hospital room they could find, and Will was pushed from the room immediately by doctors who swiftly went to work on Henry.

Will sat in the lobby for hours beside Jack and Becky, who silently comforted him. It hadn't mattered whether they had talked to him or not anyways. Will felt as if he had failed Henry, his partner he'd only met a month ago.

The lights flickered in the hospital lobby around the three of them, while Will tapped his foot in anxiety. Only his own house had been connected to a generator, but one of his plans for the town was for a power plant of sorts to be built, to give needed power to at least the essential work environments, such as hospitals and markets.

Will still struggled to take in what had just happened. Just hours before, Will had been standing beside Terrance and Henry, reminiscing on how far they'd come in the short month. It seemed as if the most difficult events were the ones that happened so quickly, that they were impossible to process.

When the doctors finally cleared, they gave the word to Will. Henry was going to live. Will sighed in relief, and the doctors continued. The wound had missed his vital organs, but he lost a lot of blood in the moment, which would prevent him from waking until at least the morning. Will nodded, and sat in a chair beside the bed to watch his friend as he slept. Jack gave Will words of comfort before leaving, and he smiled back at Jack's hope for Henry. Jack shut the door behind him, and Will sat back in the chair, closing his eyes softly.

Before he could drift off, Becky entered the room, pale faced, and Will stood to meet her. For a moment they simply stared into each other's eyes, before Becky began to tear up, wrapping Will in an embrace. Even in distress, her hair smelled of calming camomile and Will exhaled softly. They simply stood there for sometime in each other's embrace, before sitting down beside each other.

"It almost feels unreal to be going back out on the road tomorrow." Will spoke quietly, and Becky looked at him concernedly.

"Are you okay?" She asked, and Will didn't respond.

"I..." He began to speak at last. "I think I just need some sleep." And as if that were a command to his brain itself, his eyes began to close automatically once more, and his view was shrouded in darkness. The last thing he felt before losing his senses was Becky holding his hand in comfort, as everything slipped away.

••

When the sun finally rose high enough to shine through the hospital windows, Will's eyes awoke. He hadn't slept this long for a long time. He looked to his side, where Becky no longer sat. Raising his body, he stared into the closed eyes of Henry, who still lay unconscious. He stood from his chair staring out the window of the hospital, and for the first time in months, there was only one thing on his mind. *The sunrise is gorgeous.*

Will returned to his home to pack his things alongside Jack and Becky. Even after his time as leader he didn't have many personal possessions, which allowed him to pack lightly in a tote bag he found in his bedroom closet. He entered the bathroom, which had been kept as clean as always, and finally used the razor that had been left for him. With some struggle, Jack did the same, and the trio were packed to leave the town at last.

Closing the door behind him, Will looked back at the place he had called his home for over a month. Even for a short period, it was the first real home he had ever lived in. It had been incredibly different from his dorm in the rebellion, which barely made up a fraction of this house in size.

Taking one last look at the town, they returned to the hospital. Before they could enter the building, Henry stumbled in a gown out to meet them in front of the hospital doors. Two doctors hurried behind him, urging Henry to re-enter the hospital, but he ignored them. Will gave his friend a pat on the shoulder, glad to see him lively as he was.

"So this is it, huh?" Henry asked, and Will nodded solemnly. It was time for the group to return to their responsibilities.

"I actually wanted to give something to you." Will spoke, reaching into his pocket. Moving his closed hand slowly, he hovered it above Henry's own, before opening it to drop a pair of keys into his palm. "You've been with me through it all here, and I wanna thank you. I know I wasn't the perfect leader, but I believe you will be."

Henry was left dumbfounded, holding the keys in both of his hands, before tearing up subtly. He quickly wiped them away with a hearty laugh, before turning to the trio again.

"Look at me. I was a bum on the street just a month ago, and now I'm gonna be the mayor of my town. It's crazy how things work out sometimes." Henry sighed, before giving Will one last grin, alongside a map of the desert district. "You three might need this to find wherever you're off to next. Just keep something in mind for me, man. When you guys make it big and save the world, just don't forget this little old town, will you? I'll be expecting you all some day."

Will smiled back, and the three finally made their way past the exit of the old desert town, headed north with the map Henry had given them. Will traced his finger along the lines upon the map, following their instructions with each step. His curled hair blew in the wind, much longer than it had been a month before when he was still with his friends in the rebellion.

The three heroes nodded silently at each other, continuing forth toward the graveyard. As the sun hung high over the horizon, the view of the town behind them grew smaller and smaller until it was out of view, and destiny hung ahead once again.

Chapter 15

Two days later, the three heroes had been traveling endlessly across the vast desert region and were finally nearing the graveyard. Will turned to face Becky as they walked, who stared off into the distance as they traveled the sandy terrain. She had returned to silence after the events at the old town, and he was concerned.

"You ok?" he said, lightly bumping her side. "You've been quiet for a month now, and I never got to check in at the town."

She kept staring into the distance, ignoring his question.

"Beck?" Jack said concernedly.

"Hmm?" She said, snapping back into focus. "Yeah." She spoke quietly and continued to stare off. Jack shrugged, and they continued to march forward.

As the graveyard grew closer in the distance, the scorching sand of the desert-like atmosphere turned to soft soil. The three travelers were ecstatic with the newfound gentle, cold ground, and sat beside a large and shadowy tree. Jack dozed off immediately from exhaustion, and Will took the opportunity to speak with Becky privately.

"Hey." He said, scooching towards Becky. "Seriously, are you ok?" She sighed.

"I don't really want to talk about it." She said quietly, and Will looked away. "I'm sorry."

"Well, if you're looking for someone to talk to, I'm here." He said with a smile. "A-And Jack, obviously." He added, and Becky grinned.

"Thanks. That means a lot."

After thirty minutes of rest, it felt like it was around 3:30. Will had lost track of what day in the week it was, but that mattered little to him. He knew it had been a little over a month since he was arrested, and this had been the farthest away from the city he had been his entire life.

The grass was a bolder green than he had ever seen before, and the surrounding plants were thriving due to the lack of human intervention. After the extreme heat of the desert section of Pyronia, the plains outside the kingdom's borders were a breath of fresh air. Will checked his pockets and pulled out what he had left.

The group had twelve combined carchans left, although they wouldn't be needing them anytime soon. Considering they were wanted figures all throughout the kingdom, they couldn't be showing their faces inside too many stores or public spaces.

Other than the Pyronian currency he had left, there was a stone-like charm that the welcoming woman had given him just outside the city walls, and an old swiss knife Wolf had given him 3 days ago. He opened the knife and began to whittle a stick he had picked up from beside him.

Back in the Rebellion base, Will used to whittle in his free time. He whittled particularly when he was feeling contemplative. As he lay on the large, thick tree, he looked beside himself at his partners. Jack had his arm over his face, and was snoring, while Becky had her arms crossed over her stomach with her eyes closed. Will looked down at the stick he held in his right hand and began to whittle.

He thought of home. The only one he had ever come to know. He wondered what had been going on there since his departure. He wondered if his arrest had affected them in any way. Then he thought of Darla.

She must be worried sick. He thought with a frown.

He began to think about the future, and what the graveyard ahead would hold in store. He began to worry slightly, as he had no possible clue as to what could be in store for the three of them. At the previous town, he had scared the witch hunters to their knees because they thought he was some kind of god, but in reality, Will had no experience at all. Wolf trained him for a day or so, but that wouldn't be enough to help him kill an enemy with any skill in the slightest, let alone the greatest and most feared swordsman in the kingdom. He began to wonder if he was really anything without the Blade of Atlas.

Suddenly, Will felt a light tap on his shoulder. He looked to his left, and saw Becky staring into his eyes, sorrowfully.

"I… Didn't know you could whittle." She spoke quietly.

"I learned back when I was a kid. It wasn't always good, but after some time I learned my way around." He said in response. Becky sighed.

"Back in that town..." Becky started. "Those men. They... jumped me. Early in the morning. There were too many of them, and I couldn't reach my wand in my bag. They tied me up, and I was scared." She said, looking down. "They were going to kill me. Just because I was a witch." She said with a tear in her eye.

"Why... Why would they want to kill all sorcerers if we weren't evil? If we hadn't done horrible things. If that's true... I don't know if I want to be a witch anymore." She finished, and Will put his hand on her shoulder.

"You can't compare yourself to what other sorcerers have done. Just because you have the potential to cause pain with your magic doesn't mean you will." He said comfortingly. "I think that you can prove them wrong. You will." He said with a smile, and she smiled back.

They sat in silence for a few moments, staring into each other's eyes quietly. After a moment, Jack made an obnoxiously loud snore, and the two broke out in laughter.

"C'mon." Will said standing up. "Wake up Jack. We're close enough to it, let's go see what this graveyard's all about."

At what seemed to be 4:30, the trio had made it to the graveyard. The calming greenery that surrounded it was silenced by the uncanniness of the quiet graveyard. The trees rustled softly in the light breeze, and the sky closed its eyes with large sheets of cloud.

Will looked around for something that would catch his eye, but to no avail.

"What are we looking for, again?" Will asked cluelessly.

"According to the prophecy that the woman read to us a month ago," Becky started. "We are supposed to find the aid of a 'Ghostly prince'. She mentioned that Prince Jonah's grave was around here somewhere..." Will looked over in confusion.

"Who is he again? I know he was the brother to King Flint, but... Why would we ask him for help? Aren't the royal family... Y'know... Evil?" He asked.

"Well... his family is evil, for sure, but Jonah was known for his good deeds while in power." She started. "I didn't go to school for very long, but from what I had been taught, he wasn't a bad person. He apparently helped innocent people escape from his father's dungeon when they were wrongfully accused, he would smuggle his father's money for charities, and everything of the sort." She spoke, and Will shrugged.

"He sounds good enough to me. If he helps us get to the king, that's all I care about."

As the three approached the center of the graveyard, Will noticed a particularly large grave that stood out from the rest. Running up to inspect it, Will read the words engraved aloud as he ran his finger over the dust coated text.

"Jonah Strife – Beloved son and brother, Prince of Pyronia."

Will looked around the grave and noticed a hole a few feet in front of the engraved stone. It went directly downward in a very straight and particular shape.

"What's this?" Will asked Jack and Becky, as they looked.

"No clue." Jack said, kneeling to get a closer look. "Maybe it's like... A keyhole of sorts." Jack continued, looking upwards.

Suddenly, an idea sprouted in the depths of Will's mind as he stared into the dark crevice beneath Jonah's grave.

"I'm going to try something." He said curiously. He held the tip of his blade downwards, touching the top of the hole. The Blade of Atlas perfectly aligned with the volume of the hole, and Will nodded toward it to alert the attention of his friends. "Perfect fit."

He pushed the sword down into the hole, and it slid in seamlessly. After a moment of nothing happening, Jack knelt next to it in observation before piping in in confusion.

"Well... what now?" He asked, and Will looked closer. He removed the blade from the hole, and shoved it back in with more force. Nothing.

"Maybe... you have to turn it in? Like a key?" Will pushed the blade with all his might, and it turned slightly right. He shook his hands to recharge his strength and turned harder. The sword, slowly but surely, twisted 90 degrees right, and stopped with a jolt.

Almost instantly, the blade slipped through Will's hands and dropped all the way into the hole, stopping at the hilt. The Blade of Atlas began to rumble from inside the hole, glowing slightly. It began to glow increasingly more, as the rumbling grew louder.

Jonah's grave began to crack and chip in the stone, and fell apart in front of Will, Jack and Becky. Will's sword began to glow blindingly bright, and a beacon of light shot up above the blade. The ground surrounding the grave suddenly caved in on itself, and a glowing figure ascended from below.

As quickly as it happened, the ground rose back into place, and the Blade of Atlas shot out of the hole at incredible velocity, and stopped around 50 feet in the air, turning around, and jabbing into the dirt next to Will. He jumped at the impact of the blade, then turned and pulled it out from the sandy ground, slipping it in his sheath.

The glowing figure began to darken, as it landed gracefully on its feet. It held its head in confusion, and Will observed it from afar. It was wearing a dark cloak, with a torn gray shirt underneath. Around its back, it had a bow and an empty arrow quiver. Its long, worn cloak waved in the desert wind as the figure grew used to its surroundings. After a moment of silence between the two parties, the figure flipped its hood back and revealed its face. It was a tall, youthful man, seemingly around the age of twenty five, with wavy black hair and faintly red pupils. Staring before the group of curiously concerned travelers, the figure spoke at last.

"My name is Jonah, crown prince of Pyronia. Name yourselves at once."

Chapter 15

The Rebellion was quiet. Quieter than it had ever been. But not empty. Hundreds of men, who had called the base home for years, mourned the loss of privacy in the streets. Hundreds of women and children carried bags by their sides, only carrying what they could. Within hours, the king would have many men and women breaching the thought to be an unfindable base where the Rebellion had been used for decades.

Darla stood atop the tallest building in sight, watching the lamentable sorrow from above. She bit her lip and thought of what she could have done to prevent this. What her father, and her father's father would have done. She laughed to herself in spite.

They must be rolling in their graves right now. She thought. She clenched her fist, and let out a hate filled yell of anguish, slamming her bloody-knuckled fist into the drywall, creating a large hole. Rose entered the room in concern.

"Are you ok, boss?" Darla turned back coldly towards her and looked away.

"Yeah. Pack your things already."

Rose left the room, and Darla sat on the floor, and wrapped her arms around her knees. She let out a big sigh. She knew she couldn't dwell on this for too long. She wouldn't let herself.

There were underground tunnels that led to an emergency base 60 miles west. They would pass underneath the edge of the desert district of Kandachta, and beneath the rocky mountain district of Scolibus. The base resides at the far end of the kingdom, almost 80 miles away from the kingdom. It would be a 3–4-day walk.

Darla grabbed her two bags of clothing and strapped her mace around her back. She left her office without looking back and met with the mob of people by the tunnel opening.

As she and a few other men lifted the gates to the tunnel, dozens of people began to pour in.

"Walk as a group!" She yelled. "Make sure everyone gets in!" As she yelled those words, the speaker buzzed on her walkie-talkie.

"Darla, there are men approaching the North gate. Looks to be around 100 of them. Led by a woman. Dark hair." Darla didn't need to hear more.

"Run!" She screamed at the unarmed civilians. "Get as far as you can!" Hundreds of people stormed into the large tunnel in a crazed stampede, and Darla spoke into her walkie-talkie. "Men, you're excused. Get into the tunnel immediately!" Most of the soldiers she ordered were obedient, however a few dozen stayed back.

"You're not alone, sir." One spoke.

One of the men who stayed back stepped up. He was armed with a crossbow, and silver arrows in a large quiver. He had dark skin, and short, black hair. Darla approached him with urgency.

"Kendrick, take the men from your legion and protect the tunnel." She turned to the rest of the men and women. "The rest of you, come to the gates with me. We're going to give the king the fight he's been looking for."

"Amber's wondering if she should stay to supply the soldiers." Kendrick spoke, and Darla yelled back with fire in her ordering tone.

"Absolutely not! They're going to need her to rebuild at the new base. Now get going!"

As Pandora and her men approached the Northern gate, Darla approached from the other side with her men. Darla pulled a lever from inside, and the entire Northern wall descended into the ground. Darla unsheathed her mace and tightened her armor. With a loud war cry, she pictured her father.

I hope you're proud. She thought. As the gates reached the ground, Pandora spun her double-ended spear in front of her. She wore golden armor, with a matching helmet.

"Charge!" She yelled, pointing with two fingers toward Darla.

The king's men ran into conflict with Darla's, and she swung her mace upwards into Pandora, landing the first blow. Pandora stumbled back and raised her spear in anger.

Around Darla, bodies were flying constantly. King's men and women, Rebellion men and women, both getting cut down like flies. She couldn't let it distract her from defeating Pandora. She swung with more ferocity than ever before, disarming Pandora of her spear and kicking her over.

With a mighty blow, she knocked her golden helmet clean off, and raised her mace to finish the job. Before she could smash the mace downwards, Pandora rolled swiftly out of the way, and grabbed her spear, blocking a downward blow from Darla. She spun her spearhead downwards and sliced clean down Darla's leg. She flinched in pain, but she wouldn't let that stop her. They attempted to swing forward at the same time, and they locked weapons together.

"Some leader you are." Darla snarked with a grin. "Your men are dying. You have no plan. You just hack and slash and hack because there's nothing else up there."

Pandora threw her foot up in anger and knocked Darla to the ground with a shocking blow.

"Yet I still win." She said, kicking Darla's mace away from her hand. "That at least makes me smarter than you. And the rest of you scum." She raised her spear head upwards to impale Darla's chest, and Darla grit her teeth. This was going to hurt.

Before she could move the spear downward, one of the king's soldiers yelled in pain and fell back into Pandora, knocking her off her balance. Darla leaped up and took a small hunting knife from her pocket. With a forceful jab, she stabbed it through Pandora's eye. Pandora screamed and kicked Darla backwards. Taking a blade from behind her back, she slammed it downwards hatefully.

"DIE!" She screamed horrifyingly loud, and Darla slipped behind the chaos. "WHERE ARE YOU!?" She bellowed, shoving her way through her men.

Darla grabbed her mace and smashed it over the head of one of Pandora's soldiers. She picked up his spear and waited for Pandora to come into view.

As Pandora locked her one remaining eye on Darla through the chaos, she charged at her screaming. Darla threw the spear with all her force, and it broke through a crack in Pandora's golden armor, impaling her. Pandora looked at the spear in her chest and stumbled. With a whimper, she dropped to the ground. Darla began to laugh powerfully with confidence.

"PANDORA IS DEAD! YIELD YOUR WEAPONS AND SURRENDER!" She screamed with pride.

As she put one foot over Pandora's body, one of Pandora's soldiers impaled Darla's shoulder with a spear. Darla screamed in pain, and the soldier began to laugh, but he stopped with a sudden choke.

Kendrick ran up to Darla, shooting an arrow clean through the face of the soldier that impaled her. He took bandages out from his pocket and grabbed the spear.

"This is going to hurt. A lot." He warned her.

"Be... careful..." She said to him,

"It's all right. There's only around 30 of them left, but my men are on it. We've lost a lot as well. I think with me and you, we only have around 18 men and women. They came unprepared. We're pushing through." He said, and Darla grinned, but winced in pain afterwards.

"You ready?" He asked, and she nodded.

He pulled the spear out quickly, and Darla yelped. He wrapped the bandage around her until it stopped bleeding.

"Take a minute to rest." He said, but she shook her head.

"In the middle of battle? No way." She said, picking up her mace.

Darla and Kendrick charged the remaining men and took them out swiftly. One approached the two of them, and Darla slammed her mace into his chest plate, making him stumble, and Kendrick followed by shooting an arrow through the skull.

He collapsed, and Darla slammed her mace into a woman behind him. The king's men noticed their major disadvantage, and one screamed;

"FALL BACK!"

The men began to drop their weapons and run, and the remaining Rebellion men cheered. One of the king's men picked up Pandora's body and ran with the group. Darla stared coldly into the eye of her fallen opponent and turned to briefly celebrate with her remaining men. Shortly after, they entered the tunnel one by one, and Darla closed it shut.

•••

Back at the city hospital, the medics had broken the news to the king, and he looked downwards, stroking his beard slowly in thought.

"Out of the 125 men only 13 returned, my lord. Most of them are in critical condition. We've been treating them, but many of them are... hopeless."

The king turned back towards the doctor.

"Where is Lieutenant Pandora?" The doctor looked at his clipboard.

"She is in... room 26. In the right wing. However, she isn't with us now. She has a pulse, but her chances of survival are slim." The doctor spoke.

"Take me to her. And give her your best treatment." Flint ordered. "I have many questions."

Suddenly, Flint clenched his head in horrible pain. Ringing grew stronger and harsher through his ears, as he fell to one knee. Surrounding doctors and nurses ran to his side and moved him into a nearby bed.

"My lord!"

Flint could hear a doctor's voice echo behind the sirens in his mind. As the ringing silenced, a familiar, booming voice rang.

YOUR BROTHER HAS RETURNED... JONAH IS ALIVE...

Chapter 16

The year is 2245. 20 years before the birth of Will Larson. Flint Strife is 14 years old, and he wanders throughout the castle garden. This garden was much larger than his old one.

It had been three years now since his father had taken over Pyronia, and today was the anniversary. His father, brother, and the others had been celebrating in the dining hall, and Flint had taken a moment to step outside. He took a deep breath and sat on a nearby stone wall. The sun had nearly reached the center of the sky, and the king would be holding his lunchtime feast soon.

All of a sudden, Flint heard a faint laugh coming from over the garden wall. Interested in finding the source, he ran up to the wall and pressed his head against it. The voice sounded around his age, and he listened closely.

Since he had settled in the castle three years before, it had been difficult for Flint to meet new people. His father hadn't been too keen with him leaving the house, so he had only interacted with servants, and the occasional friends of his father.

Shrouded in curiosity, Flint ran to the garden corner, where there was a door which led to a slender spiral staircase. He attempted to open the door, but it was locked. He picked a small stick from off the ground and tried to pick the lock. Given he had no experience picking a lock, he failed.

Turning to the castle, he ran back inside. He snuck past the dining hall, where he could hear his father and the visitors talking over food. After passing the hall, Flint made a break for a large drawer in the pantry, where he knew that his father had kept the keys. He pulled open the drawer, and flipped through the dozens of keys, until he found one labeled "Garden Stairway".

Back outside, Flint ran to the door and unlocked it. Before stepping through, his heart jumped for a second. He knew he wasn't allowed on the wall, let alone outside the castle. In defiance, he entered and climbed up the stairs.

Reaching the top, he could still hear the laughter of the children coming from below. He peeked his head slowly over the wall, and his eyes were laid upon four people who seemed to be his age. Two of them male, like himself, and the others female.

As he stuck his head slightly higher, he listened closely. He listened to the distant bickering of the group and held his head slightly higher. One of the people made a joke, and Flint chuckled. He smiled and began to consider climbing down.

Suddenly, a noise rang from behind Flint. It sounded like a door slamming shut, and Flint leaped in shock. He cracked his head against the wall, and cried out, but quickly covered his mouth. He slowly turned his head around to see his father, who had entered the courtyard.

"Flint?" He called, and Flint was as silent as a mouse. "Foolish child." He could hear his father mutter, as he reentered the castle.

Flint, now left alone, peeked over the castle wall. The teenagers that he had previously seen were packing their belongings, bickering playfully. Flint suddenly had a rush-like feeling in his gut, one he had never felt before.

He had to go down there and talk to those people. Maybe this could be his one chance at leaving the castle and interacting with the world. He attempted to step over the wall but retreated in fear. It was a 20-foot drop from the castle walls, which would most definitely injure Flint if he failed to scale it.

Touching the stone wall was a tall pine tree, almost as tall as the wall itself. Flint stepped on top of the edge and looked down. The 20-foot drop looked a lot farther from the top. He reached out and grabbed the closest branch and closed his eyes. Without thinking further, Flint leaped from the castle ledge, and wrapped his arms around the tree.

Holy crap, I did it! He thought in pride. He began to step down lower, placing his foot on the next branch, and then repeating for the one after. When he was around halfway down, Flint looked up and saw the other teens leaving the area. In a panic, he began to drop quicker, worried that he would lose his window of opportunity to talk to them.

As he grew near six feet from the ground, Flint's foot slipped off the branch he had reached for, and he fell. He cracked against the last two branches, and slammed into the earth with a thud. The four people turned around, and one of the guys yelled something that Flint couldn't hear, but it sounded along the lines of;

'Holy shit!'

Flint held the back of his head as it ached, and attempted to sit up. His vision was blurred, but he could see a figure or two approaching him from afar. As he lifted his head back on his shoulders, his stomach became queasy in shock. As his sight came back, he attempted to get on one knee, but fell back.

Flint felt a hand on his shoulder, and looked towards the motion. One of the girls that he had seen earlier kneeled next to him, while one of the guys crouched beside her.

"Are you ok, man?" He asked.

"Do you think you broke anything? Should we call a doctor?" The girl continued.

Flint sat up, and looked her in the eyes. The girl had hazel eyes, with long black hair. She had slightly tanned skin, and wore a casual striped cotton dress. Flint opened his mouth to speak, but nothing came out. He had never spoken to someone his age. His mouth trembled in anxiety, longing to speak, but he couldn't make a sound.

One of the other men approached Flint and tapped his shoulder.

"Is he stupid or something?"

The girl frowned.

“Stop, he’s clearly in shock. You know my mom is a nurse, so I was raised to recognize stuff like this.” She turned back towards him. “What’s your name, kid?”

Flint stayed silent, and the first guy knelt next to the girl.

“Hey, we don’t bite.”

The other two people talked quietly to each other quietly behind the two that were in front of Flint.

At last, Flint opened his mouth.

“M-m... My name is Flintlock.” The two looked at him strangely.

“Flintlock, huh. That's a strange name.” The guy said, and the girl whacked him lightly across the head.

The second guy approached him, and held out his hand. Grabbing it, Flint pulled himself up. He dusted off his regal clothing, and looked back up.

“Thank you.” He started. “I assure you, I’m fine-” He stumbled forward, grabbing his side. He yelped in pain, and the others ran over to support him.

“We’re gonna take you to the doctor. See what you hurt.” One of the men said.

The city was incredible, in ways that Flint never could have imagined. Not the advanced technology, or the dazzling lights, but the people.

Flint had never seen this many people. He turned his head, and saw dozens and dozens of people, each with their own lives. Mothers, fathers, children. They each had their own day to day, a part to play in society. It was absolutely marvelous.

When they had reached the medical office, one of the girls took him by the arm, and stepped towards the door. Flint stumbled, but caught himself.

"I'm going to bring him to my mother, and hopefully she'll have time to take a look at him." The others looked at each other, and one spoke up.

"Don't worry, we'll be right out here, a'right?" The boy said as Flint turned towards the door, and the girl opened it firmly.

The lights coming from inside the building were brighter than Flint had been used too. When his eyes grew used to the room, he noticed that there were LED lights, similar to the ones in the castle bathrooms.

Flint had been a young boy when the use of technology began to dwindle, and he gazed in amazement at the sight of a fully electronic building. Looking behind the reception desk, there were multiple large computers, each of with a subtle buzz emitting from the back.

Flint sat in a soft, velvet chair next to the girl. He took a breath in relief, but grasped his side in pain. Sitting back slowly, he let the breath out cautiously. Flint could hear the noises from machines in the distant rooms, and murmuring voices walking by. As he looked down at his clammy palms in anxiety, the girl spoke.

"My name's Helen by the way. I think Flintlock is a beautiful name." Flint looked up, and sat in silence for a moment, thinking of what to say.

"I... Thank you. No one's ever told me that before." He stammered.

"It's a little long though. How about Flint? Can I call you that?" She smiled, and Flint did the same.

"That's what my brother has called me on occasion." He said, thinking it over. "Sure. I give you permission to call me Flint." He said in an attempt to seem regal with his words, but the attempt only led Helen to stare at him oddly.

She looked around for a minute, and Flint followed. Turning back to him, she spoke again.

"So... What were you doing in that tree? Were you listening to us?" Flint took a short breath. She hadn't realized who he was.

"Uh... I hadn't meant to. You see, I'm..." He paused. "A frequent... Tree climber... Yes." She looked at him strangely.

"Ok... sure."

At that moment, a nurse came into the lobby and called Flint's name, and he and Helen followed her into a bright room.

Flint had broken three ribs. He wasn't surprised, but a bit disappointed that they would need time to heal. He and Helen left the office, and regrouped with her friends. Flint gave them thanks before bidding goodbye, and as they walked away, Helen turned back to Flint one last time.

"Meet again tomorrow?" She asked, and Flint chuckled.

"Sure." He responded with a grin. As he turned away, he thought to himself. He was going to have to get a lot better at climbing trees.

As he reached the top of the pine next to the castle, Flint carefully stepped back on top of the wall and sighed in relief and exhaustion. Heading back into the castle yard, he could hear his father shouting.

"Flintlock! Where are you, boy?" Flint entered the castle, with the lookout key hidden behind his back.

"Yes?" Flint called out nervously.

Flint's father was a tall and slender, dark bearded man with a resting face that could break the strongest man in one glance. He approached Flint sternly, and exclaimed;

"There you are. It is shameful to not answer when callen." He growled while Flint apologized, and his father placed his hand on Flint's shoulder with a smirk. "You are forgiven." The smile quickly turned sour.

"There's something that is of urgent concern. It's about your brother."

Chapter 17

Flint sat with his father in his quarters. A small television rested on a coffee table in the corner, the only one in the house. His father sat in a curved, gray chair in front of Flint, who sat in a brown leather coffee chair.

Flint's father sighed, and held his hands together over his legs in a triangle-like shape. Then he looked up at Flint.

"You remember how your brother Jonah has been consistently admitted to the hospital as of recently, correct?" Thanatos spoke as Flint nodded.

"Yes. Is that why you and him have been meeting so much at night?" He asked in young curiosity, as his father sat in silence for a moment, and nodded softly and grimly.

"Jonah has been... poisoned with an incurable illness. Of course, you understand this would mean you would be next in line to be king." He spoke knowingly, and Flint's pupils shrank and he sat back in surprise.

"Jonah is going to die?" He asked, face pale as the smoke above the fireplace.

His father looked out the window in lament, and Flint turned his gaze to the ground. He couldn't believe it.

He had known Jonah his whole life, and he had always been someone he could talk to, even with the 8-year age difference. He was only in his early twenties. Flint's father stood at last.

"I am interested in discussing this further, but it seems as though you are struggling to take this in. I suppose you should take the night and rest, and we will continue tomorrow."

Thanatos left the room promptly, and Flint was left alone in utter shock.

The next morning, Flint felt queasy. He hadn't grown too close to his brother, but they had been raised together nevertheless. Jonah's death would not only be tragic for the family, Flint thought, but for the kingdom as well.

Jonah was next in line to be king, and the kingdom needed a stable change in power after their father had taken the throne by force years before. With Jonah gone, all of the responsibility would be placed on Flint, and his chest sank in uncertainty. He was definitely not prepared for this.

As the weight of the kingdom began to rest on his shoulders, Flint unlocked the watchtower door and climbed to the top. He climbed down the tree with more caution than previously, and waited at the bottom for Helen to arrive.

Flint waited for half an hour or so, and when she came, she brought two of her friends that had been with her the day before, one male and one female. She waved hello, and Flint smiled and did the same. When they met, the guy stepped forward and stuck his hand out to Flint.

"We didn't really get to introduce ourselves yesterday."

Flint put his hand out, and the guy shook it firmly while continuing.

"My name is Theodore. My friends call me Ted." He grinned, and the girl next to Helen gave him a soft shove.

"We call him Theo, and for some reason he thinks 'Ted' sounds any cooler." Flint chuckled, and she continued. "Nancy, nice to meet you."

"I'm Flintlo-" Flint paused, and looked at Helen who gave him a thumbs up. "I'm Flint. Nice to meet you both."

Flint's three newfound friends took him to a restaurant. Not any top-of-the-line restaurant like his father had always ordered from, but a normal restaurant. From the outside, it looked as if it was a pizza place. Flint had never eaten pizza, but he had overheard many things from passing guards. He looked at the name, and recognized it instantly. *Giorno's #1 Pizza*.

Flint chuckled to himself, and remembered the young newbie who had just joined the guard force a few months ago. In his first week on the job, he left and came back with a box from this place. Flint had seen the box, and wondered if this was really the "#1 Pizza". Intrigued, he followed the group through the door.

They were met with a heavy groan from the large, bearded man behind the counter. Ted walked up and rested his arm across the counter. Before he could talk, the man raised his voice.

"Kid, if ye' add one more thing to this tab of yers, I'm gonna be able to buy a condo after what ye' pay up, that's fer sure."

Ted chuckled, and looked up to the man.

"C'mon, G. I got until I croak to pay this tab off, right? Is another pie gonna hurt that much?"

Flint looked at the man's name tag, which read "Giorno". He must be the owner. The man sighed.

"Only fer you, kid." He grumbled, and walked into the kitchen.

As the group took their seats, Flint sighed. He crossed his arms over the table, and observed the busy streets outside. It was around 2pm, and the sun gleamed through the large windows. Suddenly, the girl Nancy spoke, and Flint turned his head.

"What's with you and that tree? Don't you know better than to be hanging so close to the castle all the time?"

Flint gulped, and thought of a comeback.

"Uh... Why were you all hanging in that area as well? Weren't you all having a picnic or something next to the wall?"

Nancy shot up, and Helen flinched.

"I knew it! You were spying on us!"

"Uh... Well, I wasn't... I didn't mean to..." Flint stammered, but before he could finish, Giorno approached the table with the pizza, and Ted grabbed it quickly.

"Ok! Pizzas here, argument solved." He said, slamming the pizza down in the center of the table.

The group began to dig in quickly, and Flint reluctantly took a slice. Taking a bite, his mouth was filled with flavors he had never experienced before. Taking another, he grinned in enjoyment, but changed back to a frown when he remembered his discourse with Nancy.

"Well, you were saying?" She said looking at him, and Helen interrupted.

"C'mon, he doesn't have to talk about it if he doesn't want to."

"It's ok." Flint said, raising his hand. "I want to talk about it. There's something I've been keeping from you guys. I..." He whispered. "My father is King Thanatos."

Nancy gasped, and Ted choked on his food. The cheese from his pizza fell onto his shirt, and slid onto his lap.

"SHIT!" He exclaimed in anger, and Giorno gave him a stink eye.

"I KNEW IT!" Nancy exclaimed, jumping from her seat. Ted frantically grabbed napkins from the table, and Nancy took out her handkerchief to help.

"Uh, we'll be right back." Ted said disappointingly. Flint could hear him mutter "And just when it was getting good..." As he walked away with Nancy. Flint turned towards Helen, who frowned.

"I'm sorry..." He started. "I wanted to tell you yesterday, but I just... I don't know..." She shrugged.

"It's ok. It was pretty easy to figure it out anyways. Who hangs around the same tree, right next to the castle, 2 days in a row? We had to assume you were either homeless, or..." She stopped.

"Maybe being homeless would have been better." Flint said, looking down in shame. "Do you... hate me?" He asked.

"I..." She started. "I don't know. I need some time to process this." She got up from the table, and stepped outside.

Flint sat alone at the table, and lay his head on his hands. These were the first friends he had ever made, and he had screwed it up. He could hear Ted and Nancy bickering near the bathrooms, trying to desperately salvage Ted's outfit.

Eventually, Nancy came back over while Ted re-entered the bathroom. She sat down, and looked concerningly at Flint.

"Where is Helen?" She asked, and Flint nodded toward the door. "We don't hate you. Or at least, Ted and I don't. We knew if you were half as bad as your father, you would've had us arrested or killed or something for hanging on royal territory."

Flint smiled.

"Thank you. That... that means a lot."

"Now go talk to her." Nancy said encouragingly. "Go." Flint got up, and left the restaurant.

Helen stood against the brick wall, with a tear streaming down her face. The sun reflected off the salty stream across her cheek, and Flint stood next to her solemnly.

"I didn't want to believe it." She cried. "I thought... I don't know what I thought!"

Flint put a hand on her shoulder, and she flinched.

"I'm not... I'm not like him..." She looked at him in the eyes, and he could see his reflection in her watery pupils.

"His army... they killed my dad..." She spoke through tears.

"When he first came through the city, and... and murdered the king. My father was one of General Wolf's men... he stayed behind at the castle to protect the king." She choked. "He had my dad publicly executed." She put her hands over her face and sobbed. Flint looked down towards the ground, and frowned. His father was a monster.

"I'm so sorry. I'm so, so sorry." He spoke. "I had no idea... I knew he did bad things to take the city, but... I never heard the details. I didn't know..." She sobbed, and he stopped.

"But I can be better." He spoke as she took a moment to calm down, and he continued. "My brother is ill, and the doctors... they don't think he's going to make it. I promise that when I become king, I'll do better than my father. I'll bring peace back to Pyronia, and avenge all of the people he murdered. I promise." She turned to him, tears still in her eyes, and she hugged him.

"Thank you, Flint." She said quietly, and Flint smiled. He had finally found a friend.

••

Back at the castle, Jonah lay in his sick bed. King Thanatos, his father, entered the room.

"Everyone in this room is dismissed until further notice. Go." All of the doctors and assistants left the room, and Thanatos closed the door behind them, and locked the top.

"I assume everything is going as planned?" He asked, and Jonah coughed.

"Y-Yes, father. Everything is falling in place, just as you said. W-Where is Flintlock?"

Thanatos grumbled.

"That bastard boy... I have not seen him for hours. Nevertheless, the plan is falling perfectly in place. He knows that he is to be king, and the mages have been working on the crown. The only thing left to be certain of is the Blade. You said the Southern Mages are holding on to it?"

"Yes, father." Jonah coughed. "They are waiting for the right host. This will sound absurd, but..." He coughed again. "They say it needs someone pure of heart. Someone to truly connect with it both spiritually, and physically."

Thanatos opened his mouth, but was interrupted by a servant knocking on the door. The king approached the door, and met the servant.

"Well, spit it out!" He shouted, and the servant whispered something to Thanatos. He smiled with his teeth, and turned back to Jonah, shutting the servant outside the room.

"I have just been informed that young Flintlock has been leaving the castle and spending time with a group of children his age." He snapped his fingers loudly, and the servant re-entered the room.

"Research every one of these children Flint has been talking to. Watch them. Observe everything they do. Report back next month. The results should be satisfactory." The servant nodded, and shut the door. "This is going to be very interesting..." Thanatos said, chuckling.

Chapter 18

Will, Becky and Jack stood in awe of Jonah's presence, as his previous order still lingered in the air. Taking charge, Will stepped before the ghostly figure.

"My name is Will, and these are my partners Becky and Jack." Will spoke, and held up the shining Blade of Atlas. "We resurrected you with this blade, as said in the prophecy."

"I see." Jonah spoke in thought. "Who is the current king? What is his name?"

The others still stood in shock, but Will was able to stammer out an answer despite his uncertainty of the previous prince's intentions.

"Uh... Flint. King Flint. The city is very far away from where we are, though." Will informed Jonah, and Jonah pulled the bow from around his back and fingered the string.

"Well then." He said energetically. "We must be going now, shall we?"

The three looked between each other concernedly, and looked back to Jonah.

"You... know what we are doing, right?" Jack asked.

"Of course, as I have known for a long time. You see, my brother Flint... he had always been jealous of me when we were young. One day, I was approached by a prophet. Or, more-so a mage using prophetic magic. He warned me that I would be murdered, and put a spell on me."

He pointed to the Blade of Atlas in Will's hands, and turned to the sun in the distance.

"He connected my spirit to that blade, and arranged it so that that sword could one day resurrect me. As the weeks went by, I became more nervous, and my brother grew more envious of my future status. One day, it was too much, and he stabbed me in the heart. The last thing I saw before it all faded was the grin on his entitled face..."

He paused, and turned toward the group again.

"I want to help you bring an end to the tyrannical reign of my family. My brother is tainted by the sadistic spirit of my father, and by stopping him, I believe we can bring peace to Pyronia at last. But you are going to have to trust me."

He held out a hand, with a serious look on his face. After a moment of silence, Will stepped forward.

"Well... what you said sounded sincere, man. We kind of have to work with you anyway according to that prophecy, so welcome to the team, I guess." He said unsurely.

The new group began their journey back to the kingdom, and started back down the road they had come on before. Hours passed and the group grew exhausted, and despite Jonah longing to continue, they paused and set up camp for the night.

When Jack and Will had prepared and lit the fire, the four gathered around.

"I guess I'm off to get food, then." Jack proclaimed, grabbing his hunting knife from his bag. "Be back in a jiff."

He began away from the fire, when Jonah stopped him.

"Allow me. My arrows give me more range than your knife would give you."

"Your... arrows." Jack said confused, peering around towards Jonah's empty quiver.

"Ah, yes." Jonah said remembering, and snapped his fingers. Suddenly, his quiver was filled with smoking arrows. "Just a small mage trick of mine." He smiled and walked away.

The three sat around the flames, and Becky grew excited.

"He's a magic user as well! Maybe he can teach me!" She proclaimed.

"I don't know, he seems to be around our age, so he may be less experienced. I don't think we can trust this guy very much anyways." Jack spat out, and Becky frowned.

"Come on. He's a victim of the king, like we are. He sounded so honest and sincere."

"Listen, I don't trust him either, but I have to side with Becky on this one." Will spoke to Jack. "According to that prophecy, we need him. And it seems like he knows more about the blade than we do. Maybe he can explain the glowing eyes thing that happened at Wolf's place."

Jack crossed his arms and sighed.

"Ok, whatever you two say. There's just something so off about this guy."

"There's nothing 'off' about him! He is in the same situation as us! Weren't you listening?" Becky argued.

"Have you considered that he was lying?" Jack asked in a confronting manner. "He's the king's brother. How do you know he isn't secretly siding with him?"

Becky stood up in annoyance.

"He isn't siding with him; he was killed by him! Are you that dense?" She yelled, and Will stood between them with his arms blocking their path.

"Ok, ok. Calm down, both of you. Let's just give it more time, and we'll see how we feel. Ok?" They both grunted in anger, and Becky sat back down.

Jonah returned around 10 minutes later with a deer-like creature. Nobody questioned him, and they began to prepare dinner. Later that night, Will lay awake on the ground, staring at the stars. He wondered what the true intentions of this 'Jonah' person were. Maybe that wasn't even his name.

Things were all happening so quickly, Will had grown overwhelmed. He took a deep breath, and focused on the dim, but prominent light of the distant flames across the sky. He shut his eyes, and his mind went silent.

Will was woken by shouts and loud noises, as he was yanked up from the ground by Jack. As his vision cleared, he could see flashing lights coming from a figure in front of him. As he woke himself up, he realized there were much more than one figure before him.

Dozens of armed men approached from a distance, moving towards them at a rapidly increasing speed. They wore the insignia of the king, and Will shot awake. He grabbed the Blade of Atlas, and stepped up next to Jonah and Becky, who were shooting ranged attacks toward the battalion.

"Someone must have given them a tip about where we were headed!" Becky shouted as she shot a flare of fire at one of the soldiers, who reflected it with his thick shield.

"We cannot hold them back for much longer!" Jonah shouted, as he re-strung his bow.

Will held the sword, and closed his eyes.

Come on. He thought. *Do the glowy-eyes thing.*

Nothing happened. He closed his eyes again and tried even harder, but to no avail. When the soldiers had grown too close for comfort, Will opened his eyes and took a breath.

"Damn it!" He muttered, and charged into the crowd. Wolf's lessons were about to pay off.

Will approached the man in the front and struck his spear from the bottom with all of his might. It flew from the soldier's hands and Will, holding the Blade of Atlas over his head, brought it down across the chest of the soldier. He yelled, and dropped to the ground.

Oh Shit. Is he dead? Will thought in panic.

Before he could process what had happened, another man jabbed his spear toward Will in fury. Reflecting the attack, Will continued to slash against the incoming thrusts. To Will's left, an explosion rang out, and three or four men were launched into the air.

In the commotion, one of the men in front of Will smashed the blunt of their spear across Will's head, and he fell to the ground. Before he could move, soldiers began to throw their weight on top of Will to prevent his recovery.

Suddenly, the world flashed red and Will's ears began to ring horribly. He was thrown into the air, and landed on his side around 10 feet from where he was. As he stumbled to get up, Jack ran over to help him.

As the throbbing in Will's ears left him, he remembered that the Blade of Atlas was still in the pile of men that had been covering him. Turning his stumble into a sprint, he ran back into the crowd of armored men. Sliding under the standing soldiers, he grabbed the sword and sliced up the leg of one. Lifting himself back up swiftly, Will leaped back into the fight.

When there were only around a dozen men left, Will grinned in triumph. Running back to regroup with Jack, Jonah, and Becky, He shouted over the commotion.

"We got this! Only a few more!" They were all breathing heavily, but they could all nod in agreement.

Suddenly, behind the remaining men, ran around 20 more. *Shit.* Will thought to himself. *Someone must have called for reinforcements.*

"Son of a bitch!" Jack complained, heaving for air. "I'm not sure how much longer I can do this for!"

"It's ok, we can win this battle! We have the privilege of range!" Jonah called in response. But the reinforcements were not carrying spears. Will had absolutely no idea what they were holding.

Those almost look like... Will thought to himself, before coming to a dark realization.

Each man carried a large, gun-like weapon, which looked similar to the shocker bands that the rebellion had invented. They must've taken his shocker band when he was arrested all that time ago, and used it to invent some sort of stronger, more distance-covering device. As they approached, the remaining spear users stepped out of their way.

"We need to get out of here, now!" Will shouted in a panic.

"Why? Will, what are those things?" Becky yelled in response.

"Just go!" He screamed, and the soldiers pulled the triggers in unison.

Large, metal-made nets shot rapidly from the barrels, and they landed roughly across the ground in front of the group.

"DUCK!" Will screamed as he dove for cover.

Becky blew a few of them from the sky, while Jonah and Jack rolled away like Will.

One of the nets landed near Becky and narrowly missed her. Another landed near Jonah around the same distance as the one near Becky, and it was pulled towards him almost magnetically.

Wrapping around him in a cocoon fashion, it suddenly shot a large burst of electricity around Jonah and caused him to scream in agony. Jonah dropped to the ground unconscious, and Will went pale.

"They are magnetically attracted!" He shouted desperately to his standing friends. "Drop anything metal you have!" Before they could react, another net fell and wrapped around Jack, and he screamed while clutching his chest, falling to the dirt, also unconscious.

"No!" Will shouted painfully as he looked in the sky, watching as a net hurdled toward his location.

He threw his blade to the side as fast as he could, but not fast enough to prevent the net from glazing his arm. He shouted in pain, and his arm went limp. He looked at Becky, who looked back in morbid horror.

They had failed. It was over. They hadn't even been able to reach the king, and they had failed. Becky cried out to Will as a net wrapped around her, and she dropped to the ground. Reaching for his blade, Will's legs began to shake in exhaustion.

Suddenly, he felt a scorching pain hug his body. He tried to look down, but his eyes wouldn't move. Dropping to the ground, the world around Will slowly went dark. The last thing he saw was shadowy figures approaching his body. Trying to reach out one more time, Will's eyesight faded.

Chapter 19

Will awoke to a large bump. His head hurt like hell. He tried to grab his head, but his hands were stuck. He opened his eyes and looked around. Jack and Becky lay asleep next to him, in shackles. Jonah sat in front of him, gazing out the barred windows.

They were in a carriage bed, connected to a vehicle. The walls were made of metal, and barely any light was able to fight its way through the slim holes of the windows.

"Where are we?" Will asked quietly and Jonah turned backwards to face him.

"We seem to be close to the city. They have taken our weapons. There is... nothing to be done."

Will's heart sank into his gut, and he keeled over. The men who had taken them had also taken the Blade of Atlas. Will thought of his newfound fantasies of being the "chosen one", which now seemed childish. For just a little bit, he had truly believed that Becky Jack and he had a chance at saving the world.

Will had been raised on the many stories of his mother and father, the quests they had taken in the name of the city, the amazing things they had seen. Maybe his dream had been arrogant, but he had always wished that he could matter like his parents had. That he could do more than just be some insignificant scout, or a simple pawn for the Rebellion.

The carriage hit another heavy bump, and Jack was shaken from his rest.

"Huh?" He sat up and came to the same realization as Will had moments before. "Oh."

He said and frowned in shame and disappointment.

"There is still hope yet." Jonah spoke. "Perhaps they are taking us to see the king. We can use that opportunity to attack him."

Will shook his head softly.

"Who's to say they won't just bring us straight to the dungeon again?" Will asked. "And even if they brought us to the king, we would still be in chains. And without weapons." He added and sighed.

The three sat in silence for a moment, and Jack's eyes opened suddenly.

"You said they took our weapons." Jack said quickly, and Will nodded. "Check my back pocket. The zipped one on the right." Jack said, turning to face the wall.

Will maneuvered his body to opposite Jacks, and felt around for his pocket. Grabbing the zipper, he opened it. Feeling through, he felt something cold and stiff. Pulling it out, it felt like the dagger Jack had used back at the castle dungeon.

Taking it from Will, Jack began to pick the lock on his handcuffs.

"Grandpa's dagger always comes in handy." He exclaimed with a smirk.

The handcuffs fell to the floor with a clang, and he turned to take Will's off. When Will and Jonah had been uncuffed by Jack, they huddled around the center of the carriage.

"We can't let this vehicle reach the castle." Will spoke. "There will be too many soldiers, and we are unarmed."

"So, what's the plan?" Jack spoke, looking up.

Will turned to Jonah.

"Is there anything you can do without your bow?"

"It's not very strong, and I didn't have a lot of time to learn it, but I can move an object through the air. Not a very large one, but I can move something small." Jonah responded.

"Do you think you could get a rock stuck in one of the wheels now that your hands are free?" Will asked, and Jonah nodded.

Jonah took a deep breath and held his index and middle fingers together while he did so. Moving his arms backwards in a specific movement, he began to lift his hand upwards, as if he was grabbing something.

Pulling his arms to his chest, the carriage jumped with an audible *crack!* Will could hear the men driving the vehicle shout, and what sounded like the closing of a door.

"The thing's trash. Ruined." He could hear one of them complain through the window.

"I'm gonna check on the escapists." One spoke. "Watch my back, will ya?" Will listened to the door begin to unlock, and he nodded towards it. Jack shook Becky awake, and she jumped.

"Hey! What's..." Jack covered her mouth, helping her to her feet, and as he could hear the large metal lock coming off, Will kicked the door with all of his might, straight into the face of the man who had unlocked it.

The sun shot into the bed of the carriage, and Will leaped out before his eyes could adjust. The man who had unlocked it was a guard, who now lay on the ground clenching his forehead.

Before he could react, the other guard jumped on top of Will, in an attempt to tackle him. Will struggled, trying to shake him off, and as his knees began to tremble, Jack leaped from the back of the carriage and drove his dagger into the guards back. He groaned loudly and fell off Will onto the ground. Jonah and Becky followed Jack out and the four huddled together.

"Now what? Where do we go?" Jack asked.

Will looked around to observe their surroundings and came to the realization that they were back in the capital city of *Thanatos*. A few civilian bystanders stood in shock, absorbing what had happened, and Will heard shouts from further down the road.

They were in the middle of the street on a very busy road, and vehicles were driving by slowly attempting to view the chaos. The shouts grew closer and Will turned his attention to them.

Dozens of royal soldiers were headed in their direction, armed and prepared for a fight.

"We need to get our weapons now!" Will shouted, opening the front door to the car. The group grabbed their weapons frantically and the soldiers grew closer.

"We cannot fight them, there are too many!" Jonah shouted, as the guards began to aim more of the shocker band-like guns at the four of them.

Will looked to his surroundings frantically and spotted an alleyway to his left. It was worn and graffitied, with an emptied trash bin in the center.

"Follow me!" Will shouted, as the other three nodded and ran after him.

Will closed his eyes for a moment and thought of his old scout routes during his time in the rebellion. *That's it!* He thought to himself. The rebellion. It would be the perfect place to hide while they prepared for their fight with the king. They had a chance to save the world once again, and Will smiled in pride. All they had to do was make it there.

Will vaulted over the trash bin, knocking it over. Jonah ran through, ignoring it, and Jack jumped upon the wall and leaped off of it, in an attempt to both give himself a boost and to show off in opposition to Will. Becky held her dress up slightly to keep up with the others, and cringed at the smell of the trash when she ran by it. The group emerged from the other side of the alley, and re-entered the streets.

Will could see a few soldiers emerging from the end of the road to chase them, and looked back to see more tailing them from the alleyway. He decided to turn downwards, and hustled down the steep road. Followed by Jonah, who was much more athletic than he had believed, Jack, and Becky, Will approached the end of the road and dove down the next. Taking a sharp turn down a longer, slenderer one-way road, Will looked for a place to hide from the searching party.

At the right side of the road, Will saw a small, run-down pizza joint. It was so old and out of sight that Will thought that it would be the perfect place to hide for the next hour or few. The four of them made their way quickly up the road, and scurried through the door. Will let out a slow sigh, and the door swung shut.

He looked up at the faded interior sign that hung above the register, which read *Giorno's #1 Pizza, the best pizza in all of Pyronia!* The man that stood behind the register was older, in many more ways than one. His white, dry hair drew contrast with his tan, wrinkled face. His eyes hung, worn and pain heavy, and his eyes looked as if they had lost their color long ago.

He looked up at the group, but locked his eyes on Will. For a moment, Will worried that he noticed him as an outlaw. But the look he gave Will was something different. Something that Will could not understand.

"What's with the weapons, eh?" The man asked in a parch, low voice. "I 'ont bite."

"Sir, do you think we could get something to eat?" Will asked, but the man looked at him in silence for a minute.

"That sword..." He said, lightly pointing at the Blade of Atlas. "Ne'rmind. That sword o' yers just looks... familiar..." Will smiled, not knowing how to respond.

"So how much will I owe you for a plain pie?" Will asked.

Despite everyone else loving some kind of complicated pizza, Will had always enjoyed just a plain cheese pizza. Darla had said she never understood it, but Will didn't either. It was somewhat of an instinct. The man, whose name tag read *Giorno*, chuckled.

"I'll put it on the tab." He said with a smile, and headed to the kitchen. Will did a double take, but he swore that he saw a light tear on the old man's face.

The group sat around a corner table to stay out of sight. They all sat in silence for a few minutes, before Becky broke the silence.

"What happened? And why didn't you guys wake me up, I don't know, before we tried jumping our kidnappers and barely escaping!" Will frowned in shame, as did Jack.

"Uh... I'm sorry Beck... we just..." Jack stammered quietly.

"We didn't think that plan through very much. That's our fault." Will interrupted. "I guess it was in the moment or something. Sorry man."

"But we got out!" Jack sat straight and butted in.

"Yeah, we did." Becky added. "But what's the plan now?" Will took a breath to gather his thoughts, and spoke.

"Remember when I asked you guys about joining the rebellion? I know it was a while ago, and way before all of this prophecy stuff... but I was thinking..." He stuttered. "I mean if you don't have a place to stay... Maybe we could stay there until we are prepared to fight the king. Maybe they could even help us get there!"

Becky and Jack looked between each other, then turned back towards Will. Becky nodded quickly, and spoke.

"Why not? It would be nice to meet some more people like us."

"And maybe I can get an actual weapon like you guys." Jack added.

Will laughed in joy and thought of his friends at the Rebellion that he had been away from for so long. Louie, Bella, Darla. He would finally see them again. *They must be so pissed at me.* Will thought, thinking about his attempt to take down that guard. Defenseless. On his own.

Will put his hand to his face in shame of his immaturity at that moment. He had nearly gotten Bella and Louie arrested as well. But they would forgive him in time. He couldn't wait to tell them about all of the places he had seen, all of the people he had met.

Jonah broke Will's daydreams and spoke.

"I apologize if I sound strange, but what is 'the rebellion'? There was never one when I was alive before."

"It's a large group of people dedicated to fighting the throne." Becky responded. "Will used to be part of it, before we left to find you." Jonah thought to himself for a moment, and Will did the same.

He had forgotten that Jonah was the son of the previous king, Thanatos. He had been friendly to the three of them, but Will was still unsure where his loyalties lie. He had seemed to have a strange reaction to hearing about the rebellion. Will turned to look at him, and Jonah seemed to be silently, yet subtly observing him.

Soon enough, the pizza was brought out and they began to eat together. Will spaced out through the group chatter, and stared out the window. The sun now lay over the rooftops, making its way down the horizon. When the group had finished their meal, Will stood up.

"Alright. We should head out now if we want to make it there before dark." No one argued, and they left together. Will thanked the man at the register, and he nodded back.

Will dropped some loose carchans in the tip jar, and the old man smiled. He could hear the man mumble something through the grin that sounded along the lines of 'Same old, same old'. Will smiled back, and left the small pizzeria with the others.

Chapter 20

By the time they made it to the Rebellion headquarters, the sun had completely set. The woods outside the entrance were dark and cold, and Will could hear strange wild-like noises coming from his left. The trees swayed slowly in the dusk breeze above him, and his friends were the only other thing he could see beside the path they walked together on.

Jonah walked with a calm stride on Will's right, with a neutral expression of serenity across his face. His focus lay on the towering doors of the Rebellion base, which had been seemingly forced open.

The ground before the doors was covered in metal and dried blood, and the large opened doors creaked in the evening wind.

"Oh no..."

Will spoke under his breath, but he found himself near breathless. His heart sank into his chest as if it had been tied to an anchor, as it clenched the bottom of his gut in a painful grip. He opened his mouth to speak again but the words could not be found. The overwhelming silence of his previously occupied home powered over the group, and Jack was the first to break the silence.

"What... what happened here?"

Will couldn't bring himself to respond. Taking a hesitant step forward, Will entered the abandoned base, and dust blew across his legs softly.

As he walked ahead of the others, Will lamented in silence at the barren homes of those he had grown with. It seemed as if they had all been in a rush, as belongings were strewn across the ground in front of each building. Will approached the nearest one, and knelt to the ground. He picked up a stuffed animal which had been dropped to the ground, which was now covered in a grey coat of dust. He closed his eyes as his heart clenched even harder, and he grit his teeth in rage.

He could have been here for his people. He could have finally done something useful, and died alongside those he had trusted the most. Louie, Bella, Darla, and the many others beside her. Will had no way of knowing if they had been able to escape whatever had happened.

Will stood and dropped the animal to the ground, and clenched his fist in pain. He took a long and shaky breath, and felt a hand on his shoulder behind him.

"It's not your fault, man. There is nothing you could've done." Jack said, standing to Will's right. He turned to face him, but couldn't find the right words to say in response. He simply stared coldly into his eyes, struggling to hold back tears.

Will broke off from Jack, and turned toward his old dorm room, which had now been worn and slightly damaged. He turned away quickly flinching as his chest sunk further down his gut. Will looked over his shoulder at the rest of the group, who were all watching him silently.

"Don't fear for the ones you love." Jonah said in a monotone voice. "The strong will have survived; the weak will have died. It is up to you to determine where your loved ones reside."

Will had no reaction to his attempt at calming him, and released another shaky breath. Struggling to open his mouth, Will was finally able to mutter the words "It's ok". Becky looked as if she was going to speak, but chose not to.

"Let's... Let's just start a fire. I'm sure there is something to eat around here." He said suddenly. "There is a garden next to the forge." He pointed to what used to be the forge, but had now been emptied of anything resembling one, except for a very worn obsidian anvil, which had been used countless times over many years. Jack approached Will again, concernedly.

"Are you sure you're ok? We can give you some time if you want-"

"Yes, I'm... fine." Will spoke over him sharply, grabbing a basket from the side of a dorm and starting toward the garden.

Later that night, the group were gathered around the fireside, laughing and telling stories over a fresh vegetable dinner. Will, however, stayed silent through the chatter and thought to himself more. He lightly picked at the meal that they had prepared, and stared deeply into the hearth of the fire. He closed his eyes for a moment to let the smoke brush against his face, and he held his breath through it. All of a sudden, he looked up slowly and stood from the ground. "I'm going to take a walk." He said, and no one answered beside a subtle nod from Jack. Becky watched him as he walked around the corner of the building the fire was next to, and disappeared into the night.

Will walked up to his dark room, and opened the unlocked door. It still smelled as it did before he left that morning many nights ago. He walked up to the wall beside his bed and twisted on an artificial lamp that hung beside his bed. The room was lit in an orange light, and he sat on his cold bed.

Will opened the drawer of his nightstand table, and carefully pulled out an old picture. Blowing the dust off the top of it, he examined the photo, which was of his parents. His father had his hair cut short, and wore a sheath around his back. His mother wore cracked spectacles, and held a hand over her stomach, which was far in pregnancy.

Will looked at the smiles across their faces, how happy they were together. The king had taken that from them. From him. Maybe if they had survived, they could have taught him what they knew. Maybe Will would have been more than just some scout. Will clenched his fist hardly, and put his other hand over his face in anguish. Everyone at the rebellion had always expected amazing things from Will, being the son of the great warrior Ted Larson. Now with the Blade of Atlas, the world had so much faith in him to save it from pain and tyranny.

I can't do it. Thought Will, and a tear went down his cheek.

"I can't do it." He spoke softly, then shouted. "I CAN'T DO IT!" He threw the picture next to him on the bed, and unsheathed the Blade of Atlas.

"How did you do it?" He asked, looking up. "Damn it, answer me! You haven't been there for me my whole life, and everyone wants me to be you! I'm not you! I'm not anything!" He looked at the sword that gleamed in the flaming light.

"It must be the maker's sickest joke, making me of all people, this hero. I can't even save some beggar from a couple pricks with spears, let alone save the entire kingdom from a mass-murdering maniac with an army of killers! I couldn't save my friends from those guards with the guns, and worst of all, I left everyone here to rot so I could play out this fucking fantasy that maybe I could be useful to someone!" He shouted at the ceiling, half-hoping for an answer. He looked down through tears, and chuckled.

"I sound insane. What am I doing?" He looked at the blade, and put it back in its sheath. "What am I doing wrong?" He said to himself, punching his forehead with both hands in anger. "Tell me, Maker, tell me ANYTHING!" He screamed, throwing a small stone figurine at the wall, smashing it.

As Will grabbed his hair and dropped more tears, there was a quiet knock at the door. Will put his hands by his side and turned his gaze to the source of the noise, and the door opened. Becky entered slowly, with a concerned expression on her face.

"Oh- Hey, what's up?" He stuttered, desperately trying to wipe away any visible tears.

"Can I sit here?" She asked, and Will nodded.

"How... How much of that did you hear?" Will asked.

"A little." She responded, sitting next to him.

She took off her hat, and let her long, brown hair loose for the first time in front of Will. It shined in the orange light of the lamp, and she brushed it backwards. She picked up the picture of Will's parents, and examined it carefully.

"You look just like them." She said with a smile, and he grinned softly back, staying silent for a moment.

"Jack and Jonah didn't hear what I said, right? They... aren't standing outside listening or anything?" Will asked, and Becky shook her head.

"I snuck off soon after you did. They are still by the fire relaxing." She looked up to the ceiling, then to the pile of rubble where Will had thrown the figure.

"Jack was right. None of what happened here was your fault." She spoke, and Will sighed.

"I know. But I can't help but feel responsible. I could have been here."

"No, you couldn't have. You were taken wrongfully by the king, just like we were. That isn't your fault, it's his." Becky said surely, but Will shook his head.

"I was on a scout mission. We had a routine, and it always ran like clockwork. But there was a man who was being attacked by a guard, and I... I chose to intervene. I wasn't supposed to, but I did. I made the choice to leave them, because I wanted to help others. I wanted to actually do something, like my mother and father had. But it was a selfish decision." He said in shame.

"I think it was very brave of you to try and save that man like that. It was the right thing to do, and I'm sure your parents would have been proud of you if they could have seen what you chose to do. Besides, if you never did that we wouldn't have met." Becky said, nudging him, and he smiled.

"Yeah, you're right." He turned back to a frown.

"But now what? The whole kingdom is counting on me to free them from the king, but I can't even stop a few of his men. My father couldn't even beat the king in a fight, how am I supposed to?"

"What happened back there with the kings' men wasn't your fault. We weren't ready for their new technology." She said comfortingly, and put her hand on his shoulder. "Your father would have been proud of how quickly you're learning to fight, and all the progress you've made. I promise."

Will smiled at her care, and thanked her. She gave him a firm hug, then sat quietly for a minute next to him. Will let the room sit for a bit, and then spoke again.

"Do... Do you have any idea where your family went when you ran away?" She frowned and shook her head softly. "I don't want to get your hopes up... But if everything went as planned there would have been an evacuation procedure. In the rebellion. I remember Darla mentioning a hidden hideout near the Kandachta district somewhere. Maybe... maybe they are there now. With the Rebellion." She thought for a second, and looked back at him.

"I'm not sure. I had always considered the possibility that they had joined the rebellion, but I had no way of finding out."

"There were many entire families in the rebellion if I remember correctly. Darla and I were raised by her parents, and her cousin Amber grew up there as well. I think she's the blacksmith now, or an apprentice at least."

"How are we even supposed to get to the hidden base?" She asked, and Will turned in thought.

"Well, there must be some sort of hidden tunnel that leads to the base around here. Maybe we can follow it and try to find the Rebellion." He responded, and Becky nodded.

"Yes! Then you can get the proper training to fight the king!" She exclaimed excitedly.

Right. Will thought. *Fighting the king.*

"But let's look for it tomorrow. It's really late." She turned to face the door. "We'll be out here if you want to join us, but I understand if you want to sleep here." She said to Will.

"I think I might bunk in here for the night." He responded, and Becky turned to leave. Before she went through the door, Will spoke again. "Hey Beck?" She turned around. "Thanks for coming to see me. I appreciate it a lot."

She smiled, and left the dorm room. Will the remaining dust off his blanket and threw it over himself. Closing his eyes, he switched off the lamp beside him.

•••

Will woke up late in the night and rubbed his eyes. He sat up in his bed, and got out slowly. He walked over to his window, and observed the full moon above the empty Rebellion base. Its light colored the pale terrain in a white gleam, and Will was amazed at its beauty.

Suddenly, Will spotted a human-like figure moving outside. They wore a hood over their head, and ran across the ground in front of Will's dorm. Will slipped on his shoes, and followed the figure outside. He snuck behind it so he wouldn't be noticed, and the person approached the large entrance to the base.

"Hey, what are you doing?" The figure turned toward Will sharply, and revealed their identity. It was Jonah.

"Jonah, where are you going?" He asked in a confused manner.

"It is none of your concern. I was simply... going for a jog." Will frowned at the obvious lie, and unsheathed the Blade of Atlas.

"Yeah right. Now answer my question. Where are you going?" Jonah smirked, which was something Will hadn't seen before.

"I would say that you will regret doing this, but you won't be able to remember anything by the time you wake." Before Will could respond, Jonah snapped his wrist stiffly and a crackle of lightning struck Will's forehead. Will swiftly lost all control of his body, and fell to his knees.

"I'll see you in the morning, Will." Jonah snarked as he left the Rebellion base. Will's eyesight began to fade, and he fell with a thump to the ground.

Chapter 21

The royal palace was completely silent at midnight. Flint sat by himself at a large desk, which was covered in wrinkled paperwork. His eyes were painted in dark grey bags, and he struggled to hold them open. He began to read the newest guard report. There had been a criminal breakout on Cyle Street that day. Flint thought of the location and flinched. Before he could read who the escapees were, he flipped the page over and took a deep breath.

Suddenly the palace door swung open loudly. This was impossible however, as they were locked with the strongest material in the entire kingdom. Flint sighed, and unsheathed his blood red blade. Before Flint could move, his head throbbed.

IT IS HIM.

The three words from his father rung powerfully in his head, and he re-sheathed his sword. Jonah hovered into the room slowly, and landed on his feet in front of Flint.

"Hello brother." He said quietly. "You look old." Flint sat in silence for a moment, and felt his beard softly.

"And you seem to have retained your youth. Interesting." He responded.

"Tell me brother, exactly how long have I been gone?"

"39 years." Flint responded solemnly.

"I assume the kingdom has been held stable during this time?" Jonah asked in an accusatory fashion.

"Of course. There is no doubt that I have established order here."

"Well, of course you must be forgetting the rebellion that is afoot." Flint flinched in surprise.

"I… I thought you hadn't heard of that."

"But I have, Flintlock. In fact, I have been traveling with one of their members. It is he who wields the Blade of Atlas." Jonah spoke in response.

"I am aware. I have had many platoons in search of them, including the most powerful super soldier the kingdom has ever had in control." Flint added, and Jonah looked in an intrigued manner.

"Tell me more about this 'super soldier'. Where is he now?"

"Last I heard, he was approaching the graveyard where you had been buried. He is yet to know that you have been woken. You and those rebels came in contact with one of my smaller squadrons in the desert district, separate from his. You are lucky that they did not bring you four directly to him, instead of here in the city." Flint said.

"He has been trained for years in hand-to-hand combat, mastered swordsmanship, and given titanium armor of the highest quality. He is very much the prized possession of the Pyronian militia." Flint continued as Jonah nodded slowly.

"I would like to meet this man." He spoke after a few moments.

For the remainder of the night, Jonah observed Flint as he returned to his paperwork. When he once again reached the report of Jonah's escape with the others, he opened the lower drawer of the desk and placed it down.

As he continued observing and responding to the papers on his desk, Jonah hovered close. There were criminal reports, tax collection reports, and personal requests, which Jonah had found to be absurd. Nevertheless, Flint spent the remaining few hours of the night carefully going through each one and responding in the best manner.

After it had all been filed and put away, it had grown close to morning. The bags under Flint's eyes had grown even darker, and he sighed. Before they could react, a messenger entered the room quickly.

"My liege." She spoke. "I carry a message from Kronos. He was unable to find the criminals despite a thorough search of the desert district."

"Tell him to return to the city. I would like to speak with him. I have taken care of the situation for the time being." The messenger left the room, and Flint sat upon the throne. Jonah floated in place, and glided over behind him.

"Well brother, it's been nice, but I must be going now. We'll meet again eventually. Until then, prepare yourself. Remember the plan." Jonah spoke, and Flint nodded. Jonah flew out the doors, and they both shut with a slam. Flint was once again left in solidarity.

Chapter 22

"Will! Oh crap, are you ok?" Will awoke to the sound of Becky's shouts, and tried to sit up. He was covered in dust, head to toe. He wiped off his face, and spit out the dirt that was in his mouth.

"What are you doing out here?" Becky shouted as she and Jack grew closer. Will struggled to stand up, but did so successfully.

"I..." He began, and he grabbed his head at the pound of his migraine. "I have no clue. Where's..." Jonah came running up from behind Jack, and stopped in front of Will.

"Where's who?" Jack asked, confused, and Will shook his head lightly.

"N-Never mind."

Will had absolutely no recollection of what had happened the previous night, and he had been left with a burning migraine. He began to walk away from the others in shame, and spoke.

"I... I'm gonna take a bit to clean up." He re-entered his room and grabbed a pair of clothes, and opened his own shower curtains for the first time in nearly two months. It took a long time to scrub the dust and dirt from his hair.

At that time, he thought back to his conversation with Becky the day before. They needed to find the new rebellion base, and train.

Will thought of Wolf, the man he had met outside the city while they traveled to find Jonah. Perhaps he had joined the rebellion while he was gone. Will shook his head at the thought. The poor old man had been through enough.

After he left the shower and slipped his clothes on, Will regrouped with the others.

"I feel a bit better now." He spoke. That was a lie, but he didn't want his friends to worry like they had yesterday. Seeing the others in the rebellion again would be incredibly difficult for him, but knowing that there are some he wouldn't see is even more difficult. He closed his eyes and swallowed back his emotions, and spoke again.

"The rebellion has a secret tunnel somewhere around here that leads to their panic base. If we can find the tunnel, we may be able to find the base. But we'll have to start looking now if we want to find it before sunset." The others nodded, and split apart. Before Will could walk away, someone grabbed his arm.

"Seriously. Talk to me." It was Becky. "What happened last night after I left your room?"

"I have no idea. I'm being honest, I swear." He responded.

"I want to help. You can't just magically wake up outside on the ground. What did you do?"

"I said I don't know! It hurts to think about. Believe me, I want to know too, but there are more important things to worry about right now." He tried to step away again, and she stepped in front of him.

"I'm not sure what happened, but you looked really bad when we found you. I don't understand how you don't know what happened, but I'll believe you if it makes you feel better." She said in an attempt to lower tension. "You are going through a lot right now. We all have at some point. I understand how you feel." Will clenched his teeth, and his lips quivered. Holding back a tear, he grumbled.

"No, you don't." He walked away with his hands in his pockets.

When Becky walked back to Jack and Jonah, she didn't say a word. Jonah felt his hand along the stone barrier wall, in search of a lever or button of sorts.

"At this rate, we may never find this tunnel." Jonah spoke at last. "Would it be more in our favor to fight the king now? We outnumber him anyways, which would give us a major advantage."

"No." Becky instantly shot the idea down. "Will needs time to train. We all do."

"You may have gotten royal bow training or something but we got nothin' man." Jack stepped in, siding with Becky. "We really need some work on our skills."

"I see. Very well then." He said in immediate agreement.

Jack turned to face Becky and moved closer, sliding away from Jonah to gain a small bit of privacy with his friend.

"How's he doing?" He asked concernedly.

"Not good. He's really crushed."

"I really wish I could do more, but I don't really know what to say, y'know?" He added. "What's going on between you two anyways? You've been spending a lot of time together, and-"

"Nothing." She interrupted. "I actually wanted to mention something to you. Don't you think it's odd that Will has absolutely no idea what happened to him last night?" She asked.

"He has to know. Maybe he just doesn't want to say."

"No, that's not it. He definitely has no clue." Becky responded quickly, and Jack thought.

"Do you think... Jonah had something to do with it?"

Becky jumped up, almost in an insulted manner.

"Are we really doing this again? He's one of us. At this point, we've gone through enough together to trust him, don't you think?" She spoke, and he shook his head.

"Beck, we've known him for like 3 days. Barely. Y'know how long it took for us to trust each other at first?" She looked up confusingly.

"I thought we trusted each other pretty quickly." She asked, and Jack laughed in a rude manner.

"Well maybe you're remembering it wrong, cuz I was really paranoid then. I used to stay awake until I was one hundred percent sure you were sleeping. I used to sleep on the complete other side of the room from you, even though our mattresses were next to each other. I slept on the floor, Beck, for the first month we knew each other!" Becky took a step back.

"I... I thought you just liked sleeping on the floor or something..." Jack rolled his eyes, and chuckled.

"This world can be a cruel place y'know. When I was on the streets, there was one saying people followed and one only. Watch your damn back, and no one else's." He sighed. "Of course, that's all changed since I met you." She sat in silence for a moment.

"Then... How did you trust Will so quickly? We've only known him for a month or so."

"I had a good feeling, I guess. Didn't have much choice anyways, once we found out he was the chosen one and such." She frowned, and he began to drift away.

"I'm gonna keep looking. But think about what I said, alright?" He walked away, and Becky stood in silence for a few moments before returning to the search.

After many hours of seemingly hopeless searching, Jack shouted for the others to see something he had spotted. Jack found two camouflaged handles connected to the wall on the eastern side of the base that seemingly led to a hidden door built into the dense wall before them.

"Check this out!" He called, pointing at the hidden levers. Will and Jack pulled upwards on each of the handles, and a gate within the wall began to shake and rise, revealing a long and dimly lit tunnel.

The group stared in silence into the seemingly endless tunnel that traveled forward for miles with poorly lit, flickering fluorescent lights. Will was reminded of the tunnels beneath the castle dungeon, which must have had even less light than given here.

"Well, here it is." Will spoke softly. The group scourged the houses and took any food or clothing they could find. As each group member entered the seemingly endless tunnel, Will stepped in last and took one more look at the base that he had called his home for most of his life. He closed his eyes before he could shed a small tear that had built in their crevice, and pulled the gate downwards. He knew that his life would never be the same.

Chapter 23

Darla had finally settled in the new base. It was smaller than the previous base, but it worked for the amount of people there were. It was now night time in the rebellion, and Darla looked out her small office window. Her dorm room was directly connected to her office, which only made her want to work even more. She checked to make sure that no one was around, or outside her office door, and switched the lock. She turned off her small light, and dropped to her knees. In a sudden outburst of tears, Darla began to sob.

"Will, you dumb piece of shit!" She yelled through the emotions. "Why did you go and get yourself killed! Or locked up, whatever the hell you did..." She breathed heavily. "Everyone hates me... You were their only bit of hope, and I just let you get taken... I just let our home get taken... Oh maker, our home!" She screamed in misery.

"I can't take this anymore." She whispered, burying her face in her palms.

A few moments later, there was a knock at her door. She shot up to her feet, and frantically wiped away her tears.

"W-Who is it?" She asked.

"Me, sir." It was Rose. Darla took a deep breath, and opened the door.

"Hey, I just had some questions about-" Rose started, but paused looking up at Darla. "Hey, are you alright?"

"Of course." Darla responded quietly.

"Are you sure?" Darla opened her mouth to respond, but re-thought her answer.

"I told you I'm alright, are you suggesting I'm not?"

"Well, I just... I just wanted to..." Rose stammered in response, but Darla interrupted.

"Just spill what you wanted to ask me." Rose collected herself, and took a breath.

"I wanted to ask about your plan for replenishing resources. At the old base, we had the city's supermarkets and convenience stores at our disposal. We have plenty of canned rations and a clean water well here, but they may only last us approximately 2 months. How are we going to get more supplies?"

Darla took a minute to think, and turned back to Rose.

"We need to search the perimeter. I want you to stay and keep the people calm while I'm gone, and I'll take Kendrick, Bella, and Louie to search for some kind of town or population nearby." Rose nodded, and Darla left the room. After rallying the others, they met in the new armory.

"Finally, something to do!" Louie exclaimed as he grabbed a stylized bayonet from off the wall.

"Don't get too excited. We're looking for some kind of civilization in the desert, and potentially forming some kind of alliance with them for resources." Louie frowned, but still slipped the bayonet into a sheath he had strapped around his waist.

Kendrick picked an unused crossbow from off one of the hooks, and observed it. It was unusual, as it had a roll of eight arrows that could be attached to it, rather than one individual at a time. He opened the metal latch to load it and the bottom opened downwards. He placed the roll onto the crossbow and locked it shut. Slipping a new quiver over his shoulder, he held the crossbow in the air in admiration.

"Sweet." He said quietly, as he clipped it on the quiver on his back.

Darla waited as the others got ready. She grabbed nothing more than her worn mace, and stood by the door silently with a soft frown. Her eyebrows knit together as she stared blankly toward the wall in thought. Bella grabbed a small dagger and pepper spray, and approached Darla.

"How're you holding up?"

"Fine, why do you ask?" Darla responded quickly.

"You're just being pretty quiet. More so than usual." She asked concernedly.

"I said I'm fine." She said, exiting the room.

"What's her problem?" Louie asked, walking toward Bella. Kendrick followed, and shrugged.

"She's never really been the type to talk about her feelings anyways." Kendrick spoke. "Never bothered me honestly."

As the others left the armory to meet with Darla, Bella switched off the light and shut the metal door carefully. It got stuck on the rough terrain, but shut with a thud. She twisted the safe-like lock to the right and it clicked.

After she regrouped with the others, they opened the large exit door to the rebellion and left one by one. They entered a long hallway, which was pitch black. When they had stumbled their way to the end, Darla grabbed a non visible object and twisted it. Opening slowly, the wall moved and let the moonlight brighten the hall. The group walked through the door silently, and Darla shut it, locking it with a key she took from her pocket. The door they had passed through was camouflaged, looking non distinguishable from the rocky cliffside it was attached to.

The desert was different at night. Different than Darla had ever seen before. In her previous trip, she had briefly passed through in the daytime while inside a vehicle. She and Will would have to travel with her father sometimes, and when she was around 11, they were given the opportunity to see the desert district of Kandachta for the first time. She could hardly see from outside the car window, and Will's constant complaints of boredom made focus incredibly difficult. All she could remember was the scorching heat, even through the a/c. Her father had rolled the front window down in hopes that the wind would block the heat, but it did not. At night however, the desert was cold and quiet, unlike Darla ever could have imagined.

By the time they had reached the closest town, Darla had grown uneasy. It was seemingly run down and abandoned, but there were many signs of life as well. There was a building with one of the lights on, and there was a distant noise of a metal can falling to the pavement. But the silence was more powerful.

"Be careful." Darla whispered to the others, as they nodded in response.

Walking down the empty streets, Darla looked closely at the buildings. As she observed the window to her right, she saw a face peek slightly past the curtains, then pull away quickly. She turned to approach them, but was distracted by distant chattering. She looked sharply at the source, and saw a large group of people approaching.

"Quick! This way!" She whispered sternly to the others, and they ran into a dark and slender alleyway.

The group stayed silent as mice and watched closely. The group of people began to pass by, and revealed themselves. Dozens and dozens of men and women, wearing the insignia of the crown. Darla snarled quietly, and watched as they walked by carelessly. When it seemed like they had all passed, Darla looked carefully to make sure that they were gone. Before she could step out, a towering figure walked by the alley.

It was completely covered in metal and technology, and made a horrifying clang with each slow step. Its demon-like gas mask of silver with faintly lit red pupils stared coldly ahead. Its arms were covered in blades and guns, and its torso was covered in the strongest metal possible, with a rusted scythe across the back. It was the sort of thing Will would have found badass when he was younger. But nothing about this moment was badass. The insignia of the king was sprayed across the back of the figure, and it was worn from many years of use.

Suddenly, the figure stopped in place. It turned its head slowly, and its cold, dead eyes stared into the alley where the group resided. Darla could feel its stare pass deep through her soul, and her pulse began to speed. Sweat began to run down her forehead, and her stomach felt more queasy than it had ever felt. For the first time in many years, she was genuinely horrified. Despite her gut telling her to run, she was frozen solid.

"Oh, Maker." She said silently under her breath. "Kronos."

Chapter 24

Will loomed behind the others as they walked down the dimly lit metal tunnel. The walls were colored in an uncanny beige and the dark orange fluorescent lights did them no justice. The air was dry and heavy, and Will breathed slowly to counter it, as he held his sleeve to his mouth to act as a mask.

Time passed inconsistently, and it was unclear as to whether it was day or night. Will never knew the answer to that anymore, as he always felt as if he was exhausted. It was moments like this that made him miss his life before his responsibilities were placed upon him, those nights where he had nothing to worry about but a cold pillow and a solid seven hours of sleep. Now, Will prayed for a mere four hours of sleep, but that didn't matter anyways. The nightmares he had been cursed with for the past few weeks made any notion of sleep unbearable.

Will's internal yearning for sleep was cut off by Jack, who groaned as his feet slid lazily across the floor. His head slumped, and Jonah sneered at Jack's movement.

"Oh, pick yourself up!" He spoke in defiance of Jack's childish mannerisms. "You are a grown man, like the rest of us!"

"I don't wanna hear a word from you, dipshit." Jack grumbled, before noticing that Jonah's feet had ceased to touch the ground as he began to hover. "Hey, wait a minute- you aren't even walking! That can't be fair!" Jack turned toward Will and Becky in a pleading manner. "That's not fair, is it?"

"Dude, I could not care any less." Will said monotone, as he kept walking forward.

"Alright, be that way. But couldn't he cast some spell or something to let us float too?" Jack turned to Becky. "Or you, couldn't you-"

"No, Jack." Becky said sternly. "I am not going to make you fly with magic. Now can we please focus on preserving our energy for the end of this tunnel? We have no idea what to expect."

The group looked down the endless tunnel as Becky's words left her mouth, staring upon the gaze of the flickering lights ahead. The only sound besides the echo of the heroes was a faint droplet of water, falling upon a puddle on the stained floor. The walls, made of concrete and covered with recycled rebellion steel, absorbed most of the light from the dying bulbs above until the hall was hardly lit, proving Becky's statement of uncertainty.

As the group trekked further towards the unseen destination, Will lamented his attitude from the previous day at the rebel base. Jack and Becky had been more accepting of him than most people in the rebellion itself, even though they had only known each other for close to a month and a half at this point. And after everything they had gone through, Will felt like he had returned the favor to his new friends with only more stress than they already had to deal with. Remembering his argument with Becky at his abandoned home, Will approached Becky and put a hand on her arm to get her attention, speaking in a whisper.

"Hey Beck... Can we talk?" She nodded softly and stepped back next to him. Jack walked quicker to give them space, and Jonah followed.

"Hey, uh..." Will started slowly. "I'm... sorry for being a dick back at the base. I know that you understand what it's like to lose someone. It just hurts so much, and it doesn't make it any better that it's all my fault that they could be..." He stopped and looked down.

"I do understand." She spoke after a minute. "Around a month or so after I ran away from home, I decided to return to check on my family. It was hard, but I needed to know they were safe. Re-entering my old neighborhood was one of the scariest things I had ever done, and it had changed so much in the time I was gone. There were many more flags, a guard patrol around nearly every corner... When I finally got home and stepped through the door..." Her eyes began to water, and she looked in the other direction briefly to hide it.

"You know how I told you that I ran away because the pressure of living up to my father was too much?" She asked, changing the subject.

"That isn't necessarily true. My father told me that he was a wizard at a young age, and that I had been born a witch. But he was scared. He told me that we needed to hide the fact that we were magic users. He was afraid that the king would force us to enlist in the army, or kill us in paranoia, or both. I spent my entire childhood hiding my abilities from everyone." She hunched over in pain at her memories, clenching her left arm and digging her nails into her skin in utter shame.

"A bit after I turned 17, about two years ago, I decided to run away. I wanted to find a teacher, or teach myself. It was selfish, but I did it. The irony was, it never led anywhere. I could never find a teacher, no matter how hard I looked. It was as if every ounce of sorcery or anything related had been simply... wiped from the city. For a small portion of time I began to search around the outskirts of the city, but when it hadn't provided any better results than inside the city I gave up hope, and decided to finally return home and face my parents."

"When I returned to my neighborhood, the door to my home had been swung wide open. The lights had been left on, and everything had been thrown everywhere. Some of the windows were broken, and there were scorch marks across the walls... It was horrible." She couldn't hide the tears any longer, and she put her hands over her face.

"The worst part... There was so much blood... On the couch, the tables..." She looked up to him. "I... I had a brother you know. He was only one year old when I left... Every day I think about what they could have done to them, what I could have done to protect them if I was there." She couldn't hold herself together any longer, and broke into tears. They stopped, and Will slowly put his arm around Becky in comfort. She lay her face in his chest, sobbing.

"Becky, listen to me. What happened to them isn't your fault." He whispered in her ear. "You said there were scorch marks.

Maybe your father was able to fight back. Also, there are so many people in the rebellion, it would be impossible to know the names of everyone there. They could be there, safe and protected. Darla would know, assuming she…" He paused. "If she survived."

They stood in silence for a moment in silence before Will broke away, holding his arm awkwardly. He let out a sigh, and turned back to face his friend.

"Thank you for telling me that. I had no idea that you had gone through all of that."

"I should have told you and Jack earlier. I'm just so ashamed of it." She spoke, and Will looked off ahead of them for a second in thought, before turning back to Becky.

"We can't let ourselves get hung up on the past. The only thing we can do is be the best people we can be in their honor."

"Yeah. You're right." She said with a smile, looking at him. "Hey… I'm sorry for bugging you at the base. I know what it's like to experience something like that."

"It's not your fault. At least I know there's someone to talk to, y'know? I…" He paused for a moment. "Thanks for keeping me sane throughout all this. Having someone to talk to during all this stress… It's been nice. It's been really nice." He finished with a grin, and she smiled back.

"We're rebel terrorists being hunted by every man and woman in the state. The least we can do is be each other's therapists for a bit." She joked, bumping his shoulder.

"Really, I appreciate you being here. Back at the rebellion, I didn't really have anyone to talk about personal stuff other than Darla, and she was more like a sister to me y'know? I'm glad that we've been able to just talk. Like friends."

He grinned goofily as he finished his statement, and Becky smiled brightly as she kissed him softly on the cheek in an instant.

"Right." She spoke. "Like friends." She chuckled and ran ahead to catch up with the others.

"Yeah..." Will said to himself, watching her run ahead to meet the others. His eyes still sparkling from the second before, he watched the back of her pointed hat move with each step, and a small feeling swam through Will's chest, hopeful that she would turn around so he could see her eyes again.

When the two had caught up to Jack and Jonah, they were deep in conversation. As they approached, Jack paused and turned in their direction.

"Well. Look who decided to join us." He spoke with a knowing smirk, and Becky slapped him across the back of the head playfully. "Damn, alright." He said, grabbing his head in surprise, while turning in the other direction. "It seems like we're almost there anyways. We've been walking down this path for a while now."

The group looked between each other and smiled. They would finally come in contact with others who wanted to fight back.

"I can't believe it's almost time. We're going to kill the king. Pyronia is gonna be free!" Jack shouted to the others excitement. Will smiled brightly and looked at the rest.

As the group embraced the hope, Will shared excited glances with his teammates. Turning to their newest member, Will swore he could see the smallest smirk across the face of Jonah, who stood away from the rest of the four.

Chapter 25

Darla held her breath. By the time the metallic monster had left the scene, her face was paler than flour. As the four rebels filed into the street one by one, they huddled together.

"What the HELL was that thing?" Kendrick screamed quietly. Bella shook Darla, and she stayed silent.

"Darla, are you ok? What was that?" Bella shouted. Darla could barely open her mouth to speak.

"T-That was Kronos. The king's personal serial murderer. He's built like a tank and brainwashed into ripping the first rebel he spies into a pile of flesh. I've only read about him... I've never seen him in person..." Her hands shook violently, but she swallowed her fear.

"We need to look for as many supplies as we can and get the hell out of here fast." She ordered. "Louie, Bella. Take the eastern side. Grab as much food and artillery you can from the abandoned homes. Ken, you're with me."

They nodded, and ran in their respective directions. The roads were long and dark, and they had to be careful with every turn. At last, they came across a house that was open and empty. Darla and Kendrick approached the door and they entered.

Darla dug through the fridge while Kendrick checked the cellar. The fridge had been emptied, and most of the drawers were ravaged through. There were only six or seven canned bean containers, and a few small sacks of uncooked rice. Kendrick came back up the stairs, carrying a taser and an antique pack of bullets.

"Not much luck?" He asked and she shook her head.

"We have to keep looking anyway." She responded sharply and went back to ruffling through the drawers. When she gave up at last, she turned to Kendrick who had been awaiting orders silently.

"We should split even more." She said as she grabbed an empty tote bag and tossed it to him. "Put everything you can find in here. When it's full, meet me and the others by the end of the town where we entered. Got it?" She put the small amount of food she had found in the tote bag and he nodded.

"Of course. Stay safe." He said quietly, sliding out of the house and darting across the street to the next open one he could find. Darla went in the opposite direction, slipping between two boarded-up houses that had already been ravaged.

Darla kept low to the ground as she sped through the dimly lit streets of the desert town. The streetlamps beside her flickered, briefly revealing her location each second. As she passed more and more houses, she could see dozens of shy eyes watching her from the rooftops. It was frightening, yet comforting at the same time.

After passing a few more tightly locked homes, she stood in front of a large building that stretched seemingly infinitely. A large, dying neon sign hung shakily from the front read 'Quick-Mart'.

Score. She thought as she entered the door, which had been left open. She switched on the lights inside, and they slowly grew into transparency. She grabbed a few plastic bags from the checkout station, and began through one of the isles.

The absolute silence was what she feared the most. She stepped as lightly as possible trying not to alert any who could be nearby. The seemingly endless rows contained little that could be considered salvageable. Bags and boxes were scattered across the floor frantically, as if there had been a struggle where Darla stood. One of the lightbulbs popped loudly above Darla and she jumped. Suddenly, she heard heavy footsteps and ducked down.

"You said she went in here?"

"Yes ma'am."

Shit. Darla thought in a panic. *Shit, shit, shit!* Some passerby had ratted her out. Another pair of boots stamped outside the door, quicker than the previous two.

"Madame, I uh..." He spoke shakingly. The soldier sounded young, perhaps in his early twenties.

I guess that's no younger than I am. Darla thought in contrast to her own thought.

"Well, spit it out." The woman ordered.

"T-The general would like to take care of the situation."

Darla got up from the ground so quickly, she almost slammed her head on the bottom of one of the shelves. She needed to leave that market, and *quickly.* She began to sneak closer to the back, but ducked again when she heard the large metal stomps of Kronos' metallic boots. Peeking past the end of the isle, she got a poor view of him.

Even at a distance, just the sight of his subtle red pupils glaring through the cold, lifeless mask was enough to shake any strong soldier to the bone. Kronos took another step into the store and jerked his arm up and down swiftly, making a horrid scratching noise. His arm mangled and morphed into an oversized machine gun like figure, and he aimed it towards the isles in front of him.

Darla stepped as lightly and softly as humanly possible, and set her eyes on a half open door that read 'Employees only!'. Slipping through the door, she changed her focus to the large exit door at the end of the hallway. Still treading as lightly as possible, she hurried to the door and grabbed the handle.

Turning it, Darla pushed outward as fast as she could. Before she could react, an ear-screeching loud *clang* rang throughout the air. The door, which had only opened about an inch, was locked by a small chain near the top. The footsteps of Kronos began to grow near, and Darla panicked. She searched frantically for a hiding spot, and spotted a janitorial closet to her left.

Stepping in, she lay underneath a shelving unit and held her breath the best she could. When Kronos had approached the hall, he ripped the Employees Only door clean from the hinges with a tearing noise, and crushed it until the wood blew like bullets from his fingers.

Stepping heavily down the cold concrete hallway, He came close to the janitorial closet Darla lay in. Aiming his arm toward the door, he blew it off with the loudest boom Darla had heard in her life, and her heart jumped. Bits of the door fell by her face, and Kronos walked into the small room. Steam seeped from his mask as he breathed heavily and slowly, and he looked carefully across the parameter.

Before he could find her, another soldier ran down the hallway to Kronos.

"G-General, sir. Another division has found a group of people who have been reported suspicious. It seems they may be from the Rebellion."

The last comment made Kronos flinch, as though a needle had been dug into his arm. He stepped backwards quickly, and punched the exit hard enough that it flew off the hinges and slammed into an abandoned car outside the building. When he had marched away, Darla slid out of her hiding spot.

As fast and frantically as she could, she flew out the exit and bolted toward the closest complex. Darla ran to the side and jumped up, grabbing the fire escape. As she climbed in a panic, it creaked and swayed after years of no use. Reaching the roof, she ran as fast as her legs could carry her to the edge and leaped to the next rooftop. She could hear screams of conflict, and darted even faster. She had to get there before Kronos.

Rapidly approaching the conflict, she didn't stop to observe the situation before sliding down the roof and rolling as she landed on the dirt ground.

Looking up, she saw Kendrick, Bella, and Louie fighting off a horde of around fifteen male and female soldiers. Kendrick slipped a strange looking arrow across his specialized crossbow and shot it at a crowd of enraged soldiers. It blew as it hit the ground, and dust shot in the air as the men went airborne. She ran up to the others and took out her mace.

"WE NEED TO LEAVE NOW! KRONOS KNOWS WE'RE HERE!"

•••

Sometime earlier, Bella and Louie had split off from Kendrick and Darla to search on their own. Passing through the ghostly homes, Louie filled a worn sack with cans and dried food, most of which stored in abandoned fallout shelters formed in a time of complete uncertainty. The walls were stained in darkened dust, and the floors creaked with every step taken. Louie reflected over Bella and his experience in the capital city to himself as placed cans of food into his tote bag.

She hasn't talked to me a lot since then... He thought with insecurity, but shook it off. *She kissed me. She must be interested. She must be.* Louie grinned as he pushed his thoughts away and continued his search. As Louie filled the last bit of his bag, he heard Bella shout in the distance.

"Bella, are you alright?" He spouted in response, and when she failed to respond he ran immediately in search of her. Unsheathing his bayonet, he approached Bella, who was struggling to fight off a royal soldier who had noticed her. With a thrust, he impaled the soldier from behind while they were turned toward Bella.

"Thank you." Bella spoke breathlessly, and Louie nodded in response.

"Of course." He started. "I, uh..." He struggled to piece together what to say to Bella, as she turned back to face him interestedly.

"Yeah?" She asked, and he gulped.

"I was just," He stammered. "I had to ask you something, that's all-" Before he could continue, a swarm of seven or eight royal soldiers caught eye of Bella and Louie, who still stood behind the body of the fallen soldier.

"Rebel scouts!" One shouted, as more surrounding soldiers were alerted of Bella and Louie's presence.

The soldiers swarmed the two instantly, and after twenty minutes caught in a fight larger than they could handle, the two rebels struggled to keep the mob of armored soldiers at bay. Bella, who had only brought a dagger and pepper spray, kept on her feet to avoid the slashes of spears and blades in her direction. Louie countered the strikes against him with his bayonet and took the lives of a few unlucky soldiers who stood in his path.

Bella slid beneath one of the attackers and slit across their leg, forcing them to scream as they dropped to their knees and tumbled across the sandy terrain. Before she could react, another soldier smashed the butt of their spear into Bella's head, and she fell on her back. Hitting the ground with a groan and a thud, her dagger slid across the ground just out of reach.

Desperate to help, Louie ran toward Bella with his bayonet in hand. Distracted by her cries, a sharp pain shot up the back of his left leg and he collapsed instantly. Another soldier, who had surprised him from behind, stood over Louie who was now just as helpless as his partner. As sweat dripped from his forehead in the desert heat, Louie swallowed the dry air and braced for more pain as the soldier raised their blade.

All of a sudden, a jolt of force blew Louie through the air, and he landed on his shoulder, screaming on impact. As a ringing shot through his ears, a hand reached down to help him up.

"Need a hand?" The voice asked, and Louie recognized it as Kendrick.

Taking his offer, Louie stood shakily holding his shoulder as the ringing faded from his mind.

"Better pick yourself up quickly. More are on the way!" He shouted, as he reloaded his crossbow with another explosive.

Bella groaned as she struggled to stand and grabbed her dagger and pepper spray. She stumbled backward, still dizzy from the blow to the forehead she had taken. Before she could react, what seemed like dozens of soldiers were approaching her, Louie and Kendrick, and she noticed the injuries across Louie's body and winced.

As she prepared for battle, a figure that seemed like Darla slid from a rooftop nearby and landed on the ground in a roll. In a frantic voice, she screamed the absolute worst news she could have given.

"OH SHIT!" Louie remarked valiantly, and he bolted past the remaining soldiers with the others in tail.

Booking it into the desert, Darla didn't look behind her. Kendrick shot another grenade arrow from his crossbow as they left the town, knocking a building down in between them and the soldiers.

By the time they all made it to the disguised entrance to the base, they were all exhausted. Most of the supplies they had found had been taken or destroyed, except for Darla's small plastic bag which contained a few cans of soup.

Kendrick took notice that some of the spikes on Darla's mace had bent and snapped in the conflict, and gave a gaze to catch her attention. Darla saw what he was staring at and shamefully hid the mace in her sheath.

"You're gonna have to take that to-"

"I know." Darla interrupted.

"You got a problem with her? She's your cousin." He asked in shock at her sudden response, and Darla simply grunted.

"I know that." Darla spoke. "She's unorthodox. But I suppose I'll need her to tinker with it. It's what she's good at anyways." Darla continued forward before Kendrick could continue, dodging the conversation.

As they entered through the door, Darla took a deep breath and held it for a minute. The four of them had barely survived the encounter, and now she was aware of what the rebellion would have to face. Kronos was looking for them, and he was getting close.

Chapter 26

Will's legs trembled as they approached the silver entrance to the hidden rebel base at last. Jack grabbed the rectangular handle in the center-right, but it failed to open. Taking a deep breath, Will stepped to the front of the group and knocked firmly on the door.

"This is it, guys." He spoke quietly, and the others nodded.

After a few minutes, there was a loud click which was followed by nothing at all. Confused, Will attempted to open the door, and it opened seamlessly. Stepping inside, he noticed that all of the lights were off, and the area was completely silent.

"Hello?" Will called, but to no answer.

"Maybe they're asleep? It could be nighttime." Jack suggested.

"No. The Rebellion is incredibly cautious. Something strange is going on." Will said quietly in response as he drew the Blade of Atlas.

Taking another step, a snap in the distance made Will stop in his place. Before anyone could react, a pole-like object pushed against Will's shoulder, and flashed next to his face. Paralyzed, Will fell onto his back on the cold, dirt covered ground. Before his eyesight faded to black, he could have sworn he saw someone he had not seen in a long time...

••

After what seemed like an eternity had passed, Will opened his eyes. He awoke in a medical facility, and he observed his surroundings. He noticed that the machinery seemed incredibly familiar, and he sat up in his bed. Becky, Jack, and Jonah were nowhere to be found.

"Hello?" He shouted, getting up from his bed.

Whoever had taken him captive had changed him into clean clothes, and his sword was missing from sight. Opening the door that left the room, he was faced with someone whom he hadn't seen since he left the rebellion base that fateful morning months ago.

"Rose?" She looked him in the eyes for some time and then responded.

"I couldn't believe it. I had to go see you for myself." She embraced him and laughed. "We thought... We were so worried!" Will smiled for a moment but remembered his newfound friends.

"Where are the others I was with?" Rose frowned. "We couldn't tell if they were royal spies sent using you as bait. They're in the prisons. I'll take you to them right away."

There was only one cell, which held a concerned Becky, a nonchalant Jonah, and a resting Jack who lay on his back with his legs crossed. When Will entered, Becky ran to the cell door to meet him.

"See, I told you he was alright." Jack spoke, getting up from the ground. Rose unlocked the door, and the three exited from the small holding cell. Becky pushed through and wrapped Will in an embrace, which he gave back.

"We were so worried, we thought maybe we had gone to the wrong place, or that there was some kind of royal presence, or that..." Becky spoke before stopping, and Will held her hand through the bars. "It's okay. Everything's going to be okay. We're here." He said with a warm smile.

"I apologize on behalf of the rebellion." Rose started. "We can never be too careful."

"Don't worry about it. You must be Darla, right? Wills talked a lot about you." Becky spoke in response and Rose chuckled.

"Not quite. She's been resting after her last outing. I'm not sure how well she's doing at the moment." Will stepped in between the two girls.

"What?! Is she ok? Take me to her now!" Will shouted concernedly.

"I... I'm sure she'd want to see you anyways." Rose turned to the other three, who stood patiently. "I'll send Terri to get you all situated."

"I won't be long. Promise." Will added, leaving the room with Rose following behind.

The door to Darla's quarters was shut and guarded by a few armed men. When Will reached the door, they dropped their weapons in shock.

"Will!" One exclaimed. "Head inside immediately. The general has been awaiting your arrival." Will entered quickly and shut the door behind him.

Darla sat with her hands in her palms on her desk, seeming perfectly able physically. Mentally however, she seemed as if she had drained all her spirit since Will's capture. Slowly turning to face Will, her face immediately lit up. She shot up from her chair almost instantaneously and stumbled on her weak ankle. Will caught her before she could fall and she embraced him firmly, tears falling from her hazel eyes.

"I was so worried..." She spoke, and Will hugged her in return.

"I missed you too." As the words left his mouth, she broke off from her and slapped him stiffly and swiftly across the face, causing him to recoil and step backwards.

"You ignored orders! You don't get to do that, dipshit!"

"I know." Will spoke shamefully. "But there's something I need to tell you. While I was gone, I found-"

"I know about your damn sword!" Darla shouted before he could finish. "I know you went out there, digging on this fucking fantasy of living up to your dad and killing the king. Have you ever considered that maybe I was holding you back because you weren't ready for something like this?" She screamed, more tears streaming from her eyes.

"I... I'm so-"

"I don't want to hear it." Darla interrupted.

"Rose mentioned that you were recovering from something..." Will spoke.

"Yeah. Do you want to know what we saw?" She asked quietly.

"Kronos is looking for us. He's pretty damn close too. At first I thought it may have just been a patrol, and we had gotten pretty damn unlucky. But he was looking for someone. And now that I know what happened to you, I understand why he's here." She spoke, and Will looked down in shame.

"Darla..."

"And who were those they found with you? Wait, let me guess. You found out about the prophecy after finding that sword, gathered a group of ragtag underdogs and thought you could actually kill the king just like that? Did you even hear the entire prophecy, or just some story book bullshit?" Will and Darla sat in silence, and Darla spoke again.

"I'm sorry. I just... I was so scared that I had lost you, and then we lost our home... everything is falling apart around I feel like I have no control..."

"Listen. I may not have understood it then, but what I did was the wrong decision. If you really want, I'll… I'll drop everything and stay here in the rebellion. There's nothing I can do to fix what happened to our home, but I can dedicate my life to making sure it never happens again." Will spoke.

"You can have the sword if you want. It was a dumb fantasy anyways." Will continued as he slumped against the wall, and slid until he sat on the ground. Darla sighed, and kneeled behind him.

"As much as I would love to go back to the way things were before, you made this decision on your own. The entire kingdom is counting on you, and it's my responsibility to make sure you can fulfill that. I'm sorry for lashing out at you. This is just… A stressful time. And I'm glad you're back safe." She smiled, and gave him a pat on the shoulder. Will smirked back.

"Now come on." She began to speak. "Lets go pay those friends of yours a visit."

••

In the rebellion infirmary, Louie lay atop a rock solid mattress, and struggled to keep his eyes shut. Sitting up slowly, he observed his surroundings. Bella lay to his right, sound asleep. He attempted to slide out of the bed, but slipped on the edge and hit the ground with a thud. His head rang from the impact, and he placed his palm upon his sweating forehead. Even in his sleep his thoughts had continued to race, most of them regarding the one beside him. Shakily getting up, he noticed that Bella had woken from the noise.

"Are you okay?" She asked.

"Yeah, I'm fine." He replied quickly, and sat next to her. Louie sat in silence, staring into Bella's diamond eyes.

"So much has been going on recently. We haven't really had time to think about... Us. You know what I mean?" Bella's confused face betrayed her as she looked at him, and Louie leaned in, kissing her on the lips. She jumped back, surprised, and pushed him away.

"Woah, what the hell are you doing?"

"What... I thought..." He said in a hurt manner. "After we nearly died in the city, we kissed, and I... I thought that meant..." Louie mumbled in his shaken words, and Bella looked around in thought before speaking. Her bagged eyes sank deeper than the sleep deprivation had already made them, as she held her arm in shame.

"I was half asleep, and didn't know how to feel. There's been so much going on, I just... I'm sorry, Louie." He put his palm over his mouth in thought and disappointment.

"I just... Why would you kiss me? Why would you do that if you didn't like me?" He said confrontationally, and she jumped with shaky pupils.

"I don't know! I just don't know..." She grabbed her hair in distress, and Louie held his hand out to comfort her before pulling it back hesitantly. "I shouldn't have. It was so dark, and I was so close to unconsciousness, it just... reminded me of something else."

"Something... else?" Louie asked, backing in betrayal. "Like some*one* else?"

"No! No, I… It's nothing." She winced as she spoke. "I haven't brought it up because I'm so scared of losing you too, but I think I've ruined that already. I don't want you to be upset-"

"I'm not upset. I'm just… confused. I really thought we kinda had something, you know?"

"We do, I promise, it's just… not in that way." She whispered, and Louie jumped from his bed.

"Listen. We've been through so much together, nearly died like six times, and through all of this I've realized one thing. I wouldn't wanna do it with anyone else." Louie smiled as he spoke, and Bella turned to hide her tears.

"I love you, Bell. I love your voice, your wavy hair, the way you scrunch your eyebrows when you think. I love the way you fight, the way you always get a job done, y'know?" He begins to tear up. "You're talented, funny, so incredibly sweet, and I would give up everything just to make you smile. I love you, Bella."

Bella smiled, but her tears wiped away her fake smile like chalk in the rain. She buried her face in her palms, and Louie put his arm around her in comfort. She pulled away, and looked into his eyes.

"Louie, I… You're such an incredible person, and you deserve the world, I just… I don't know how to feel right now. I've always viewed you like a brother of sorts, never in that sort of way. I just don't know what to do." She sobbed, wiping her tear soaked eyes as Louie contemplated for a moment.

"You say I deserve the world, but you are my world. I'm sorry Bell, I just... I don't know what I'd do without you by my side. Would there be anyone nearly as perfect?"

"I'm not perfect, Louie, and I never will be." Bella said in defiance, but Louie scooched closer, placing his hands on hers as he laughed.

"Bella, you don't understand. To me, you *are* perfect. Every little thing you do, every little thing you say. For me, you are the one. I will never find anyone else like you, and it scares me."

"Well maybe... maybe you don't need to find someone like me. Maybe you need to find someone new, you know?" She responded,the room sat in silence for a few moments. Louie gulped as he stood, and sighed as he looked into Bella's wet eyes.

"I'm sorry, Bell, I don't know what came over me. I should have thought before I did anything, and honestly I should get myself checked out because there's gotta be something wrong with me-"

Before he could finish, Bella wrapped Louie in a warm embrace, crying into his chest. Louie opened his mouth to speak, but decided against it. For just a moment, they both sat in complete silence, embracing each other.

"I'm being such a jerk, aren't I? Listen Louie, you matter so so much to me, I just... don't feel that way." She cried, and Louie smiled.

"I care about you a hell of a lot, too. And that's why I hope you'll stay friends with me." He spoke, and Bella smirked.

"Of course, you big dunce! I just told you that I care about you, didn't I?"

"You know Bell, I meant everything I said. About you, that is." She smiled, and then it slowly turned to a frown.

"Hah. I don't deserve you, do I?" She said, getting up to leave the room. As her hand turned the doorknob, Louie stood and stared into her eyes one last time. "I'm so sorry."

"Hey, wait!-" He shouted with concern, and she slammed the door behind her before he could see the tears staining her rosy cheeks.

Bella's boots splashed against the puddles of dew beneath her feet, born from the humidity. Her shaking arm rubbed the tears that blinded her vision, as she charged for her dorm room before anyone could spot her. Catching her foot in a ditch, Bella tripped and kissed the earth beneath her. Blood dripped from her lip as her teeth sank inside, and she bit the wound with her lips to cease the bleeding the best she could. She continued to run in a stumble, until she reached the locked door to her dorm. Shakily twisting the doorknob, she threw the door open and slammed it shut behind her. The moment the door closed against the wall, Bella's legs gave way and she curled in a sob against the steel behind her.

Why couldn't I just feel the same? She asked herself, dropping tears upon her clenched hands as she grit her teeth in rage with herself. Except, she knew the answer to the question she had been asking herself for months now. She reached for her chest, clenching the religious charm she wore around her neck, in the shape of the Maker's sigil. She tore it from her neck, holding it tightly in her hands.

"Oh, Maker." She pleaded to the skies. "Why can't I just move on? Why can't I love someone who loves me back? Someone who's not..." Her hands began to shake even more, as Bella threw the charm across the room. She stood, walking past the halls of paintings and sketches until she reached one that resembled a man. He wore dark boots, and fabric straps across his chest. A line of yellow glare ran up the torso, until it touched the tip of the man's curling brown hair.

In an instant, Bella's fist went through the painting, tearing it to broken pieces across the floor of her room. As she threw the stand holding the remnants of the painting to the ground, she fell against the wall beside her, using only her palm to hold her body up as her soggy black hair swung in front of her eyes, shielding the world from their pain. She fell to her knees one last time, crying a desperate sob as she wrapped her arms around herself, left completely to her lonesome by her shallow surroundings.

Chapter 27

Will opened the door to the holding cell room slowly, and Darla switched on the flickering light above the cell door. Jack lay on his back, with his leg resting over his right knee in a tranquil pose. Jonah sat in the corner, tapping his foot seemingly impatiently, and Becky paced by the iron gate locking them behind the steel bars.

"Will!" She shouted as Will entered behind Darla, and Jack shot up from the ground.

"Took you long enough." He remarked while approaching Will, but Becky shoved him out of the way.

"What did she say?" Becky whispered to Will, who chuckled as he opened the metal jail cell door.

"Welcome to the rebellion."

"Quite the warm welcome, huh?" Jack remarked, wiping his clothes off as he stepped out the door.

"I apologize, but you have to understand the safety precautions we take." Darla spoke to him.

"And you are?" Jack asked, crossing his arms.

"Name's Darla. I lead things around here, so I'm not the person you want to be a prick to. Will here is also the only reason I'm even considering setting you free, so you better be grateful." Jack gulped and stuck out his hand.

"Woah, sorry. Didn't mean to sound rude. I'm Jack, and I sort of lead things in my group as well." He chuckled, and Darla refused the handshake, scoffing in disapproval. Becky whacked him across the back of the head and began to approach Darla.

"Like hell you do. I'm Becky, pleased to meet you. Will's talked so much about you!" She shook Darla's hand firmly and kindly.

"Yeah, nice to meet you too." Darla remarked coldly, and Becky looked confusingly at Will, who shrugged. Jonah levitated, gliding toward Darla and bowed deeply.

"Prince Jonah, at your acquaintance." She squinted her eyes in response, calculating his odd warmth.

"Hmm." She spoke. "Allow me to show you all around." She said turning out the door.

As Darla hesitantly spoke about the rebellion and the important locations, Jack slowed and pulled Will back a few paces.

"Hey dude, what's up with your friend?"

"What's wrong?" Will responded confused, and Jack scrunched his eyebrows.

"She's acting pretty stuck up for someone you said would be welcoming."

"Just give her time. She's... cautious, to say the least. I don't know what else to tell you man." Will and Jack caught up with Darla and the others, just as she was describing the garden area.

"It's not as big as our previous area, of course, but we'll work with what we have. The woman working there is Terri. She's quite talented, and if you have any botanical questions I'm sure she can answer them." Darla pointed out a woman with short, blonde hair working over a mount of small sprouts. She wiped her sweat covered forehead with her leather glove, and continued on with her work.

As the group passed the edge of the garden and the line of the training grounds, they stopped to observe a few rebellion soldiers that were training with sharpened iron blades against wood dummies.

"How many soldiers would you say you have protecting the rebellion? In the case of an invasion or attack, there would need to be sufficient preparation, correct?" Jonah spoke without prompt, and Darla approached him.

"You make a good point. But that is confidential information." She began to circle him like prey. "Where did you say you were from?" She asked.

"Prince Jonah of the royal court, ma'am. I have been resurrected by William here to lead his group to the royal throne, as stated in the prophecy. You've heard of it, haven't you?"

"Of course I've heard of it. Now what reason do I have to believe you aren't just going to lead them to their deaths?" Becky stepped forward to intervene, but Will held her back.

"Let her talk to him." Will whispered, and Jonah spoke while floating in front of Darla.

"Why, you do have a point. I did side with my father in many of the decisions he made. But I have reason to believe my brother was the sole reason for my death, and I intend to take revenge against him. Even if it may not give me power in the court, having passed on, it will give my soul clarity. I shall be able to leave the purgatory and move on at last."

Darla listened carefully, and put her head down for a moment in thought. Coming to a decision, she fearlessly stared at him in his cold eyes.

"Okay then. Why don't I have Kendrick show you to your rooms, and I'll take Will aside for a moment to discuss logistics." Darla ordered, and Will stepped forward and whispered in Darla's ear.

"The others can come as well. I trust them completely."

Darla thought for a moment, and looked back up.

"Fine. You two come with us." She pointed to Jack and Becky. "You stay. I am still skeptical of your honesty." She looked at Jonah, and he shrugged.

"That is fair. I will go with this 'Kendrick' and get used to the quarters." Kendrick approached behind Darla, and she sent him toward the dorm rooms with Jonah on trail.

Closing the door behind her, the group stood in Darla's office, which was silent except for the light hum of the AC machine in the corner. Darla stood against the wall with her arms crossed while Jack paced quietly in the corner, and Becky sat with her legs crossed upon the floor while Will sat in Darla's office chair. Breaking the silence, Darla looked at the group.

"I don't trust him. Not one bit." She spoke, and Jack threw his hands in the air.

"Finally! Someone agrees with me!" He exclaimed, and she shot a look of disapproval in his direction.

"I don't trust you either, so don't get giddy. I just trust him less." She said to his disappointment. "Why are you traveling with him? You have the sword, you could have come here and prepared on your own." She asked Will accusingly.

"Listen, the prophecy said that we needed the aid of a prince to successfully defeat the king. I would rather have come straight to you, but we had no choice."

"Oh, did you now?" She said to Will's annoyance.

"With the aid of a ghostly prince, and the Blade of Atlas, they will vanquish the tyrannous monarchy from the castle, and bring peace back to Pyronia." Becky spoke from memory. "The prophecy was very clear about what we had to do."

Darla laughed obnoxiously at the remark.

"I apologize for the rude response, but that is absurd. What version of the prophecy did you read, some fairy tale version?" She asked, and Will's face went pale.

Uh oh. He thought with a gulp. He had never previously considered that the prophecy they had heard had been for a younger audience, or sugarcoated. Jack stepped up and looked between Will and Becky's anxious eyes.

"Oh come on. You guys seriously believed that was the original prophecy? Had you never heard of it before?" Darla taunted, and Becky stepped forward defensively.

"My parents had never let me hear it because they were afraid I'd get ideas." Becky said, and turned accusingly toward Jack. "Besides, *you* were the person to claim we were the people from the prophecy in the first place!"

"Woah, I may have had the idea but that was not the first time I had heard that. I'd heard of the ghostly prince part before, but many versions are different. Some don't even mention that he's a prince, or that he had died." Jack responded quickly, and Darla stepped between them.

"Calm down, will you?" She shouted, and they both looked down in shame.

"I've known my whole life that Will was the person from the prophecy. But my family made a vow to keep the prophecy concealed within rebellion walls, so that Will's life would not be at risk. That gave me possession of one of the most valuable items in the entire kingdom." She said, as she removed a cracked mirror from her wall and flipped a switch underneath it.

The wall opened and revealed a secret room that held a tainted piece of paper that stretched very long. At the very top, in neat handwriting, it was titled;

'THE PYRONIAN PROPHECY'.

"I had to hide this in my bag when we escaped from the previous base. It was harder than you would think. But there's a reason every rebel base has a secret room in some area, and that's to conceal this." She spoke as she moved her hand along the rough texture of the ancient paper.

"Now, let me tell you what *really* happened in the prophecy."

Chapter 28

Set in an older Pyronia, over fifty years before the birth of Flint and Jonah, the capitol kingdom is lit by dazzling torch light, and thousands of excited onlookers stand in the streets, peeking over a string barricade. There is a long, velvet carpet laid across the streets, leading up the castle stairs to the front entrance.

A golden throne sat at the top of the marvelous display, with a group of decorated religious figures beside it. The sky was clear as glass, and the ruby covered pillars outside the castle doors reflected in the sunlight. Behind the throne and out of sight, sat the most ornate crown, tinted with silver and diamond, with the points at the top sharper than the tip of a needle.

As roars from the crowd grew, a limousine plated with gold approached the end of the velvet carpet. The doors opened, and a young man with black hair and pale skin was lifted from the vehicle. Every sophisticated step he took seemed as if he were being lifted by doves, as the long purple robe he bore flapped in the breeze.

He raised his right hand with a grin to the audience, who were clapping and applauding his presence. He began to laugh in joy, but stopped himself in formality. Stepping up the covered stairs to the golden throne that awaited him at the top of the stairs, he took a deep breath. Today was the day he had been waiting for his entire life. He stared into the promising eyes of the audience, who had their complete faith in him. Each set of eyes stared back into his, giving him hope. These were the people that would make this job worth it.

Before he could react, something grasped his arm firmly, and pulled him back.

"Prince Malcolm..." A raspy voice called from behind him, and the young prince turned around.

He was faced with a shriveled man, with a dark rag draped over him. His eyes were white, insinuating he was blind.

"Heed my words..." He spoke softly, and Malcolm could do nothing but listen breathlessly. "An era of darkness will befall the kingdom under your rule... A great betrayal will fall upon you... The tainted crown will be worn..." He spoke with urgency and fear.

The man trembled as Malcolm tried to pull away, laughing awkwardly. The man's grip tightened on Malcolm, and guards began to run over.

"You must listen, Malcolm... Something grave is near, for you, and for Pyronia..." The man was pulled away aggressively by the guards, but Malcolm stared into his eyes still. His raspy voice echoed deep in the prince's head.

As he sat on the throne at the top of the stairwell, Malcolm's face had lost the joy it carried before. It only wore pure shock. The voices of the priests were blurred by the thoughts of what had been pronounced to him just minutes before. He snapped from his trance as the crown was placed on his head, and the crowd burst into a series of shouts and applause.

He stood in pride and waved to the thousands before him, forgetting what had been bothering him before. He looked at the faces throughout the crowd, young and old, cheering his name. Thinking of them, he took the crown from off his head and stared deeply into it. The words of the man echoed throughout his head as he stared into the reflecting diamonds on the crown.

The tainted crown will be worn.

Would accepting the position be worth it if it would endanger the lives of the kingdom? Malcolm knew that he had no choice, and put the crown back upon his head.

Later that night, Malcolm sat in the throne room with no one but his personal servant and a few guards. He rested his head on his palm, with his fingers impatiently tapping against his cheek.

"My liege, you should rest. It is quite late." The servant spoke, and Malcolm smiled.

"I will make my way there. I just have a lot on my mind. I appreciate it, though." The servant nodded, and exited the room. Malcolm let himself be lost in thought.

How was he to know if this man had been an oracle, or an insane man with no clue what he had been saying? With this on his mind, the newly crowned king realized that the following day would be long, and that it would be beneficial to get rest. As he entered his quarters and laid his head softly on the padded pillow, his eyes shut slowly. The last thought that lingered on his mind before his conscience faded was; *Am I really to doom the kingdom?*

••

Forty-five years later, Malcolm still sat on the throne of Pyronia. His hair had now grayed from stress and age, and his king's robe had been worn from many years of use. His servants had all retired or passed away, as with the guards also. He had forgotten the fateful words of the old man he had met those many years before, and lived his life in constant servitude to his kingdom.

One morning however, something had caused his mind to wander back to that day of his coronation. A young man, seemingly around his early twenties, had run urgently into the castle halls.

"My lord, my lord there is something I must tell you." He stopped to breathe, and Malcolm looked down to him in focus.

"What is there I can do for you?" He asked calmly.

"My great grandfather is dying, and says he needs to speak with you."

"I apologize, but I have a long list of other needs to attend to before I can go with you, son." Malcolm spoke in a lamenting tone, knowing it would be too late.

"But sir, it's urgent. He's an oracle, and says he's spoken with you before."

At the remark, Malcolm's eyes shrunk and his face went pale. Turning to face the boy, he opened his mouth to speak but was unable to think of the right words to say.

"Well? I promise it will be worth your time, my lord."

"O-Of course. Yes. Take me there at once." Malcolm responded quickly, and left the castle behind the boy with some guards following. The car ride there was short, but felt like an eternity for the worn king.

When they arrived, Malcolm stepped carefully from the vehicle and observed the surroundings. He was in front of a beaten alleyway, covered in graffiti and cracks. In the center, there was a tent made of ripped fabric and wood.

"My lord, I would advise against entering... that." One of the guards spoke, but Malcolm held his hand in the air to quiet him. Stepping slowly into the tent, all light around him vanished in an instant. He was in a void like atmosphere, and all he could see was the man he had met so many years before sitting on a rectangular bed.

"Good morning, my lord." The man remarked calmly. "My great grandson did not lie. I am close to death. Before I move on to meet the creator, I have something to tell you." Malcolm was shocked at the statement and moved closer.

"What do you mean? Why now? Why didn't you tell me so many years ago?"

"It was not clear then. Only blurred visions. But now, I know the truth. Rather, I have the ability to know. As an oracle, I can bring prophecies from the creator. Or so I thought. You see, there is a price to each prophecy given. A small part of one's soul is taken each time. And now, being so close to death, I am on my last one. I am having frequent visions of the future of the city, and I must tell you what is to happen." Malcolm was speechless, and sat in pure concentration. Before the man could speak, Malcolm opened his mouth.

"Wait, sir. Before you begin, where are we? How am I to return?"

"We are in the domain of my soul. An ability nearly impossible to learn, one that requires an absurd amount of power." The old man spoke, and Malcolm jumped back.

"If we are in your soul, then what is to happen when you die?"

"You are safe. You will simply be returned to where you entered from. Now, my time is nearly spent. Are you ready?" Malcolm nodded slowly, and the old man took a deep breath. He began to mutter words in a language Malcolm could not understand, and slowly the man's body began to twitch.

As he finished the last sentence, his entire torso lunged back, and as his head recentered his eyes began to glow incredibly bright. The worn king covered his eyes with his hands as the old man's eyes grew blinding. They began to simmer, and a powerful wind began to swirl around Malcolm and the man. As the old man opened his mouth, the thunderous voice that came out was not his.

THE FATE OF PYRONIA WILL SOON BE REACHED

THROUGH CORRUPTION'S HOLD IT'S LIFE IS LEECHED

TWO GENERATIONS OF DEMONIC SUN

VANQUISHED WITH AID FROM A TYRANT SON

SHROUDED IN DARKNESS FOR AGES HENCE

FROM THE HEAVENS THE MAKER SENDS

THREE SHINING HEROES, TO TAKE THE THRONE

FROM ANGERED DEMONS AND HEARTS OF STONE

A GOLDEN BLADE, FORGED DIVINE

A SKILLFUL TOOLSMAN, AND WITCH ALIGN

TO KEEP THE PEACE, THERE IS A PRICE

FROM ONE OF THREE, A SACRIFICE

ONLY THEN WILL LIGHT RETURN

AND THE AGE OF DEMONIC RULE WILL BURN

Malcolm sat in utter shock for a moment, and watched as the light disappeared from the eyes of the man. Before he could speak, the realm around Malcom began to tear and disappear, and he watched life slip from the old man's face.

Suddenly, he was thrown backward into the street, and landed in front of the car he arrived in. As the world spun around him, Malcolm could see a figure run up to him.

"My liege, are you alright? What happened in there?" As he stood shakily, Malcolm saw something laying on the ground where the tent used to stand.

Approaching it, he picked up a long piece of paper, which read exactly what the old man had spoken to him. It was titled "The Pyronian Prophecy", and Malcolm rolled it up into a scroll.

"Shall we head back to the castle then?" He spoke in an unfazed tone, covering his absolute shock with a look of control and serenity.

"O-Of course, my lord." The guard spoke, and Malcolm entered the vehicle. Driving off into the sunset, Malcolm thought over what he had just witnessed.

Less than a year later, a mysterious man marched toward the city with an army of hundreds. He wore a hood, a devilish grin, and wielded a blood red sword. His army wore a special insignia on their torsos, and walked in unison. Malcolm gathered his army in response, but knew it would be no good.

As the foreign army marched upon the castle stairs, the man in charge removed his hood to reveal a scarred face with dark hair and yellow eyes. The man's name was Thanatos Strife, the soon to be father of Jonah and Flint. This was the man who would kill the king, and change the lives of every Pyronian citizen forever.

Chapter 29

"Holy shit..." Jack remarked as he slid back against the wall in shock.

"What I just showed you is the only real copy of the Pyronian Prophecy to exist in the entire world. All the other versions have been spread through word of mouth or, as you guys found it, fairy tale." Darla spoke to the group. Will stared at the ground deep in thought, with his arms crossed. Everything had made sense to him except one part.

TO KEEP THE PEACE, THERE IS A PRICE, FROM ONE OF THREE, A SACRIFICE.

Will let those words bounce in his head as he stood in concentration. If he was understanding the words correctly, that could only mean one thing. Either he, Jack, or Becky would have to make some sort of sacrifice to bring peace back to Pyronia.

As the thought lingered in Will's mind, a knock went off at the door to Darla's office. The group exited and shut the secret room just as Bella entered quickly, looking around.

"Hey Darla, I-" She stopped as swiftly as she had begun, seeing Will staring back joyfully into her eyes. "Oh, thank the maker!" She exclaimed, running into Will's arms as he embraced her firmly. "I'm so glad you're okay." She spoke under her breath as she pulled away from Will, and he smiled.

"I'm glad you're okay too. Where's Louie?" He asked, and her grin faded.

"I-I don't know. Probably still in the hospital room." Will jumped back and Darla stepped in front of him.

"It's a long story." Darla said to Will, and turned to Bella.

"Find him and tell him that Will's returned. I'll take the others to the dining hall to get situated."

Before Darla could step away, Becky grabbed her arm to get her attention.

"Wait, I'm sorry, I just... had a question." Darla crossed her arms and listened. "You wouldn't happen to know if... anyone by the name of 'King' is part of the rebellion would you?" Darla thought for a moment, and looked back to Becky.

"There are so many in the rebellion, and most of them never share their last names. If I could tell you I would, but I can't." She responded disappointingly, and Becky nodded.

"I understand. Thank you though." She turned to walk back and Darla spoke.

"Wait. I don't want to get your hopes up, but it may be worth looking around the base. Especially during dinner tonight." Becky smiled, and thanked Darla.

"Thank you, really. I appreciate it."

Entering the dining hall, Will's ears were instantly flooded with endless cheer and laughter, with dozens and dozens of men and women keeping each other company. Rows of tables were set and decorated with all kinds of simple delicacies such as rice and beans, and the entire rebellion sat around them feasting in unison. The electric powered lights hanging above the dining hall flickered occasionally from the worn generator, but it hardly removed the light that was emitted from the room.

Will took a seat at a table where Kendrick resided, who was deep in hearty conversation with Jonah. Their bellows of laughter echoed across the dining hall, and attracted the attention of others who surrounded them, interested in the good tidings brought by the ghost-like newcomer.

Becky wandered between the endless sea of joyous people, locking eyes with every man and woman in front of her. She observed each article of clothing and listened closely to each voice around her for signs of familiarity.

After visiting each corner of each table, she finally took a deep breath and started back toward the table where Jack and Will had sat. As her face sank in disappointment, she had to fight to hold back tears. As she took another step, she felt a bump against her leg and nearly fell.

"Sorry Miss!" A high pitched voice rang, and a small boy with brown hair scurried past Becky. Suddenly, a million memories flooded Becky's mind, with that brown haired boy at the center of them. He looked scarily familiar, and she did an instant 180 and began chasing the boy.

"Wait, come back!" She shouted, and the boy ran faster.

"I said I'm sorry!" He shouted while jumping over a chair left in the center of the floor.

"Wait, I'm not mad I just-" Becky stumbled over the chair that the boy had leaped over. "I just want to ask a question!"

The boy ran up to a young man, seemingly of late twenties or early thirties and hid behind his back. The man was joking playfully with a group of other young men, and they all held worn cans of alcohol, most likely beer.

"This crazy lady's trying to kill me!" The boy shouted while pointing at Becky, who stood in breathless shock.

"It's okay, bud. I'll handle this." The man said while standing to face Becky. He had hazel eyes, and a strawberry blonde buzzcut. He had a scar that ran down his cheek, like a teardrop of skin. "Excuse me ma'am, I apologize for his behavior, he-" He stopped, locking eyes with Becky for a moment.

"No. Way." He spoke softly, and they both began to laugh.

"Orion?" Becky asked and he nodded.

"In the flesh. Good to see you, whiskers."

"Don't call me that!" Becky yelled through laughter, and turned her attention to the young boy, who had become comfortable enough to step out from behind Orion.

"Aries?" She asked with tears in her eyes, and he gave her a quick hug, grasping tightly around her waist. His stout legs shook in emotion as he looked up with his youthful eyes.

"Hi Becky." He spoke through tears with a smile, and she smiled back. "Orion told me about you. Mommy misses you." He continued, and Becky looked toward Orion.

"Is it... Is it just you two?" Becky asked while her gut sank down her spine in anxiety.

"Everyone is here." Orion spoke happily, and Becky laughed in pure joy.

"Your parents are in their dorm right now. They came to the hall earlier."

"Could you take me to them?" She asked eagerly, and he handed him a pair of keys.

"Room 128. You can find them yourself." He said with a grin, and she grinned back. "Tell 'em I said hey." He shouted as Becky ran into the distance.

Will, Jack, Jonah and Kendrick sat at the dinner table, laughing together at each other's humorous remarks. When the laughter had died down, Will felt a tap on his shoulder. Turning around, he was met face to face with a tall, strawberry blonde haired, pale skinned boy whom Will hadn't seen in ages.

"Hey Louie!" Will exclaimed, giving him a quick embrace. "How's it been, dude?"

"It's been..." Louie spoke, and Will turned his head awaiting a response. "Alright." He finished after a moment, and Will smiled. "We thought you were a goner. I was so scared, man. We all were."

“I’m okay. I ran into a close call with the king, but I’m okay.” Will said to his worried friend. “It’s been too long. I’m so glad you’re all okay.”

“We barely made it, but we always do.” Louie cracked a grin before sticking his hand out toward Jack.

“My name's Louie, nice to meet you." Jack smiled and shook his hand.

“Jack. How's it going?” He said as Louie turned to face Will, and pulled him aside.

“Hey, I dunno if it’s a bad time or anything, but could you talk for a bit?” Louie asked as Will looked back concernedly.

“Of course, man.” Will and Louie left the dining hall, where Jack and the others sat confused.

“Okay, then.” Jack remarked in a hurt manner, and continued to eat.

Chapter 30

Becky stepped up the concrete stairs of the dorm building and was left face to face with the metal door. The corroded numbers on the right side of the entrance stared into Becky's soul with a sense of finality. She would see her father again at last. Her hand, shaking, grasped the doorknob and slipped the key into the slot. She took a deep breath, and twisted the key to the right until she heard a click.

Stepping through the door, she held her breath as the floor softly creaked beneath her. She heard muffled voices coming from a nearby room, blocked by a wooden door. The two voices, one male and one female, spoke in disagreement with each other. Becky recognized them as her parents immediately.

Opening the door slowly, she walked forward and the voices silenced.

"Who's there?" The man spoke softly, and Becky was met face to face with her father, who had changed in the years since she'd seen him.

He leaned against a crutch, with his bony arm shivering as he gripped it. He had lost a lot of weight, and grown a dark beard that complemented his scruffed hair. Her mother wore a gray dress with dark boots and a necklace over her neck. Holding its emblem in her hand, she met eyes with Becky and began to tear. She ran to give Becky a long embrace, crying into her shoulder. Becky took another deep breath as she lay her head on her mothers stout shoulder.

"Hey." She spoke, and her mother pulled away.

"'Hey'. Is that all you have to say?" She spoke through tears. "You run away, disappear for years- We thought you were dead!" She yelled and Becky's father stepped up slowly, putting his arm in front of his wife.

"Let her talk, Ellie." He coughed, and she stepped back. "Now where were you?"

Becky explained everything she had gone through in the past few years, and her parents listened earnestly.

"It was destiny that I met them." She spoke. "We're going to restore freedom to the kingdom."

"Why do you have to do this? Why can't you just stay, you just came back!" Becky's mom shouted.

"Mom, the fate of the kingdom lies on our shoulders. I can't just sit at home while they have to risk their lives!"

"I can't let you do this. It's too dangerous." She spoke with her arms crossed, and Becky fumed.

"This is why I ran away. I have abilities most aren't blessed enough to have, and you just hold me back!" She yelled and her mom grit her teeth.

"You are a kid! You don't know how to use your powers, and that fact will get you killed!"

"I have been practicing! I know what I'm doing!" Her mom stomped her foot, and Becky went silent.

"You don't know enough. You are staying. That's final."

"Mom... I'm sorry." Becky said, stepping toward the door.

"Wait." Becky's father spoke, stepping toward her slowly with his crutch. "If you are going to go no matter what..." He continued. "Let me give you lessons to prepare you. Please." Becky smiled and gave him a long embrace.

"Thank you, dad. I promise I won't disappoint you." Becky's mom Ellie stepped between them.

"Woah, we aren't seriously considering letting her go, are we Fred?" She asked her husband, and his gaze turned to her.

"She is old enough to make her own decisions, and she wants to save the world. If she believes that is her destiny, then... Let it be so." Ellie nodded, and Becky's father Fred turned back to her.

"Tomorrow morning, 9am sharp. Okay?" Becky jumped in happiness.

"I won't let you down!" She shouted, running out the door.

••

Jack sat at the table alongside Jonah and Kendrick, watching as Will left with the young man whom he had just met.

"Who was that?" He asked, and Kendrick set his drink upon the table.

"Louie." Kendrick responded slyly.

"Yeah, no shit. Who is he?" Jack responded.

"He and Will used to work together. They grew up together too. He's a good kid." Kendrick continued to sip his ale, and Jack looked around him. After a moment, Jack decided to converse a bit more with the man he was left with.

"How long have you been here for?" Jack asked, grabbing another drink from the center of the table. Kendrick leaned back in his chair, resting the ends of his boots on the table.

"I'd say for as long as I can remember, but that'd be a lie. I moved here around ten years ago, when I was a little younger than you, around eighteen or so. I used to live in Spiral city with my brother, before he went." Kendrick took another laid back sip of his ale, and Jack questioned further.

"Where did your brother go?" Jack asked, and Kendrick shrugged.

"Missing. Went out to grab dinner one night, and he wasn't there when I returned. Never saw him again." Before Jack could ask any more questions, Kendrick sat up in his chair.

"So Darla's a nice girl, ain't she?" Kendrick spoke sarcastically, and Jack refocused his attention in another direction.

To his left, he spotted the girl he had just met, Darla, sitting with a group of other men and women. She laughed heartily as she downed a pint of some sort of liquor, over a plate of steaming rice and freshly picked beans.

Jack hadn't considered the possibility of talking to women very much in his confinement, believing it would be impossible to talk with anyone other than Becky. He had always wondered if something could happen between the two of them, but she had always felt more like a sister to him.

Standing in the rebellion, the idea of talking to someone floated across his mind once again. Jack stood from the table slowly, slicked his hair back, and cracked his knuckles.

"Where are you going?" Kendrick asked. Jack said nothing as he turned around, eyes set on Darla's table.

"I'll be right back." He spoke, starting toward her.

"I hope he's not doing what I think he's doing." Kendrick laughed. "Bless that kid."

Jack approached Darla confidently, who stopped laughing and turned to face him. Jack stuck out his hand and smiled a toothy grin.

"I think we got off on the wrong foot. Darla, right?"

Darla chuckled and gripped his hand tightly. As she shook it Jack had to pretend to not wince at his underestimation of her strength. He kept a poker face, but Darla could tell he was tense.

"At ease, soldier." She joked, and he grinned again.

"You see, Becky and I had been in the dungeons for about a year before Will showed up. We had found this series of tunnels, they were impossible to decrypt until Will pulled that sword. I thought we'd never get out." Darla's eyes shone at the mention of the tunnels. She cleared her throat to hide her excitement.

"You found the old rebel tunnels, huh? They were created to be impossible to solve without help. I suppose the blade was able to guide you. I've always wanted to see them for myself."

"Well maybe I could take you there sometime." Jack blurted out without giving a second thought.

Darla's table sat in silence, and she began to chuckle. The chuckle grew into a bellowing laugh, which was followed by the others at her table. Jack chuckled awkwardly, stepping back a step.

"I'm sorry, I'm sorry." Darla spoke through tears of laughter.

"It's just... you just asked me to go to the royal dungeons with you... as a date?"

"Well, no I-"

The table burst in laughter again, and Jack's face grew slightly red in annoyance. Darla yelled for them to be at ease, and the table quieted.

"I appreciate the offer, kid, but I have more important things to worry about right now." Jack flushed in embarrassment.

"I swear I didn't mean it like that, but if you wanna be an asshole about it, then be my guest!"

Jack stormed off, and the table was left laughing hysterically while Darla tried to chuckle alongside, hiding her surprise at the new recruits outburst. As the laughter subsided, she breathed a long sigh.

"Interesting." She spoke.

•••

Will entered Louie's dorm alongside him, and they sat on the worn grey couch placed along the back wall. Will stretched and cracked his stiff back as he laid back upon the pillowed surface with a long sigh. Louie reached for a pack of diet sodas he had left out on his coffee table, and handed one to Will.

"Couldn't bring half of your clothes, but you had to bring the soda." Will remarked, and Louie let out a soft chuckle.

"It was here when I got here." He crossed his arms as he laid backwards, releasing a deep breath. The room went silent for a few minutes, as Will stared at the ceiling in thought.

"I actually wanted to ask you about something." Louie spoke, breaking the silence.

Will nodded, and Louie told him about what had happened between him and Bella in the city with Dave, and what occurred in the hospital room after. Will listened earnestly at each detail of the story, surprised at how much had happened between his friends in his absence. As he finished, Louie crossed his arms in an elongated sigh, as Will processed the news.

"So, she kissed you in the city?" He asked.

Louie nodded, and Will thought for a moment.

"Maybe she does have feelings for you, but just isn't ready to commit yet. And if she doesn't, who cares?" Will said, and Louie looked at him in an insulted manner, but Will held his hand up. "You're a great person, Lou." Will started. "Bella's a good person too, but you gotta understand that you deserve someone who loves you back. There's a ton of girls in the rebellion, and they're all sweet. Or, most of them." Will continued as Louie stood in interruption, and spoke.

"But you don't understand, Will. I've never loved someone like I've loved Bella. We've gone through so much together. Even if I do find someone else, I don't know if I'll be able to live with seeing her every day..." He put his face in his palms, and Will put a hand on his shoulder.

"It's hard to deal with, but she either loves you or she doesn't. If she does eventually, that's great. But if she doesn't, there's nothing you can do to change that. One day you'll move on, like all people do, and eventually..." Will sat in thought over the people he had met these last few months.

He remembered how he believed he'd never find someone to love, and how Darla used to tease him for it when they were kids. There was one year, Valentine's Day in primary school, where he had made the foolish decision to give a girl in his lecture hall a flower he had found along the wall. She held it for a moment, before running away sobbing. Will had never been so embarrassed in his life. He remembered how he eventually lost any motivation to find someone at all. Then he remembered the kiss Becky gave him in the tunnel, and how his entire perspective had been changed by that one miniscule action. How his hopelessness could turn into hope in mere minutes.

"Someone will fall into your hands, just like that." Will finished with a grin grinned at Louie, and after a moment, Louie grinned back.

"Thank you, man" Louie spoke through a smile. "I really missed having you around here." Louie looked over Will's shoulder, noticing the Blade of Atlas strapped to his back. "Wait a minute." He took the blade carefully from off Will's back, and Will's pupils dilated at the realization that he hadn't told his friend.

"Right." Will spoke under his breath. "There's a bit more of the story that I haven't told you yet."

Chapter 31

While Will, Becky and Jack grew comfortable and trained vigorously to face the king, Flint waited impatiently in the meantimes. The minutes seemed like hours, and each drip of water from the ceiling triggered Flint's senses just as he would fade into an exhaustive rest.

Late one night, Flint sat upon his throne as he usually did and his butler Argus entered the throne room. He wore a dark suit down his slender body, and held his hands behind his back in a suitable manner. His dark, lengthy hair was slicked back with a gel, and he stood in composure by the foot of Flint's throne.

"Good evening, my lord." He spoke. "Lieutenant Pandora is recovering swiftly from her conflict."

"This is good news. Have her promoted to general at once, and when she is capable of moving, have her come to me. I have another mission for her." Flint spoke in a monotone voice, and Argus nodded.

Flint sat on his throne as he watched the light slowly dim from the stained glass window above the grand entrance to the castle. Instead of switching on the led lights he had been graced with inside the royal walls, Flint chose to sit in absolute silence as the room became increasingly dark.

As the last bit of light disappeared from Flint's sight, he closed his eyes. Breathing in and out slowly, he felt the summation of all the stress and pain on his shoulders begin to sink into his gut.

As the room was left completely barren at last, Flint could no longer keep himself together. Stripped from the requirement of appearing professional, Flint allowed the built agony of twenty years to release a single tear, which he let roll down his cheek in a slow movement. As it dripped to the floor, Flint took another deep breath, just as his head began to clench in pressure and pain.

WEAK.

He heard the ghastly voice of his father sting through his mind, and he ripped the jeweled crown from his head.

"Leave me be!" He shouted, as he threw the crown against the castle doors with all of his might. As it slammed against the metal trim of the grand doors, the sharp pain only strengthened in Flint's mind.

YOU ARE TREASONOUS...

"You are the traitor! I am the king! Leave me be at once-"

Flint was thrown from his seat in pain, and he hit the castle ground with a slam. Soldiers began to flow into the room, alongside Argus.

Flint was raised and carried into an enclosed room, and laid upon a bed. Doctors entered frantically and attached metallic items to Flint, and his head shook with even greater pain.

As the agony began to grow unbearable, a figure that resembled Argus approached the foot of Flint's bed. Placing his hands on Flint's chest, the pain finally began to subside as the world around him went darker than the throne room. As Flint's eyes shut, a final sentence rang throughout his mind.

WE WILL MEET AGAIN, MY SON...

••

Flint woke to the sound of bluebirds chirping along the great pines that lined the outside of the castle walls. The window to Flint's left had been left open, which had allowed the sounds to enter his hospital room. He sat up in his bed carefully, and rubbed his bagged eyes. His back ached as he stepped from the hospital bed, and stripped from the gown the doctors had placed over him.

Placing his cloak across his body and his crown back upon his head, he stepped out the door and was met with multiple frantic doctors, who stopped in their place at his appearance. As he stepped back into the castle corridors, he found Argus, who had been waiting for him.

"How long have I been asleep, Argus?" Flint asked concernedly.

"Not too long, my lord. A day, at most." Argus responded.

"What has happened in my absence?" Flint spoke, as Argus turned toward a door that had been opened.

Out stepped Pandora, who seemed different than she had been before. Her upper-left chest shined dimly, and light escaped through the corners of her golden chestplate, which had been replaced. Her left eye was replaced with a metallic prosthetic that glowed in an artificial rage, but calmed as she knelt before Flint.

"Good morning, my lord." She spoke in a low voice.

"Pandora was injured critically near the heart, and almost died. Our cyber-technicians have been hard at work replacing it with a gamma core, but they completed their work. She will be ready to be deployed again very soon." Argus said, turning back toward Flint.

"Very good work, Argus. You are dismissed." Flint responded, and Argus left. "Come with me, Pandora. We have a lot to talk about."

Re-entering the throne room, the doors were locked shut and guarded in the king's absence. Flint ordered them to stay that way while he met with Pandora, and the guards nodded. He sat upon his throne, resting his hand upon his chin. His head had felt the most clear that morning that it had ever before, yet he couldn't understand why. Turning his focus toward Pandora, he spoke.

"You are lucky, Lieutenant Pandora. The wound in your heart should have been fatal, but you are strong."

"I have failed you, my king." She responded solemnly. "I failed to kill the leader of the Rebellion."

"However you now know who she is, correct?" Flint asked with curiosity.

"She was a woman, red haired. They called her Darla."

"Interesting." Flint responded in thought.

The Rebellion had been able to escape the conflict, but Flint knew that they hadn't been able to go far. There must have been some backup base, not too far from the original glade.

"I have a new mission for you. General Kronos has been sweeping the desert region of Kandachta for any trace of rebels, and he brought back the most pleasing news. His forces laid eyes on a group of rebels, one of which with red hair. I want you to join him in his search, and locate the rebel base. It's time the rebellion is brought down at last."

He finished his order, and Pandora nodded obediently. Her gamma core shined in rage as she thought of Darla, and her glowing eye flashed brightly in agreement. She exited the throne room, and Flint was left alone once more.

Chapter 32

Will stepped out from his dorm and stretched his arms. He had gotten better sleep the few nights they had been in the rebellion than he had for many weeks. It was still barely dawn, as Will could tell by watching the sun rise slowly on the weather screen by the gathering square. He heard noises coming from his left, and identified one voice as Becky's.

He approached the source of the noises, and observed quietly. Becky stood alongside an older man, and the two of them held wands towards each other, in a battle ready stance.

"Alright, try it again." The older man spoke, nodding toward Becky. She took a breath, and gained her balance.

"Crystal Thunder." She spoke confidently, and swirled her wand, gathering dark thunderous clouds before striking fiercely toward the man.

Will held his breath as the spell released, remembering her failure the first time she had attempted the spell at Wolf's home. To his shock, a gargantuan bolt of lightning struck against the other man's wand, and he caught it with a counter spell, reflecting the bolt into the ground with a crack.

"You're improving." The man spoke, and to Will's shock he seemed hardly impressed. "Again."

Becky cast the spell once more, and it struck the opposing man's wand with even more force than before. The man stepped back from the impact, but kept tranquil in the moment.

"Again."

Becky grit her teeth in annoyance, and began to cast the spell again. She swung the wand above her head this time, and a great dark cloud formed above, with the lightning swarming so strongly that it leaked from the edges.

As she struck her hand down, she yelled as the weight of the lightning slammed upon the wand of the man, who barely caught the blow. The opposing force was so strong that he was unable to deflect it, and he held his wand in the air to direct the lightning upward. The bolt struck the air with an ear piercing crackle, and the man stepped back again in opposition to the force.

"Very good, but you can do better."

Becky shouted in anger as she stamped her foot into the ground below her, nearly knocking her purple hat from her head in fury.

"We've been doing this for an hour, and that was my strongest one yet! Why can't you be happy with my progress?"

"I'm worried about you. If you're going to face the king, you need to be prepared. Until I say you are, I will not be comfortable with you going." He responded.

"Will you ever be comfortable?" She shouted.

Will walked toward the two of them, and Becky began to storm toward Will.

"Hey, I thought you did pretty-"

He began to speak, but Becky kept walking past him in rage.

"-Good." He blurted as she ignored his praise.

Will was left speechless as the man approached him. He had scruffy brown hair, bushy eyebrows, and a dark beard that accompanied it. He leaned against a crutch that Will hadn't noticed in the man's swift movements from before.

"You must be the kid. Will." The man spoke, sticking out his hand. "I've been here for years, but we've never formally met I suppose."

Will stuck his hand out to shake his, and the man firmly gripped Will's hand in a dominant gesture. Will awkwardly attempted to match his grip, but only made the handshake more uncomfortable.

"Are you Becky's father?" Will spoke in assumption, and the man nodded.

"You can call me Frederick. It's good you showed up actually, Darla told me to speak with you." He said, and his gaze turned to the Blade of Atlas, which was sheathed at Will's side.

Frederick reached for the blade, and Will flinched.

"Darla said your sword is magic. Lemme hold it." Frederick spoke, and Will let him hold the hilt and unsheath the sword.

Frederick moved his hand up the blade, feeling the edges with genuine curiosity.

"Interesting." He spoke. "How interesting..."

"What's that?" Will asked in wonder at his remark.

"This blade is infused with incredibly powerful spiritual magic. It should be incredibly dangerous, but it's locked to a specific bloodline. Yours." Frederick said, poking Will in the chest.

Will took the sword back, and stared at his reflection in the gem connected to the bottom of the hilt.

Why me? He thought carefully.

"I knew it was somewhat connected to Jonah, but I hadn't considered that it was connected to me..." Will spoke to Frederick. "Is there any more you can tell me?" Will continued, and Frederick took the sword back from Will.

"To tell you the truth, I can't." He answered to Will's disappointment. "Like I said, it's locked to your bloodline, which means only you can unlock its powers."

"Would it be possible to remove the lock? Just temporarily, so you can understand it more?" Will asked, and Frederick shook his head.

"It is technically possible, but it wouldn't be temporary. It would take an immense amount of power, much more than I could generate. It would open a whole can of worms anyways, so I'd keep this power to yourself kid."

Frederick pat Will on the back, and began to limp away. As he went further, Will turned to stop him.

"Will you teach me how to use it? The power?"

"I was hoping you'd ask that." Frederick spoke with a grin. "Let's get to work."

•••

"Focus, boy." Frederick spoke to Will, who was sweating in deep focus.

"I am." Will said in response, as he closed his eyes.

The two had been working for hours, but to no avail. They had tried many different tactics, but Will struggled to unlock the magic on command. Frederick stood in focus with his arms crossed, while Will stood calmly with a tight grip on the blade's leather wrapped hilt. Will took a breath, and closed his eyes as shut as possible.

"Nothing's happening." Will spoke, and Frederick rolled his eyes.

"What are you trying to do?" He asked.

"Feel the power, I guess. In the past, it's always awakened in emotion, y'know?" Will responded, and Frederick shook his head.

"Magic isn't something you just expect to feel. You need to really try and reach in, not just in the sword, but inside you. If the magic is activating in times of stress or high emotion, that means you have a strong mental connection to the power that you need to be able to locate." He instructed, and Will listened keenly.

Will sat on the ground with his legs crossed, and held the blade in his lap. He breathed slowly, and tried to ignore the crowd that had formed around the two of them. He thought of why he had activated the power before in the first place.

With Wolf, Will had been wrapped in emotion and anger, and he let that control his mind. The second time had been in urgency, when Becky had been nearly killed. Will felt his fingers rub against the hilt of the sword, and tried his hardest to feel the magic inside. When that failed, he began to search his mind.

He thought of his responsibility, his destiny to kill the king and restore peace to the kingdom. The fate of everyone he has ever loved, and the legacy of his family before him, rested now on his shoulders.

He thought of Jack and Becky, Louie and Bella, and Darla. They were all counting on him to live up to his responsibilities and use the magic inside him. Will thought of the maker, the being said to have created all of life.

Maker, give me strength. He pleaded in his mind.

As Will's mind went completely empty, he poured his soul inside the sword. As the world around him went deaf, a voice whispered in the back of his head.

I am proud of you, my son. You have unlocked the sword.

Will's eyes emitted a radiating white immediately, glowing brighter than they had even before. The sword grew an impenetrable aura that pushed the bystanders back in awe. Will began to levitate, holding the blade above his head.

After a few seconds, Will regained consciousness, and his eyes began to glow less and less. He remained in the air, and observed the onlookers below him.

"It worked!" Will shouted in joy, as Frederick nodded proudly below. Will began to return to the ground, and he was given a round of applause as his feet touched the ground again.

He began to feel greatly lightheaded as the power left his body, but kept on his feet despite stumbling. He felt something wrap around his body, and turned to see an excited Becky beside him.

"You did it! You controlled your power!" She exclaimed, and Will smiled.

"You watched?" He said happily, and she nodded. Becky's father approached the two of them, and her smile faded.

"Becky, we need to talk." Frederick spoke, and she frowned. "But first, we must celebrate. I believe with this power controlled, Will is ready to face the king at last."

Will took a deep breath and let the moment sink in. Rather than the expected wave of anxiety, Will felt a surge of confidence. He was ready to face the king.

Chapter 33

As the weeks passed, Will continued to train with Frederick and attempt to understand the power of the Blade of Atlas more. Despite all of his effort, however, he was unable to hear that voice he had heard the very first time he controlled his powers. When he successfully activated the powers for a second time, he heard nothing but a sound similar to blowing dust flow through his mind.

Becky, on the other hand, had practiced very little since her argument with her father. The bit of practice she was given was done independently, and was difficult to achieve without disrupting the peaceful setting.

Growing tired of her lack of practice and improvement, Becky approached her father at last, who was instructing a glowing-eyed Will.

"Alright, center yourself. Move your focus into the tip of the blade."

Will gripped the blade firmly, and closed his glowing eyes. He swung the blade behind him with one hand in a bat-like fashion, and leaped before striking the ground below him in an arch. As the blade struck against the rocky ground, energy built in clumps at the tip.

When he completed the swing, he ended the arch with the blade facing toward a stack of tin cans, and the energy released from the blade in a glowing slash that smashed into the tins at blinding speed, sending them scattering.

"Good, very good." Frederick spoke, and Will's eyes returned to normal.

"I'm getting the hang of this, I think." Will spoke in confidence, and Becky approached her father at last.

"Dad." She spoke, and Frederick hesitantly turned to face her. "I want to keep practicing. I want to be better."

"You understand that if I am to continue teaching you, you have to let me push you." He responded.

"I just want you to appreciate the progress I've made." She asked, and he shook his head.

"Beck, listen. If I start praising you for where you are now, you'll never have the drive for perfection." He said back, and she frowned. "But you've improved a lot since I first met you. I am impressed with how quickly you've advanced." Becky's face glowed at the remark, but he turned away again. "Don't let that get to your head."

"I won't. I promise."

Will said hi to Becky, but left to leave her with her father. Frederick held his wand by his side in readiness while Becky got into her stance with confidence.

"What're we doing first? Crystal Thunder? Do you want me to try *Gelida Flamma* again?" She asked in impatience and he shook his head.

"I'd like to try something new today. Balance your stance."

Becky balanced her stance and kept her focus on her father. Frederick put his weight against the crutch on his left side, and began to swirl his wand slowly in the air.

"There are going to be situations where you are not the one attacking, but the one being attacked. I want to teach you how to defend yourself and others in that case." He spoke as he continued to swirl his wand. "I'm going to unleash a small bolt of electricity in your direction, and I want you to catch and redirect it."

"How do I catch something that fast?" She asked in worry.

"All you need to do is focus on the source of energy, and truly feel the magic through your wand. Your reflexes will catch it on their own."

"How am I supposed to-"

He released the small bolt before she could finish her sentence, and she desperately attempted to catch it. The bolt deflected off the tip of her wand and struck her in the foot, and she leaped in shock and pain.

"Shit! I wasn't ready!" She complained.

"The enemy will not wait for you to be ready." Her father spoke, and began to swirl another strike. "Truly focus on my wand, the source of the magic. Try to feel it with your wand, even from far away."

Becky lightly swirled her wand in a similar motion to her fathers, and could feel the tingle of magic upon the tip. It wasn't her own, but more of a sense of the nearby energy. When her father released the energy, Becky caught the bolt of lightning in a swift catch, and the energy sparked at the tip of her wand.

"I caught it! Did you see that!" She said excitedly.

"Now redirect it, quick!" Her father shouted in response.

"What-"

Before she could finish, the energy began to push in opposition to Becky incredibly forcefully, and grabbed the wand with her other hand to keep the bolt from blowing off the tip into her forehead. With a rough swing, she redirected the rapidly growing force into a small hill of dirt beside her, which cracked at the incredible speed of the small shock.

"When you catch the attack, no matter what it is, you must continue to swirl your wand while stationary so that the energy is not condensed. If you hold it still like you did, the energy grows in speed rapidly and begins to push with immense force. This can be very helpful as a retaliatory attack, but can be very risky." Frederick spoke, and Becky sighed in shell shock.

"I wish you had told me that before I tried to catch the bolt." She responded, and her father chuckled.

"Let's try one more time. A real spell this time."

He began to swirl his wand with incredible force, creating a large cloud of thunder above the wand.

"I don't know if I'll be able to-"

Before she could finish, he released the large bolt of energy and Becky hardly caught it at the tip, and began to slowly swirl her wand while the energy jittered and pulled its weight in all directions. With a harsh thrust, she deflected the spell in the direction of the ground to her right, and it struck with a loud crack. Frederick nodded his head in pride, and sheathed his wand.

"Very good. You seem to have picked up on that technique very quickly. I'm proud."

Becky shined in pride and sheathed her wand. She had received her fathers acceptance, and was content for the day.

••

Jack wandered through the weapons hall, and went through the many options hanging from the wall in front of him. His eyes set on a silver Xiphos that sat on two wooden support beams. Jack grabbed the blade and ran his hand along the edge.

He swung it around to get a feel for it, and grinned at his reflection in the gleaming silver. As he stared into the image of his intrigued face, he saw a figure approach from behind him and jumped. Darla put her hands in the air as Jack put the Xiphos to her neck.

"At ease, soldier. It's just me." She spoke, and he lowered the weapon.

"My bad. I guess I've just been a bit jumpy."

"Listen, Jack was it?" Darla asked and he nodded. "I was rude a few nights ago. I shouldn't have been, and I'm sorry for that."

"No worries, I guess." Jack responded dryly and turned back to focus on the blade.

"You're interested in a Xiphos?" She asked, noticing his interest in the sword. "Why don't I teach you a few things? Stances and stuff."

"Right now? In here?" He asked, shocked at her interest in teaching, and she shrugged.

"Why not?" Darla responded, and Jack nodded.

"Okay, sure." Jack swung the sword playfully and balanced his stance. "Hit me."

"If you say so." Darla spoke, and took a sword from the wall.

She struck down upon Jack's Xiphos with immense power, and his legs shook as his strength briefly faltered. She began to spar with Jack who very clearly struggled to keep up with her rapid blows.

"Shit, chill!" He shouted and Darla cackled in joy.

She continued to swiftly strike against his continuously loosening grip until the blade swung from his hands and hit the ground with a clang. Jack fell onto his backside, and Darla crossed her arms in triumph.

"Is that all you got, Jack?" She asked with a grin.

"Pretty much." He said as he rubbed his aching back with a groan. "What was this supposed to teach me, anyways?" He questioned, as Darla cracked a hearty laugh at Jack's response to her taunt.

"Nothing, I was just having fun." She responded, sticking her arm out to lift him up. He accepted, and stood shakily. "You got your ass beat like a champ."

"Shut up." He said, stifling a chuckle.

"But enough screwing around. How's about I teach you something real? Maybe you can learn a bit of how I kick ass so easily."

"Sure!" Jack nodded with a grin, and she got back into her battle stance with a smile.

Jack did the same, and spun the Xiphos in his wrist to get a feel for the silver blade. Taking a breath of exhilaration, Darla opened her mouth to speak.

"Show me what you got."

Chapter 34

Darla stood before a large group of people in her office, with a note covered poster beside her. Will, Jack, Becky, Jonah, Louie, Kendrick, and Bella stood in front of her, as she paced across the room in calculated thought. Her eyes hung from stress and her undone hair waved in the light breeze that came from the small fan beside her desk.

"Thank you for gathering here this morning." She started, and rooted herself beside the poster she had prepared, which mapped a roughly drawn multiple step plan. "It's been close to three weeks since you three arrived in the rebellion, and began training to fight the king." She said while gesturing in the direction of Will, Becky, Jonah and Jack. "I've seen and heard of nothing but incredible progress, and I think I'm finally confident in your abilities."

"So that's it, then?" Jack spoke in a disappointed tone, and Darla tried to ignore his remark by looking in the opposite direction.

"I've decided that I want you four to leave for the capital city tomorrow morning. I've also decided that Kendrick, Bella and Louie will be accompanying you on your trip."

"I'm sorry, what?" Louie spoke in shock, but Darla wasn't affected. "You want *us* to-"

"You three are going to need all of the support you can get, while also staying quiet and out of sight." Darla spoke, turning toward the board behind her. "The plan is for you to sneak unseen through the back skirts of the city, until you reach the castle walls. Kendrick is going to rig an explosion by the east wall that will go off exactly two minutes and thirty seconds after being set. When the guards move to the source of the noise, Louie and Bella will use shocker bands against the remaining guards at the entrance to quietly enter."

"I can do that, but..." Kendrick spoke. "You don't expect us to fight the king, do you?"

"Of course not." Darla answered. "That's for Will and the others to do. You three are only meant to help from the sideline."

Kendrick nodded, and the group began to stand to leave.

"That's all. Meet me by the tunnel entrance first thing tomorrow." Darla finished, and everyone began to exit her office into the blinding lights outside.

Before Will could exit, Darla pulled him aside.

"Do you... Can you stay back for a second?"

"Sure, what's up?

"I just..." She spoke anxiously. "I know I didn't sound like it, but I'm scared. For you."

"I'm going to be okay, Darla-"

"You don't understand," She interrupted. "The king is one of the strongest bladesmen in the entire kingdom. He will be incredibly difficult to kill without... casualty." She frowned, and he put his arm on her shoulder.

"I won't let that happen. I promise you."

"But you can't promise that, Will!" She shouted. "Especially if Kronos is there. If the king is able to contact him fast enough... You will not be able to defeat him. You're not invincible, Will."

"I just don't understand." Will said to his friend. "If you are concerned about our ability to kill the king, why send us now?"

"I'm not concerned about your ability, I just..." She mumbled. "I don't want to lose you again. Not so soon."

"Then why send us so quickly?" Will questioned, and Darla spoke through her teeth.

"I'm being pressured by the people. They are wondering why we're keeping you here, why we haven't just sent you to kill the king already. They don't understand how dangerous it is."

"I... I'll be careful." Will said in response. "No matter what it takes. I'll make sure we win."

"I..." Darla started in protest, before stopping herself and wrapping Will in a sisterly embrace. "Thank you. And good luck."

"I don't need it." He said with a grin. "But, thank you."

• •

When Will exited the office, he found Louie standing outside with his arms crossed in thought.

He wore a white tank top, and brushed his short, strawberry blonde hair back in retaliation from the heat. Noticing Will, he stood back on his feet.

"Hey." He said. "Can I talk to you, man?"

"Of course." Will responded. "What's up?"

The two began to walk through the rebellion square together in conversation. The center square was lively as it had ever been, and sunlight came through the camouflaged windows above to brighten it.

Terri had a cart full of freshly picked vegetables that she was handing to a line of hungered rebels, and two younger boys played catch with an old baseball in a grassy patch to Will's right. Wild flowers had begun to bloom at last along the sides of the stone and metal coated road, and worn sprinklers began to go off in sputters in the fields to keep them growing.

"I've been thinking." Louie started. "These past couple weeks I've been doing that a lot. Thinking. And I've been kinda working on myself, y'know?"

"Yeah? That's good, man." Will said with a smile.

"It is. I've really tried to reflect on everything that's happened with Bella, and figure out how I can grow from it." Louie grinned pridefully. "I think things are gonna get much better. They will be."

Will grinned back to his old friend as they continued to walk through the rebellion square. They made their way to the food court, and grabbed a tray of freshly prepared food before sitting next to Jonah and Kendrick, who were talking amongst each other.

“It is quite an odd feeling.” Jonah spoke. “I haven’t been in that castle for so long.”

“Well, you’re about to be there again.” Kendrick said with excitement. “We’re going to restore balance to the kingdom. Now that’s a crazy feeling.”

“Exactly,” Louie piped in. “Especially after fighting for so long. What are we even going to do afterwards?”

“Probably settle down at last. Have a family, all that.” Kendrick responded dreamily. “Always wanted to have a kid of my own, but never felt comfortable placing one in the middle of all this, y’know?”

Jonah said nothing, but Will could have sworn he saw the slightest smirk break out from the corner of his mouth.

“What about you?” Kendrick said, turning to Jonah.

“Oh, I don’t know,” Jonah started. “I’ve never been one to plan too far.”

“Come on, if you could do anything at all afterwards, what would it be?” Kendrick pushed, and Jonah thought for a moment.

“I suppose there are many things that I could do. So many things that my father did... So many things that he left. So many loose holes. If I could only...” Jonah cleared his throat. “If only I could go back on everything that my father did.”

"True that." Kendrick responded while continuing to eat. "How about you two? Any future ambitions or something?"

"I suppose having a family would be nice." Louie thought. "I've always wanted to join the military, though. It's impossible now, with the king in charge and all, but when he's gone I'd love to be on the royal guard. It would give some personal clarity, y'know? To know that I'm important, and that my presence matters. Without me, who'd protect the democracy we fought so hard to restore? That's just my perspective."

"Deep." Will thought in response to his friends' hopes. "I don't know what I'd do. I..."

Will remembered the prophecy, and its echoing statement that had ceased to leave his mind.

TO KEEP THE PEACE, THERE IS A PRICE, FROM ONE OF THREE, A SACRIFICE.

Those lines had rocked in his mind since he had first heard them weeks before, but he had refused to let them bother him. In this moment however, thinking of the future that his loved ones longed for so much, Will realized the fact that he may not have one. The thought scared him.

He enjoyed the life that he was given. But he also knew that he would give anything for those around him. Will knew that if it came down to it, he would give his life to make sure his friends could keep theirs. He didn't know how to explain it, but each time the Blade of Atlas activated its powers, it felt as if it was taking part of Will's soul with each flash of power. It was almost as if it was trying to tell him something. The further into the power of the blade Will sank, the more it felt as if someone was trying to talk to him. To warn him of something. Staring back into the eyes of his friends beside him, he could think of no response beside what he had described before. He didn't have the heart to tell the truth of how he saw his future.

"I don't know."

Chapter 35

As the sun rose upon the weather camera, Will sat anxiously beside Becky and Jack, who all looked back with similar fear. Jonah hovered carelessly beside them in conversation with Kendrick, and cracked his knuckles audibly.

Darla approached the group from behind, with Bella and Louie on trail. Louie sheathed his two blades across his back, and Bella wore shocker bands across her wrists. Jack had decided to bring his Xiphos, and when Darla noticed a small smile broke in the corner of her mouth just for a moment. Kendrick had filled his quiver and loaded his revolving crossbow, as had Jonah with his own quiver and bow, which he had refused to replace with a newer one.

"Are you all ready?" Darla asked, knowing it was a dumb question.

"How could we be?" Louie remarked back.

"You're going to have to be." She spoke solemnly and the group nodded. She opened the door and the seven figures began to enter. Darla stopped Jack before he entered, and whispered in his ear.

"I like you. You better not die out there, chump."

She gave him a shove across his chest as Jack chuckled, and glowed in pride. Darla nodded as the rest of the people entered, until Will stood as the last to enter.

"This is it." Will spoke, and Darla checked to make sure no one was watching before embracing him tightly.

"Be careful. Promise me you will."

"I will. Thank you, Darla." He responded, and she smiled before slapping him across the back.

"Stab the king a couple times for me."

••

Flint sat uneasily upon his throne, while Argus paced across the room. Light had barely begun to peer through the tinted castle windows. It had only been a day since Pandora had left to assist Kronos, and he had yet to hear a report back.

This morning had felt more odd than others, and that feeling was seemingly felt across the entire castle. Argus paced in thought, trying to complete necessary tasks while also watching Flint to ensure another accident didn't happen.

"You don't have to stay here, Argus. You are free to leave if you please." He spoke to his loyal servant.

"I appreciate the thought, my lord, but I'd rather stay and keep watch over you." He responded.

"Don't mind me. I am fine."

Argus thought for a moment, and decided to respect the king's wish.

"As you wish, my lord." He exited the throne room, and Flint sighed in anxious thought.

Kronos' squadron had been searching for many months, and were unable to find the rebel base. Pandora was now to join him in the search, but Flint feared that it was too late. He had a deep feeling in his chest that his time was running out, like sand dropping inside an hourglass. But there was nothing he could do about it. He closed his eyes in his helplessness and took a long, extended breath.

The light breeze from outside the castle's regal interior blew in through the slightly opened window, and grazed Flint's forehead. As time on the invisible watch inside his mind ticked each second, he gave his absolute earnestness to stay in complete mindfulness, absorbing the moment of tranquility he had been given. And time went on.

••

After hours of walking, the group began to reach an exit to the endless tunnel. Stepping outward, Becky let the warm rays of the open sun press upon her skin, as did the others.

"It's strange." Becky remarked. "After weeks of being cooped inside, I thought it would feel nicer to be outside again."

"It's probably just nerves." Jack responded with a sigh. "I get it."

They continued to walk through the edges of Kandachta, until they reached a small desert town, one that Becky had not seen before. The town was another abandoned area, with dust and tumbleweeds blowing between each ghastly building.

In front of one of the houses, there was a large metallic object that was completely covered in dust from many years of no use. Kendrick approached the machine and wiped the dust off the glass cover that curved across the front, revealing an elegant interior.

"No way, man! No way!" Kendrick spoke excitedly. "Darla told me we could find one of these out here, but I didn't think we'd actually be able to do it!"

"What is it?" Louie asked in genuine interest.

"It's a car." Jonah spoke, stepping forward. "They weren't common, but there were still some around when I was very young. My father used to drive one. It was quite long, called a limousine."

"Can we use it?" Bella asked and Kendrick nodded.

"Of course we can. I just need a little time."

After a close to half an hour of Kendrick poking and twisting the small lock on the door, first with his arrow and next with Jack's dagger, it opened and he stuck the dagger inside a hole-like object beside a wheel that must have been meant for steering the vehicle. After a moment of turning, the car jumped to live with a thunderous roar and Becky jumped at the noise.

"Well, what are you all waiting for?" Kendrick yelled to the others. "Get in!"

The group slowly gathered into the vehicle, and sat upon the soft, coated seats. Becky grabbed the seat to feel its texture in curiosity, and rubbed its dark leather exterior, moving her finger through the groves. As they all settled in the car, Kendrick put his hands upon the wheel and rested his feet upon two lever-like objects near the bottom.

"Let's see if I remember how to run one of these."

He pushed down on one of the levers, and the vehicle jumped and began to rapidly accelerate backwards, into one of the rotting buildings behind it. The car stopped with a jolt as Kendrick removed his foot and sighed in shock.

"Wrong way. Sorry guys."

He pushed an object that seemed like a joystick forward, and pushed his foot upon the floor lever once again, but instead of going backward like previously, the car began to move forwards. Kendrick sighed with a chuckle and put his hands upon the wheel, as Jack squealed in excitement. The car began to accelerate rapidly, shooting out of the deserted town at mach speed.

"Why didn't we find one of these things earlier? At this rate we'll be in the city in an hour at the latest!" He yelled across the vehicle, and Becky shushed him despite her own excitement.

She had never been in a vehicle like this one before, and the pure speed that it moved at gave her goosebumps. Each time the vehicle rocked she slightly moved from her seat, but she was too distracted by the pure joy in the vehicle to be scared.

All she could hear around her was the nervous laughter that brought a bit of light to the incredibly tense feeling shared amongst them. Becky looked between them all with a grin, but it faded when her eyes landed on Bella, who sat beside Becky with her eyes locked on one of the seats in front of her and a grim expression painted upon her face.

"Is everything okay?" She asked, and Bella nodded. "Are you sure?" Becky frowned in concern for the girl beside her.

"I just..." She took a slow breath, and Becky listened. "A lot has been going on, and... things just feel like they are going too quickly. I have a really bad feeling about all of this, and I'm scared. I feel..."

"Cold." Becky responded. "I feel it too. But look around you. We all feel that, but we're trying so hard to enjoy the time we have."

"I'm sorry, I know I'm being a buzzkill right now."

"Don't be. This is scary. I get it." Becky responded, and Bella smiled.

"This car is pretty cool, I'll admit." She spoke, and Becky grinned. "I would have loved to do this as a kid."

She stared out the windshield into the road ahead, which blew with dust in the rising sun. She smiled softly, taking in the precious moment. And so the worn vehicle drove on, carrying the prophecy closer and closer to inevitability.

•••

As the clock struck noon, the aching feeling in Flint's gut grew even more. He could feel conflict brewing, but he didn't know where or when it would occur. Unsheathing his ancient blade, he stared into his tired reflection in its blood red shine. He felt as if he could see the crying soul of every man murdered by his fathers weapon staring back at him through its blinding glare. Flint frowned back, condemning the actions done with the blade. And then he realized that he had done the same.

In comparison to his father, he had committed similar atrocities. Even if it had been against his wishes, or in the name of his father, there was no excuse. Flint sighed deeply and held the blade in his lap, as Argus entered the room.

"My lord, we have received word from Lieutenant Pandora. She has made contact with General Kronos, and their squadrons have combined in the search." He spoke calmly. "They are currently observing the North sector of the Kandachta region, close to the grave where your brother was buried."

The mention of his brother made Flint slightly flinch, knowing that he too would be arriving alongside the prophecy heroes.

"I see," responded Flint. "Thank you, Argus."

"At your service, my liege." Argus responded with a light bow, covering a thin smile.

As he turned to leave the room, an earth shaking explosion shook the castle walls, throwing Argus to the floor and nearly knocking Flint from his throne. Rubble began to crumble and fall from the impact, before the castle ceased its shaking and returned to silence.

"King Flint, we must vacate immediately!" Argus shouted, and held a hand to a speaker in his ear. His thin face went pale as he listened earnestly. "My lord, there has been a terrorist attack! We must leave now!"

Flint sat for a moment before closing his eyes and shaking his head solemnly.

"Argus, my loyal servant," Flint began. "Alert Kronos of the disturbance. The time has come. The prophecy arrives at my doorstep, and I must accept its beckon. I suggest you leave."

"But, my lord-"

"This is my decision. And I am ordering you to leave. For your own safety." Flint commanded, and Argus could do nothing but nod.

"As you wish, my lord." He began to leave, head held low beneath his shoulders in concern. "Be careful, my king."

Argus left the room with his head hung in shame, just as the grand castle doors finally opened. A young man, seemingly eighteen or nineteen, stood in charge of a group of other young individuals. His eyes glowed brighter than the core of a star, and his golden blade sent chills up Flint's aged spine. The boy's hair blew in the wind as dust swirled surrounding his stature, and his eyes began to dim, returning to normal. The face of the youth before him sent echoes of a thousand memories through Flint's aging mind, and his eyes winced in silent agony at the youthful reminder. The golden blade, unscathed as it was many years ago, held Flint's lamenting face in its piercing reflection.

"Your reign of genocide and corruption is over, Flint!" The ethereal leader shouted in a scarily familiar voice, and Flint closed his eyes in remorse for the young soul.

"So it is." He responded lamentingly, as he stood from his throne. He took a deep, slow breath of air, and eyes shaded in pain, Flint unsheathed his blood red blade synchronistically with his heavy exhale.

Chapter 36

The castle was calm and serene. Much different than Will had ever imagined. The walls were built from the foundation with beautifully molded concrete, and the floor was coated in an ornate marble. Each stained glass window was coated in an illustrious array of gorgeous colors, letting just enough light into the throne room. The throne itself was plated in gold and silver, and was formed as though for a god.

Will stood in absolute awe before the monstrous king. He tried to keep a fearless exterior, but the tip of the large man's blood sword left a fear so pure and deep that Will felt like dropping to his knees and weeping. He was unable to see, but he could tell that the others had the same feeling. Thinking of his friends, Will caught his breath and readied his stance.

I need to do this. For them.

He spun his blade into position and began toward the king. Flint leaped from his elevated throne, with his regal robe fluttering in the air, and landed on the marble floor with an enormous thud.

Regaining his balance, he held his long blade toward Will, and stared into his soul with a lamenting glance.

"It didn't have to be this way, boy. But you leave me no choice."

As Flint prepared his long, murderous claymore for battle, Jonah held his right hand behind his back. His legs went limp as he began to hover, moving between Louie and Kendrick, then past Jack and Becky.

The group watched as he slowly inched to the front, with his hand cracking in strange movements behind his back. Dark red lightning began to form upon his palm, like none that any had seen before. It grew rapidly in size, as did Jonah's smirk, as he began to float higher than everyone before him.

Flint and Will were too focused on each other's presence to notice, and Jack watched as Jonah stuck his hand before his chest, now coated in lethal lightning. Thrusting his hand back, he aimed to the center of the conflict. The head of Will Larson.

"Will, look out!" Jack cried desperately as Jonah shot the bolt violently toward Will.

Will jumped at Jack's yell, and rolled out of the way. The bolt grazed the sole of Will's boot as he dove from the strike, and it struck Flint in the chest, gripping around his golden chestplate like vines around an old oak.

The old king dropped to his knees in pure agony, letting his blade fall to the ground beside him. He clenched the air in pain as Jonah used his left hand to levitate his brother, and slammed him against one of the stone pillars. Flint's plated armor cracked as his body smashed against the dense pillar, and he dropped to the floor with a pathetic thud. His crown rolled from his limp body, stopping with a small clang.

The heroes were left speechless. Will stood his ground shakily, getting back up from his near death. Louie and Bella began to back away toward the door, which Jonah flung shut with a flick of his wrist. He shot a beam of lightning at the handle, forming a lock of pure energy in front.

"What's the rush, heroes?" He cackled, flying toward the crown that lay before the throne. He placed it upon his head, and chuckled in joy. "We won! The king is no more."

"Jonah..." Will fought to speak. "We didn't agree to this. The monarchy was supposed to be destroyed. A new king was meant to be placed in power."

"Exactly. Me." Jonah floated up to the throne, and sat carelessly upon its seat. He checked his nails in boredom, and looked back up toward the betrayed heroes. "You know, I had grown so bored of acting so prim and proper. 'My evil father' this and 'save the kingdom' that. What was I to get out of it?"

"You... You asshole!" Jack shouted, pointing his finger. "You weren't supposed to get anything out of it! None of us were! We had to do it for the prophecy! For the people!"

"The prophecy?" Jonah cackled at the remark. "Can't you see? It was a fake. The whole plan was a fake. 'Three heroes to save the kingdom'. Hah! Did you really think that cliche bedtime story was *real*?"

Becky began to tear up as she whipped her wand into ready position and aimed it at Jonah.

"Take that back. All of it." She shouted through tears. "Take it back, damn it! I defended you! I..."

"Oh, boo hoo." Jonah mocked Becky, who grit her teeth. "Your fairy tale quest didn't have a happy ending. Well guess what, princess? Not all stories have happy endings. Sometimes the good guys win, and sometimes..." He cracked his knuckles in taunting. "Sometimes the smart people win."

Will clenched his fist at Jonah's malevolence, and stepped forward, Blade of Atlas in hand.

"It's over, Jonah. Like I said, the murderous reign of your family ends today." He spoke with rage. "Whatever it takes."

"Whatever you say, kid." Jonah mocked, charging an electric volt in his palm.

Will closed his eyes and began to activate the power of the blade, but before he could react Jonah shot the blood red lightning toward Will, who barely caught it with his sword. The impact pushed him back a few feet, and Will nearly fell over.

"Alright, 'heroes'," Jonah spoke as he levitated, lightning sparking and cracking violently from his hands. "I've waited a long, long time to do this. So, let's see what you got."

Jonah shot another charge of electricity toward Will at light speed, which he struggled to catch. Jonah continued to fire an endless array of attacks in Will's direction, who began to falter with each powerful blow.

Come on! Will thought, arms shaking in fear. *Activate the power!*

Will closed his eyes with a big inhale, but Jonah interrupted with another hate-filled shock. Will grit his teeth as Jonah's bolt struck powerfully against his blade, and he began to lose his grip on the sword. The electric force pushed even greater against the Blade of Atlas, as Will struggled to counter its incredible strength. Will's hands slipped from his sword as sweat dripped down his face, and the blade was thrust across the throne room in one fell swoop.

Will stumbled backwards with a shout as Jonah charged another shock. Shooting the lethal bolt at Will, Jonah cackled in delight. Will flinched, but before the bolt could hit him Becky shoved him aside and barely caught it with the tip of her wand. She groaned as the power surged in her wand, and she swirled it shakily above her head to contain its force.

"Wow!" Jonah laughed. "That old cripple knew the power of redirection. How interesting..."

"Becky!" Will shouted, and she winced in pain.

"I'm okay, it's just," She regained her footing. "A really powerful spell! I don't know how long I can-"

Her arm swung in the direction of the castle wall, and the blood colored bolt struck the wall with immense force, causing its dense concrete to crack and deteriorate from the blow.

"Come on!" Kendrick whispered to Jack, as they began for the door. Jack took his knife from his pocket, and Kendrick took one of his arrows.

They began trying to pick the lock of energy Jonah had placed, and Will grabbed the Blade of Atlas with a roll while Becky continued to redirect Jonah's flurry of attacks.

"This is cute!" Jonah remarked. "It's been fun watching you struggle, but I have a job to do."

He lifted Becky into the air by the throat and she gasped loudly, clenching her chest. She kicked her legs while he held her midair, until she began to lose her breath and ceased her effort to escape. Will screamed in anger, and gripped his blade tightly as he approached Jonah.

"Put her down, now!" He roared, and Jonah chuckled. He slammed Becky into the wall as he did his brother, and she fell to the ground unconscious.

"Look who finally decided to man up." Jonah mocked Will, and Will growled.

"I trusted you. I let you in our team, in the rebellion..." Will's eyes went wide with the realization. Jonah knew where the rebellion base was. There was no other base, and the rebellion had been cornered. If Jonah gathered the king's army, he could... *No.* Will thought in rage.

"I'm sorry, Jonah." His grip on the blade tightened even more, and he closed his eyes.

"Yeah, I don't think so." Jonah spoke annoyingly, as he shot an unpredictable volt of lightning at Will, which wrapped around his body, forcing him to drop to his knees in shock.

Bella and Louie ran up toward Will, helping him to his feet. He shook as he gained his balance, and Jonah took the bow from behind his back.

"I forgot I had this. Might as well use it." He removed his quiver that had been filled with old rebellion arrows, and emptied it to the ground with a sneer.

He snapped his fingers, and the quiver filled instantaneously with dense, red arrows of pure energy. He levitated four of them, and strung them all into his bow, which was now glowing in power.

"That's what I'm talking about." He laughed, as he aimed the arrows at Bella, Will and Louie. "Let's put a little more energy into these, shall we?" He cackled as the arrow tips began to glow white, and Louie held his swords between Will and Bella protectively.

Jonah released the arrows and they hit the ground between Bella and Will, creating a forceful blast that split the three apart. Will's ears rang with a piercing screech as he slammed into the ground, sending the Blade of Atlas sliding across the floor. Blood ran down his cheek as the world around him blurred shakily, and he saw Becky's unconscious hand laying beside his face.

Bella flew in the opposite direction, landing on her shoulder with a painful crack. Louie was launched backward and landed on his back, but stood upwards as his knee wobbled in shellshock. Jonah looked down at Louie and turned his head in curiosity.

"Interesting. That was quite the explosion, but you are back up just like that." Jonah remarked, and Louie stood his ground neutrally, unaffected. "Not much of a talker, huh? I like you." Jonah taunted as he shot a bolt of fatal lightning at light speed, and Louie caught it with his two silver blades, grunting as the force pushed him back.

"Louie!" Kendrick shouted. "Be careful!"

Jonah shot another bolt at Louie, who hardly caught it. Jonah shot another, and another, and Louie's arms swung from each impact. But he stood his ground, sweat dripping down his tired face.

"That's it!" Kendrick shouted, dropping his arrow and picking his revolving crossbow up from the ground. "I thought you were cool, Jonah! We were cool!" Jonah laughed, grabbing his gut in entertainment.

"You thought... You thought I would be friends with someone like.." Jonah continued to cackle, and Kendrick flushed in rage.

"Someone like what?" He grit his teeth. "Rot in hell, you bastard." Kendrick fired a barrage of explosive arrows at Jonah's head, and Jonah stopped them with a light flick of his right wrist, just before they made impact.

"Real cute." He spoke, launching the arrows back in the direction of Kendrick and Jack.

The array of explosions sent the two flying, and the door cracked and split from the impact. One arrow entered Kendricks left shoulder, and he yelled in agony as blood dripped down his arm. Louie was pushed by the force, but continued to hold his ground. Suddenly, Bella held her hand out toward Louie, and groaned his name.

"Louie..." She spoke softly and weakly, and Louie looked to where she was pointing. One of Kendrick's reflected arrows had lodged itself in his upper chest, and he winced at the realization.

His legs began to shake in exhaustion, and Jonah watched the interaction between the two.

"Aw, she cares about you kid." Jonah taunted the weakened Louie, who turned his attention back toward Jonah with a jump.

Jonah shot another arrow of pure energy at Louie, who sliced it away with a slash of his swords. Jonah shot another, and another, each reflected by Louie's cat-like reflexes. Jonah shot a powerful beam of blood red energy toward Louie, who deterred it with his swords, groaning from the force it was placing against his weakened body.

As Jonah held the beam of energy, he turned to face Bella, who was struggling to stand from her hands and knees. While holding the beam of energy with his right hand, Jonah held an energy arrow between his fingers on his left hand.

"This one amuses me. She didn't even bring a weapon. Was she just expecting to kill the monstrous king of Pyronia with a kiss?" He cackled maliciously, and aimed the arrow at her skull. "Say goodbye to your girlfriend, kid!" Jonah shouted gleefully, and Louie went pale.

Louie deflected the energy beam with a slash and ran toward Bella. Blood dripped from his worn chest, and his legs limped in agony with each step. Jonah launched the arrow with a forceful slam, and it flew through the air toward its destination. Bella raised her head in fear, and Louie threw himself in front of her swinging his blades to deflect the arrow.

His thrust missed the arrow, and it lodged gorily in his center chest, cracking his heart covering from the impact. Blood dripped like a fountain from the piercing, and he stumbled backwards in shock. Louie fell backwards beside Bella with a thud as blood began to run to his mouth and his eyes went bloodshot. He turned his head to face her, mouth trembling.

"It's happening... Isn't it?" He asked weakly, and she nodded, tears in her eyes. "I'm sorry-" He broke out into a cough, and she put her hands on his chest. "I'm sorry I made your life worse in the end."

Bella shook her head in denial, tears streaming down her pale face. Louie mouthed indecipherable words to Bella's eyes, and she shook her head again, laying it on his lap in agony. He coughed blood to the ground beside him, unable to move his face. Slowly, he laid his head back against the marble wall behind him, and used his remaining strength to look toward Bella and stroke her hair softly with his shaking hand.

"I saved you though, didn't I?" He spoke slowly, coughing between words as blood began to fill his tired lungs, and his pierced heart ceased to beat any longer. "At least... At least I did something right in the end."

"No, no no no..." She sobbed, and his body went limp at last, and his eyes lost their seemingly constant light. "No!" She roared in pain, and Will shook from his unconsciousness at the painful wail of his childhood friend.

His vision remained blurry as he grabbed the marble floor in silent rage. He pulled his shaking body to the ground, and his sight cleared. Becky lay beside him, blood draped elegantly across her forehead, and across the room, Bella sobbed into the lap of his silent friend. Tears dripped from his bagged eyes he grit his teeth, and breathed more heavily than he had ever before.

He had failed to fulfill his responsibility, and now his friend was dead. The Blade of Atlas began to shake from the distance, and flung itself across the room into Will's rageful grip. His eyes immediately glowed brighter than the sun itself, and levitated as the air cracked around him.

"You're dead." Were all the pain filled words Will could speak, and Jonah smirked.

"What now, special boy? You're gonna cry-"

Before Jonah could finish, Will moved before him in a burst of incredible speed and gripped Jonah by the neck fiercely. He grasped his throat so hatefully that his fingers left imprints on Jonah's ghastly neck, and he began to wince in pain. Tears ran down Will's face in streams, as he exploded forward and smashed Jonah's body against the throne, which cracked from the pure power.

Will flew immediately to the right wall of the castle, moving at such speed that he smashed through the stained glass. Still holding Jonah by the neck, he turned back around and flew back into the throne room, slamming Jonah into the left wall of the room with a loud shake. Will breathed heavily as Jonah groaned from the impact, and put his hands around Will's arm.

"Put me... the hell... down-" Jonah spoke before being interrupted by Will's swift movement.

Will threw Jonah with all of his might toward the marble floor, and his back cracked against it with great speed. Will followed, picking Jonah's body back up again, and throwing it into the concrete support of the right wall.

Will held him against the wall with his foot, and held the Blade of Atlas at Jonah's neck as he coughed blood from his weakened body. Will grit his teeth as Jonah formed a small grin, and Will held the edge of the Blade closer to his neck.

"Well? Are you gonna-" Jonah coughed more blood into his arm. "Are you gonna kill me or what? Just do it. Show that you're like your father. Do it!"

Despite wanting in all of his being to slit Jonah's throat in that moment, Will hesitated. The ceiling continued to crack above them, and a large chunk of concrete broke off with a snap. It began to fall heavily, straight toward the spot that Becky lay unconscious.

Without a moment more to think, Will threw Jonah back toward the throne and flew as fast as possible toward the sleeping Becky. He caught her just in the nick of time, and carried her body toward Jack, who sat leaning against the wall with a bloodied face. His eyes suddenly went wide, and spoke weakly and desperately.

"Will, look-"

Before Jack could finish, Will felt what felt like fire surging through his body, scratching at his veins with a fiery grasp. His whole body stung in agony, as his arms clenched to his side and his body began to levitate, turning to face the enraged Jonah who floated before him, swarmed in dark red electricity. The same electricity surrounded Will's body, gripping him tightly and fiercely.

"This has been fun, but that fucking hurt." Jonah said in anger. "I'm gonna enjoy this, kid."

The energy began to strengthen, and Will's agony increased. He could feel his insides burning and tearing in the power, and he dropped the Blade of Atlas to the ground with an echoing clang. Kendrick lay half unconscious from the explosion, and so did Jack. The castle doors had been blown open, but had been abandoned by the surviving guards. Becky still lay unconscious, and Bella lay sobbing over the body of her friend. Will was alone, and Jonah grinned maliciously as the power surged painfully throughout Will's body.

"At last, the end of the 'prophecy'." Jonah spoke mockingly, and Will's vision began to fade.

Suddenly, Jonah was knocked aside by an explosion, which had come from behind Will. Jack stood shakily, holding Kendrick's revolving crossbow. He had shot the last explosive arrow into Jonah's chest, who clenched the wound in shock. Will regained his sight as he fell to the ground, losing the wind in his lungs as he hit the floor with a thud.

Jonah's eyes went bloodshot in rage as he picked Jack into the air with electricity, wrapping it around his body until his limbs were imobile. Jack grunted in pain, holding back the complete agony he felt across his body.

"Fuck... you..." Jack choked out, as Jonah increased the surge and Jack began to black out.

Before Jack could fall from consciousness, Jonah was wrapped in white lightning, similar in power to his own. Jack hit the ground with a roll and regained his breath. A slender figure stood in front of the King's body, whose hands crackled in the white lightning that had saved Jack's life.

"You shall pay for your tyranny against the throne!" Jonah broke free and screamed to Argus, who kept a neutral expression. "I am your king!"

"You are not my king." Argus responded calmly, and his lightning clashed powerfully in the air against Jonahs. The force wore on Argus's strength, but he kept a straight face. "Run! Leave at once!" He screamed to the rebels, who struggled to stand. Kendrick jumped up and grabbed Bella, who refused to let go of Louie.

"Bella, we have to go now! We don't have much time!"

"No, I'm not leaving him!" She cried, and Kendrick pulled on her arm.

"He's gone, Bell." He said with tears in his eyes.

She sobbed as she ran out the door beside Kendrick, and Jack ran to the door before stopping for Will.

"Will, we need to go!" He screamed, and Will turned to him.

"I'm not leaving without Becky!" He screamed back. "I won't!"

Jack nodded, and stepped out the door.

"Grab her quickly! We'll wait for you outside the castle!" He shouted, and Will nodded.

Jack ran after Kendrick and Bella, as Will ran for the unconscious Becky. He sheathed the Blade of Atlas behind him, and knelt next to Becky's slowly breathing body. He slipped her wand in his pocket, and threw her body over his shoulder. He looked back as he ran toward the gargantuan entrance, and saw Argus, who looked back to Will in pleading.

Go. He mouthed to Will, who listened to the man. It was pouring rain outside the castle, and each step Will took made a splash in the blood stained mud beneath him. Exiting the castle walls, he met with Jack, Bella, and Kendrick who ran beside him.

"Where do we go?" Kendrick shouted to Will. "I lost the car keys in the castle!"

"To the old base!" Will shouted over the rain, and the others nodded.

The group ran through the rain, wiping the smeared blood from their eyes with each step. The forest outside the capital city was the quietest it had ever been, and so were the rebels. No one spoke a word until they reached the old base, stumbling through the door into its abandoned plaza. Vines had begun to grow along the unused buildings, and weeds grew across each square foot of the ground.

Will collapsed upon the ground, laying Becky beside him in exhaustion. His body ached more than it had ever before, as rain pattered across his bloodied wounds. The others followed in his footsteps, with Jack and Kendrick collapsing pale faced. Bella took a breath before dropping to her knees and sobbing, wrapping her arms around her head in pain. Will began to tear up as well, as the weight of what had just happened dawned upon his shoulders.

"I..." Will began to speak, but stopped himself. Jack put his hand on Will's shoulder, and swallowed a tear back before speaking.

"It wasn't your fault, what happened." Jack spoke softly to Will, and he shook his head.

"I could have killed Jonah earlier. I could have..." Will began to cry into his palms, and Jack kept his hand on Will's shoulder in comfort. Images of what Will could have done in the moment flashed through his racing mind, filling him with more and more regret. If he had only stopped holding himself back, maybe Louie would still be standing beside him. If Will had only acted sooner, perhaps he could have seen his friend's snarky grin once again. But that was impossible now. His friend was dead.

As Will's pain-ridden eyes swelled more than they had ever before, a large metallic scratching sound came from outside the protective walls of the base. The noise sent shivers down Will's spine, ringing with the likeness of nails on a chalkboard. The group of rebels twisted in terror at the sound, until they were left in the uncanny silence once again. Will's heart sunk into his chest as he went completely silent, before moving to face his palefaced friends.

"Someone's watching us."

Chapter 37

Will ripped the Blade of Atlas from its sheath as the group went silent. After a moment of utter silence, the sound of a twig snapping echoed outside the rebellion walls.

All of a sudden, a prolonged, scraping thud rang against the rebellion door, which Will had locked behind him while entering. A low humming noise began, and grew louder with each passing moment. Before anyone could react, an ear piercing explosion commenced, blowing a large hole through the seemingly impenetrable rebel walls. As the smoke cleared, the shadow of a tall and mangled figure stepped through inside the old rebel base. Each of its heavy steps made a clang against the dry, yet rain coated ground, as the figure came into view.

Steam seeped from its gas mask as it breathed roughly, and its red eyes stared bloodthirsty into Will's beating heart. It stopped where it was, and began to scan the area around it in a series of slow turns, its metallic eyes widening as if to absorb every detail. It turned back to face Will, who shakily held the Blade of Atlas. The sun began to set behind the grand castle far in the distance, as the figure made a sharp movement of its arm, releasing a thin and jagged blade that was built into it. The tip ran down his cyborg arm and past his rugged hand, which he clenched into a fist.

"Rebels..." He spoke with a painful wheeze, and chills were sent down Will's spine. He had heard many stories of Kronos in the past, but had never seen him. No one who had ever seen Kronos in person had ever lived to describe him, until Darla's recent encounter. Will had imagined Kronos to be a sadistic, murderous killing machine with a relentlessly horrifying persona. Standing before him, Will saw a deep pain in its metallic veins that he never could have expected. A sense of pathetic aching radiated from his slow and agonizing movements, that chilled Will to the bone all the same.

"I'll give you one chance to leave." Will spoke in a deep, tired tone. He gripped the Blade of Atlas and focused all of his will into the blade. Kronos made a movement as though he were to laugh, but it translated into a slow, ghastly exhale that sounded like the last, whimpering breath of an old man. Will's legs shook in fear and disgust as he stood his ground, and took a deep breath to calm himself.

Kronos' eyes began to glow brighter than the light left in the sky, as a dark red liquid began to flow through vein-like tubes connected underneath his metal shell. A ghost-like clicking noise rang as Kronos' limbs began to crack in subtle movement, before lunging toward Will in indescribable speed.

The jagged blade attached to Kronos' arm clashed against Wills with incredible force, nearly knocking the blade from his hands. Will knew that Kronos was stronger than him, and struggled to counter the force inflicted by him. Will grit his teeth in focus as he looked up to Kronos' beady red eyes, that seemed even more horrifying up close beneath his towering stance.

"Run!" Will grunted to his friends as he held Kronos stationary.

"We're not leaving you with this thing!" Jack screamed back, and Will winced.

"Just go! I'll be fine! Take Becky!" His eye twitched in struggle as the Blade of Atlas began to glow. Kronos made a soft grunt in confusion as Will's strength began to grow exponentially, and his eyes began to glow brighter than Kronos' own. With a powerful thrust, Will swung the Blade of Atlas upward, sending Kronos' blade into the air. Leaving an opening, Will kicked Kronos with the bottom of his boot, sending him backward a few feet unexpectedly. Kronos tilted his head slowly to the side in silent curiosity, as Will stared back hatefully.

When Jack, Kendrick, Bella and Becky had been moved from the line of conflict, Will lunged at the idle Kronos with a shout. Will slashed down at Kronos with the blade, and Kronos blocked the blow with his dense, metal left arm. Kronos' chest began to glow, and fired a burst of energy into Will before he could react, launching him airborne. Kronos leaped into the air with horrifying force, and raised his sword to smash down upon Will's body.

Will swiftly dodged the attack, and grabbed the iron ribcage surrounding Kronos' energetic core as if they were handles, swinging him with ferocity into the rebellion wall. He grunted as his large body smashed against the metal, and he began to slide toward the ground. Will flew at mach speed, readying his blade to pierce Kronos. Kronos predicted this, and gripped the metal wall behind him to slow his descent, blasting Will as he approached with another shot from his core. Will spun in the air, but found his balance quickly.

Kronos pushed off the wall powerfully, and flew toward Will with a menacing glare. He tried to grab Will as they collided, but Will was able to move out of the way, and Kronos began to fall to the ground. Before he could collide with the dry dirt beneath, his gigantic boots released a surplus of steam that slowed his fall, and he hit the ground with a thud as he caught himself with his hand.

Before he could regain his balance, Will approached from behind quickly and kicked him with such force that it sent Kronos airborne once again.

"Is that all you got?" Will screamed in exhausted pride as he exploded through the air on the tail of Kronos' flying body. "After all the stories I heard, all the pain you caused, and this is what you are?" Will continued. "Pathetic."

Kronos screamed deeply and scratchily in rage, as he caught himself on the ground again, regaining his balance. He lunged toward Will, metallic claws extended, fueled by pure rage and malevolence. Will flew faster, and grabbed Kronos' rib cage before he could slash him. Will kept flying, and smashed into the rebellion wall with Kronos' with a revolting crack.

Kronos grunted as his eyes flashed for a moment, before recentering on Will. With a vicious thrust, Kronos swung his clenched fist at Will, who caught it with his own hand before it could strike his head.

"I needed this." Will spoke through a breath. "Jonah won because of me. One of my closest friends died because of me. The first girl who's ever loved me almost died, because of me. If there's anything I needed at all today," Will continued. "It's something to punch as hard as I can."

Will punched Kronos with all of his might, and he winced deeply with a jolt as the metal behind him split from the impact. Kronos looked around frantically in a panic, and twisted his head just as quickly back toward the enraged Will. With an unstoppable movement, he clenched his hand around Will's neck and squeezed until the glowing light faded from Will's eyes, and he returned to a normal state. Will grunted from Kronos' rageful strength, and tried to pull his giant hand off his neck. Kronos jumped from the rebel wall, and swung Will behind him before throwing him through the air. Will flew a huge chunk of distance from Kronos, as he slammed into the ground and cracked his jaw against the ground as he tumbled and slid until he reached the area where Jack and the others had hid, and they swarmed him immediately.

Becky woke from the loud sound, and blinked slowly to regain her vision.

"Where..." She spoke quietly. "What's going on?"

"It's a long story," Jack shouted. "But we escaped back to the old rebellion, and were followed by Kronos. Will has been able to hold him back, but he just got hit with a pretty bad blow."

"You were followed by *who?*" She screamed as Kronos began to approach the area where Will had landed to finish the job.

Will weakly took Becky's wand from his pocket and held it out to her, and she took it from him. Kronos began to increase his speed, red energy pumping through his tube-like veins. Becky swung her wand above her head, and Kronos slowed, recognizing the spell. She shot a beam of crystal thunder toward him, and Kronos avoided it by crossing his dense arms to deflect the attack. She held the beam up shakily as Kronos began to stomp forward slowly, pushing through the electric force. Becky grunted as she held the spell intact, but it was not strong enough to stop the beast of iron.

Will leaned on his knee as he stood shakily, wiping blood from the corner of his mouth as he lightly felt his stinging jaw. He picked up the Blade of Atlas and watched as Kronos approached Becky and knocked her over with a swing of his arm. She fell to the ground with a shriek and Jack stepped in front of her, holding his Xiphos.

"Back off, y'hear me? Back off!" He shouted defensively, and steam poured out Kronos' facial vent as he shot out the sword attached to his right arm once again, and raised it above his head. Will's heart jumped as he watched Kronos strike down with such force that Jack's Xiphos split in two before his eyes. Jack fell beside Becky from the impact, and put his arm defensively in front of her as Kronos raised his blade once more.

Will moved so fast he felt as though he were phasing through time itself, punching Kronos' chest with his bare hand to defend his friends as his eyes flashed for just a moment. The skin on his knuckles ripped open as it scraped against Kronos' iron core, and Kronos was sent far backward from the blow, landing on his back with a painful thud. Blood began to pour from Will's hand, and he collapsed upon the ground before Jack and Becky.

"Oh, shit!" Jack shouted as he put his hand on his friend's chest. Becky pushed past him and placed her hands on his chest, muttering in tongue.

"What are you doing?" Bella shouted, but she ignored her question and continued to speak softly. Becky's eyes suddenly shot open, and she looked into Will's eyes, which stayed shut in silent pain.

"I tried to use healing magic I'd learned from the spellbook, but it's no use. His soul is too closed off after returning from the blade's control." She spoke grimly, and Kronos began to stand again, locking his eyes on the disabled Will.

"What are we going to do?" Kendrick shouted. "We can't fight that thing!"

Becky sat in thought as her friends panicked around her, until her sight moved to the Blade of Atlas, which rested in Will's hand.

"I have an idea." She spoke quickly, placing both of her hands upon the edge of the Blade of Atlas. She closed her eyes, and sat in complete silence as Kronos approached increasingly quickly with each thunderous stomp. As she began to speak in indescribable tongue, a small light shone down from the heavens upon the Blade of Atlas. It continued to grow until it enveloped both Becky and Will, and Will began to levitate while holding the blade. Becky stepped from the beam of light, just as Will's eyes exploded in a blinding display of diving glow.

His eyes cringed at the sight of Kronos, who had stopped his movement to observe the glowing figure before him. Dust blew around will in a spiral-like fashion, and his hair blew in the self created wind. Will moved with incredible speed and rammed himself into Kronos, smashing his metallic shell into the ground beneath them. When Kronos tried to push himself up from the ground, Will slammed him downward with even more force as the dry ground cracked ferociously. Kronos' suit began to tweak slightly from the damage, and his eyes began to flicker once more. Will clenched his right fist in the air, scarred knuckles still covered in dry blood, and it began to glow. It looked as if Will's skin was melting from the inferno of light that grew around his raised fist, and it smashed with colossal force against Kronos' iron rib cage, shattering it instantly. A crater formed beneath the two of them from the constant impact, and a wave of dust blew around them.

Will grabbed Kronos by the neck and threw him with immense strength to his left, and Kronos was sent smashing through what used to be the blacksmith house, as the building collapsed upon him. Will blew into the rubble and picked Kronos up again, throwing him with even greater force through the old dining hall, and he slammed against the metal wall behind it. Will flew over before Kronos had time to move an inch, and punched him with so much power that it left a huge dent in the dense metal wall behind them. Kronos groaned in agony as red steam coughed from his facial vent, and Will grabbed him by the leg, slamming his body into what used to be his dorm room building, now emptied.

The ceiling collapsed upon the old room, and Will smashed down on top of Kronos, who wheezed from the incredible damage done to his suit.

"Is that... All... You got?" Will spoke as he breathed heavily on top of the aching Kronos. Will raised his glowing fist once more, and slammed it down on Kronos' damaged chest.

"This is for my parents, who I never got to meet because of you!" He raised his fist again, and repeated. "This is for Louie, who wouldn't be dead if it weren't for you!" He slammed again on Kronos' core, which began to vibrate from damage as he coughed violently. "Let this be a message to Jonah. Let him see that I'm not weak!" Will screamed as he grabbed Kronos by the neck and began to fly with incredible speed toward the east wall. With a cry, he threw Kronos with all the force he could muster against the metal, and his body shattered with a loud crack. His eyes flicked as he dropped to the ground, before fading to black as he leaned back against the damaged ground, resting idly on the shaken ground.

Will's eyes began to flutter as he dropped to the ground, landing on his knees. He dropped his hands to the ground as tears fell from his bloodshot eyes. The others ran to check on him, and Becky knelt beside him. Will broke down in tears of anguish as he saw what he had done to his home.

Nearly every building had been demolished as dust flooded the air around them. The walls previously believed to be impenetrable were covered in holes and dents from the conflict, and the ground cracked all around. Worst of all, the entrance to the tunnel system that led to the other base had been destroyed and mangled in the battle, and was unusable.

Will grabbed the ground beneath him in anger as Becky put her hand on his back in comfort. Because of his inability to control himself, it would be impossible to return to the base. He looked over toward Kronos' mangled body and retched in disgust of his own actions.

How could I do this... Will thought to himself through silent tears.

The sun was now near set over the horizon, and the sky turned darker than the pit that had formed in the bottom of Will's soul. Will collapsed in tears, and Becky caught him, closing her eyes and rubbing his back in comfort. As the sun finally set beneath the skyline and the castle lights faded in the distance, the day of inevitability had finally ended, and the holocaust was complete.

Chapter 38

Flint opened his eyes slowly and sat up. He once again sat in a hospital bed, however it was late in the night rather than the day time. He stood from the bed and observed his surroundings. Unlike last time, his royal robe and crown were nowhere to be seen. All that resided on a small table beside his bed was his long, murderous blade that he despised with his soul.

"Good evening, lord Flintlock." A nurse spoke to him as she entered the room. "The king is waiting to speak with you."

"The..." Flint spoke in confusion of the nurse's news. "The king?"

The nurse nodded, and left the room after handing Flint a pile of spare clothing. It was elegant clothing but nothing regal. It was more similar to the wardrobe he had used when he was a boy, before the death of his father.

Flint donned the dark clothing, and left the hospital room toward the throne room. Entering the room, he was shocked to see it in devastating condition. Dozens of construction workers climbed amongst the castle walls, filling and repairing large holes that had been blown through.

What did I miss? Flint thought, rubbing his forehead in exhaustion and confusion.

Upon the damaged throne, sat Jonah, wearing the ornate crown that Flint had worn for many years, as well as his purple robe. He sat with his arms crossed in boredom as he watched the workers fix the damages in the night. Noticing his brother, he sat straight and met his glance.

"Come here, brother." He ordered. "Kneel before your king."

"My..." Flint spoke in utter disbelief. "I am the king!"

Jonah laughed tauntingly as Flint moved before the throne to face his brother in the eyes. Flint's expression changed from confused to angered as he watched his brother sit where he had sat for centuries.

"You are not the king anymore." Jonah explained. "In case you forgot, I am your elder. And with my vitality, that makes me legally king of Pyronia."

Flint clenched his fist in fury, but calmed himself quickly. His brother was right. Even though he had served the kingdom for many years as its king, Jonah legally had the right to claim the throne because he was no longer dead.

Flint changed his focus to the scurrying servants, which there were now many of. Flint had always only kept one servant, and Argus was incredibly loyal to him. Their relationship eventually formed into a sort of friendship, rather than an employment. Jonah, however, surrounded himself with dozens of hardworking, slave-like servants, with whom he hardly communicated with. With Argus on his mind, Flint noticed that his loyal servant was nowhere to be found in the sea of quickly moving servants behind and before him.

"Where is Argus?" Flint asked his brother, who scoffed at the question.

"Firstly, you must now ask questions formally, as I am your superior." Jonah began, and Flint's face grew red in annoyance. "However, your servant is deep in the royal dungeons at the moment for his act of treason."

"T-Treason?" Flint spoke with his mouth open in shock. He felt his beard in surprised thought as he processed the news Jonah broke to him. Jonah simply nodded without giving a look in Flint's direction.

Before Flint could ask more, one of the scurrying servants approached Jonah and knelt before him.

"My lord, I carry urgent news!" He spoke, and Jonah interrupted him before he could continue.

"Well, what are you doing stalling? Give me the news at once!"

"Yes, well, Kronos chased after the rebels as they escaped the castle, but he outran the soldiers in his squadron. When he found them hiding in the rebel base, he was unable to defeat them in battle. His suit released a distress signal before he went offline, but it's not looking good. When his squadron found him, he was nearly dead and his suit was completely destroyed." The servant spoke nervously, and Jonah scoffed.

"That imbecile, facing them alone." Jonah started, and turned to face his brother. "You said he was the strongest supersoldier ever created in the kingdom, brother. What is the meaning of this?"

"Impossible..." Flint remarked, staring into the ground in shame. After a few moments, the servant left, and Jonah stared down at Flint.

"Nevermind that. Now, you have work you must be attending to, don't you?" Jonah asked, and Flint stared back unknowingly. "Well, you must explain to the people that I am the king now, correct?" Jonah continued, and Flint flushed in anger. But there was nothing he could do. His brother had outsmarted him, and now he was powerless.

"Yes..." Flint began, and hesitated in annoyance. "My lord."

Jonah cracked a malicious grin at his brother's submission, and Flint forced himself to walk shamefully from the throne, toward the outside of the castle, where he was to address the situation in front of the thousands that feared the news to come. Flint had lost, and now was his moment of retribution.

••

The sun beat down achingly on Will and the others as they wandered North through the Kandachta district. Nobody spoke a word, and they continued forth in the boiling desert in complete silence. Will hadn't gotten any sleep, and neither had the others. His jaw still ached from the fight, as did the rest of his weakened body.

At last, Jack, who was leading the line of silent march, stopped in his tracks. He turned to face the rest of the group, who stared back at him.

"Okay, now what? We have no water, we have no food, we didn't get any sleep, and we're in the middle of the desert. It's boiling hot out here and we have no idea what we're doing!" He shouted, and the others grimaced.

"Alright, Jack. What's the plan." Kendrick spoke annoyedly, and Jack slumped.

"I… I don't know" Jack spoke hopelessly. "I don't know."

The group was left to silence once again, as they all ceased movement and sat upon the steaming sand.

"When Will, Jack and I first escaped the dungeons, we stayed at this kind woman's home for the night." Becky spoke quietly. "Maybe we could go back there? I'm sure her town is close by."

"I'm not sure what other choice we have." Will responded in monotone. "We'll die out here if we don't find resources soon."

The others nodded and they continued to walk forward in the beating sun, searching for a source of hospitality. As the group continued to march on in the heat, Will loomed back from the others to think to himself. Dishonoring his silent wish, Becky followed and looked into his eyes concernedly, and he refused to meet her stare.

"Hey." She spoke. "How are you feeling?"

"I'm not." He responded to her confusion. "I haven't felt anything for some time now."

"It's not your fault." She said comfortingly, and he looked away. "Nothing was."

"You don't understand." Will growled. "I hesitated. I could have killed Jonah. He killed Louie, he almost killed you and Jack, and now he's going to kill countless others because I failed."

"Will, none of that was-"

"And then at the base, I lost control of my powers. I thought I had control over them, but I don't. I did horrible things, and I destroyed my home." He choked in pain, and Becky put her arm around him.

"Will." She spoke in his ear, and he took a breath. "Everything is going to be okay."

It wasn't. Louie trusted Will with his life. They had spent so much time together, told each other every little secret. And now he is gone, because Will wasn't strong enough. Jonah won, because Will wasn't strong enough.

"Okay." He responded to her, ignoring the thoughts that rushed through his head. She gave him a soft peck on the cheek, and he felt nothing.

Then he had an epiphany. Everything *was* going to be okay. He was going to make sure of it. It didn't matter the cost, even if it meant giving his life. Jonah and his bastardly bloodline would pay for the pain they had cost, no matter what. Will was going to become more powerful than they could ever imagine with the blessing of his divine sword, and he would bring them the inevitable retribution they deserved. Locked on the memory of his lost friend, Will closed his eyes and continued on, wandering into the vast restlessness of the endless desert before him with nothing but determination. As Will felt the light breeze brush against his skin, a booming voice echoed in the chamber of his mind.

I am so very proud. You are strong, my son. You are strong.

Epilogue

Kronos' squadron entered the gargantuan hole left by their general in the old rebellion base with caution. They had no idea what powerful being they could find behind the walls that had slain their seemingly invincible general.

As they observed their surroundings nervously, they stood in shock at the destroyed rebel base that they had longed to find for decades. Vines grew up the sides of the torn and cracked walls that once camouflaged the hidden glade, and the remnants of the crumpled buildings that once housed rebels blew around in the wind.

"Do you think he's even here?" One of the soldiers spoke. "Maybe he was taken."

"No, that couldn't have been it." Another responded. "The general's distress signal goes off every hour, giving a location. It was last located at this location."

The squadron continued their search for their missing general, and decided to split into groups. A young, male soldier made his way toward the eastern wall, pointing a flashlight into any dark crevices. The young soldier shone his light underneath the rubble of a rebel building, seemingly a blacksmith's shop based on the anvil that had been tilted over in the conflict.

The young man was about to turn around and search elsewhere when he stopped at the light sound of dripping. He turned to the source of the sound, and jumped in horror when he laid his eyes upon the remains of his general.

Kronos' blood dripped slowly from the torn tubular veins that rain up his shattered rib cage, and his energy core lit dimly, blinking as if it were a distress light. Kronos said upon the ground wet with blood, and slumped against the wall as if he were a deactivated robot. Kronos' terrible red eyes sat dormant for the first time in the young man's life, and he could do nothing but stare into the corpse of his powerful general.

As the young man signalled the other soldiers, they approached his location and gave the same reaction. After a moment of shock, they all knelt before their fallen general in honor.

"Whatever it was, he fought it back pretty damn hard." A female soldier spoke.

"Y'know," One said. "He may have been a little intimidating when alive, but I can't help but feel bad now."

"Me too. He looks like he suffered a lot before he passed." The young man spoke up. "May the maker bless his soul."

The others nodded, and turned to leave his body to rest. Before they could step away, a scratching noise stopped them dead in their tracks. The young man turned back to watch the general, who was still laying stationery. Just as he was about to give up and leave Kronos, the scratching sound rang again.

All of a sudden, Kronos' eyes flickered briefly before going back to darkness. The soldiers watched in shock, expecting him to stand unexpectedly, unscathed. But he remained silent and idle.

"Maybe he really is gone." One of the soldiers spoke. "That could have been a malfunction."

As the soldier finished speaking the scratching noise went off one more time, alerting the squadron. It was the most subtle movement, one that none of the other soldiers were able to see, but the young soldier did. Kronos' finger twitched beside his limp body, ever so slightly.

"No." The young man spoke. "He's alive."

Acknowledgements:

There are so many people I want to thank for the creation of this novel, so I am going to do so here. Firstly, I'd like to thank my parents, as well as the rest of my family, for raising me in a loving household that supported my insane storytelling and oddly prominent creativity (Wearing a bucket on my head and pretending to be a hero when I was 8).

I'd like to thank Dylan Trumpis for being the kindest, most supportive friend I could have met when I was young, and I'd like to thank Dylan Langler for being the coolest, most trustworthy friend I could have met in these last couple years. I'd like to thank Molly Alcock for creating stunning character concepts using my god awful character designs. I'd also like to thank Audrey Cruckshank for creating astounding character concepts, drawing the incredible cover art, and for supporting my journey in writing this novel.

I'd like to thank Toby Fox and his works, which inspired me to create this novel nearly seven years ago at the time of writing this. If you know of his work, there are very clear inspirations from his incredible characters and story that I will always cherish creating while listening to his amazing music.

I'd like to thank my theater teachers at Sturgis West, Mrs Botsford and Mr D'innocenzo, for being way too kind and supporting my novel, as well as my plays that I wrote too many of. I'd also like to thank Ms Trayer, for helping me with the process of editing and reviewing my novel, and for being a supportive figure whom I can always trust.

Lastly, I'd like to thank my dog Puddles, just as I did in the very first (shitty) draft of this novel I ever made back in fifth grade. And for everyone else that I missed, thank you all so much for the support. It meant and still means so much to me and I will always cherish it deeply. This has been quite the ride.

About the Author

Robert Rotondi lives in Sandwich, Massachusetts with his family of three siblings, a dog, two bunnies, and other assortments of animals.

He has loved reading and writing since he was young, constantly writing comic books with his colleagues until he was in 5th grade, and decided to write a full length novel.

He is currently attending Sturgis Public Charter School's West Campus, participating greatly in the school's theater and English departments. He has written two One Act plays, *Baby Blue* and *Eternal Bliss,* and one Two Act play, *Gatsby*, at the time of writing.

www.ingramcontent.com/pod-product-compliance
Lightning Source LLC
LaVergne TN
LVHW020700110826
845149LV00012B/2061

* 9 7 9 8 9 9 4 7 1 8 8 0 3 *